.

SACRIFICIAL LAMB

SACRIFICIAL LAMB

KARIN HOFLAND

FIVE STAR
A part of Gale, Cengage Learning

GALE
CENGAGE Learning™

Detroit • New York • San Francisco • New Haven, Conn • Waterville, Maine • London

GALE
CENGAGE Learning

Set in 11 pt. Plantin.
Printed on permanent paper.

LIBRARY OF CONGRESS CATALOGING-IN-PUBLICATION DATA

Hofland, Karin.
    Sacrificial lamb / Karin Hofland. — 1st ed.
      p. cm.
    ISBN-13: 978-1-59414-774-6 (alk. paper)
    ISBN-10: 1-59414-774-4 (alk. paper)
    1. Women television producers and directors—Fiction. 2. Murder—Investigation—Fiction. I. Title.
    PS3608.O4795S33 2009
    813'.6—dc22
                                            2009016128

First Edition. First Printing: September 2009.
Published in 2009 in conjunction with Tekno Books and Ed Gorman.

Printed in the United States of America
1 2 3 4 5 6 7 13 12 11 10 09

For Corey

CHAPTER 1

"Hey, Magnussen, there's a hooker here to see you."

I looked up from the stomach-churning array of crime-scene photos on my desk. So much blood, so much suffering, so much hatred. The case involved a series of slasher killings in Ohio that had gone unsolved for eight years, until a disgruntled ex-wife crawled from the woodwork eager to rat out Hubby.

Lucky me. I got to choose which images were gruesome enough—but not too gruesome—to rivet a television audience. Jaded by cable TV and the Internet, viewers tend to greet crime-scene photos with a yawn. Not these. Even Mona the receptionist stuck a finger down her throat and pretended to gag.

"How do you know she's a hooker?" I asked, grateful for the interruption. Another few minutes and I'd have had to put my head between my knees.

Mona slouched against my cubicle doorway in a suggestive Hollywood Boulevard pose. "Straight out of Central Casting."

"Oh, come on. You can't judge people by their appearances."

Turned out she was, in fact, a hooker.

Mona had stuck her in the conference room, where she sat bobbing a foot up and down, sucking a hard candy or maybe a cough drop, surveying her surroundings with the bored air of a teenager who's got way better things to do. She could have passed for a kid waiting outside the principal's office for yet another talking-to—except for the purple leather miniskirt, the leopard-print halter-top, the glittery gold sandals with platform soles thicker than an L.A. phone book. Come to think of it, that's how some of the girls at my son's school dress.

If you scraped off all the makeup, got rid of the hard edge to her mouth, she'd probably look old enough to drive. With the cosmetics overlay, she looked closer to my age—thirty-nine, at least for another seventeen days.

"Hello, I'm Harmony Magnussen." The conference room possessed that rare feature of modern office design, an actual door. I closed it. "I'm an associate producer with *Cold Case Chronicles.*"

The young woman aimed a dubious glance at my hand, then shook it as though it might break. "Harmony. Cool."

"Credit my mother, the ex-hippie. Well, I shouldn't say ex. Last year she changed her legal name to Rainbow. Just Rainbow."

"You mean like Pink?"

I flashed on a neon-haired pop star gracing one of the plastic CD covers my son Dane was in the habit of strewing around the house. "Exactly." I opened my notepad and sat next to her at the conference table, bringing my nose within range of cheap perfume and stale cigarette smoke. "And your name is . . . ?"

She hesitated. Her hair was an unlikely shade of blond that fell in long straight curtains from a center part. She twisted a few strands around her finger. "Leilani."

"You mean like Pink?"

That pried half a smile from her. "Actually, um, my real name's Layla. Layla Schultz. Totally boring, huh? That's why I changed my name to Leilani when I came to Hollywood."

"Hollywood. Are you an actress?"

"Yes . . . well, no." She transferred the candy to her other cheek, releasing a whiff of peppermint. "Not yet. But I'm trying to be."

"Good for you. I think Layla's a pretty name. So, how can I

help you, Layla?"

"Uh, well, like I told that chick out front . . ." More hair twisting. "I was wondering if you could maybe . . . if you might be interested . . ."

"Does this have something to do with a crime?"

"Yes!" Her face dimmed. "Well, maybe. I'm not sure, see. That's why I . . . I don't really know how to . . ."

Part of my job—besides sorting through gory pictures, scheduling shoots, booking travel arrangements, acting as general dogsbody for the show's producer—is screening ideas for new episodes. Ninety-five percent of the time this means weeding out letters and e-mail from cranks and wackos who insist their festering grudges and paranoid conspiracy theories are raw material for a ratings blockbuster, if only we had the guts to hear them out and reveal to the world what really happened.

The majority of useful tips come from law-enforcement agencies around the country, anxious to trumpet their cleverness in solving cases that lay dormant for years.

Occasionally, a private citizen brings an intriguing story to our attention. Odds seemed long that this would be one of those occasions.

"Why don't you start at the beginning?" I suggested, striving to keep impatience from my voice. I had a hundred and three items on my To-Do list this morning, and so far I was on number four.

Something in this young woman's eyes caught my attention, though. I've interviewed prostitutes before, even played a couple during my starving-actress days. You see the same expressions in their eyes. Resentment. Defiance. Desperation. Fear. Embarrassment, sometimes, if they're brand new. Once in a while the eyes are simply vacant, dead, as if nobody's lived there for a long time.

This girl's eyes were the saddest I've ever seen. Big, green, sad eyes that made me want to bake her some cookies.

She combed her lipstick with her teeth and stared down at the bulky handbag parked next to her feet. Alligator or some other species of reptilian leather. After struggling with what appeared a momentous decision, she dove into the handbag and retrieved an envelope. "I guess the beginning was when I got this."

You don't work for a true-crime show without absorbing certain reflexes. Like the voice inside my head yelling, "Don't get fingerprints on potential evidence, you idiot!" But I hadn't brought any latex gloves with me, and I figured the chances it would turn out to be significant were approximately zero. Besides, Layla's prints would be all over the paper.

Just to placate the indignant voice, I held the envelope and its contents by their edges, as gingerly as I handled Dane's gym socks on laundry day. The envelope, ripped open along the top, was addressed to Layla Schultz at an apartment on Argyle in Hollywood. No return address, just a blurred L.A. postmark.

The single sheet inside had been torn from a tablet of cheap writing paper. Unfolded, it revealed one sentence block-printed in blue ballpoint pen.

YOUR NOT THE ONE WHO KILLED HIM.

I frowned. "Who?"

Layla/Leilani gnawed a fingernail. "No clue. They didn't even sign it, see. Or put their address on the envelope."

"No, I mean, who—whom are you supposed to have, uh, killed?"

"Oh." Color stained her cheeks beneath the thick coat of foundation. She winched up a shoulder, let it drop, looked away from me. Her reply was so soft I barely heard it. "My brother."

Caught off guard, I blurted out the first thing that came to mind. "Well, did you?"

She wiped her palms back and forth on her leather miniskirt. "I—I guess so. That's what they always told me, anyway. But now, this letter . . ." Hope flickered across her face. "Maybe I didn't kill him. Do you think that's possible?"

"Whoa. Let's back up." What was I dealing with here? Drug-induced hallucinations? Mental illness? A cold-blooded killer? I threw a nervous glance at that big purse. "When did your brother die?"

"I was like, four or five? So, about fifteen years ago."

"You supposedly killed your brother when you were four? How old was he?"

She blinked rapidly. "Just a baby. Less than a year, I think."

Dear God. Very, very carefully, I folded the note back into the envelope. "Do you remember what happened?"

"Not really." She gave a dainty little smoker's hack. "I mean, I remember him a little bit. He was so cute. I used to tickle his belly button and he'd laugh." Something akin to a smile brushed her mouth and vanished. "Then he just . . . wasn't there anymore. I remember being sad. Missing him. But it's all kind of vague, you know?"

In as gentle a voice as I could muster, I said, "Who told you that you killed him?"

"Dunno." Another shrug. "I just grew up, like, knowing. Probably my mom told me. I remember one time when I got older, I asked my grandma about it, but she wouldn't tell me shit." She reddened. "Sorry. She said it was something we were never supposed to talk about. Like the whole thing was this deep, dark secret everyone tried to pretend never happened."

"It must have been awful for you. Growing up under that kind of cloud."

Sympathy made her squirm. "Yeah, well. We all got problems, right?" *Crunch*, went the shrunken peppermint. "I just thought, I mean, I catch your show sometimes, and I thought, hey, maybe

11

we can help each other. You figure out did I really do it, and then you get to make an episode out of it." She watched me with the calculating scrutiny of an embezzler who's just discovered a bank error in his favor. "So would I get any money for this?"

I tapped the pen against my notepad and put on a starchy schoolmarm face. "We don't have the budget to pay people who submit ideas to us."

"Oh. Bummer." She brightened. "Maybe I could be one of those whaddya-call-ems, consultants."

"We don't have the budget for that, either." Sympathy was starting to wear thin. "Look, if this is about money—"

"No, no, no." She waved her hands as if flagging down a bus. "It's just I'm a little shy of cash right now. I figure, no harm asking. Right?"

I checked the envelope again. Postmarked September 13. "This note came last month?"

"Uh-huh. What's freakin' me out is, how did they even know my address? I mean, it's gotta be somebody who knew me when I was a kid, right?"

"Or someone your mother or grandmother discussed it with later."

"But how would they know where to send it? See, my mom and grandma don't even know my address."

"Oh." I made a note, like I was a real investigator. "Why's that?"

She studied her manicure, which needed refurbishing. "It's sorta like, they don't bug me; I don't bug them."

Uh-huh. "We'd need to speak with them, if we decide to investigate your story."

"Hey, no prob. It's not like I don't know my mom's address. And Grandma lives with them."

"Them?"

"Her and my stepfather."

"Was your mother married to your stepfather at the time your brother died?"

"Nah. She hooked up with him later."

"Do you think your mother would agree to talk to an interviewer?"

Layla snickered. "Sure. Long as you bring a bunch of TV cameras."

I ransacked my brain for more questions, positive I was forgetting crucial ones that my producer would sneer at me for not asking. "Where were you living when your brother died?"

"Actually, I'm not exactly sure." She fished through her purse. "Shit, I thought I had another mint. Can I smoke in here?"

"This is California. You're lucky you can still smoke outdoors."

"Oh, wait! I found one." She popped the mint in her mouth, tossed the crinkled cellophane on the table. "Mostly all I remember growing up is living in Orange County. But I'm pretty sure there were places before that." She poked the candy into her cheek. "One time I overheard my mom and grandma talking . . ." She rolled her eyes. "Well, yelling, actually, which is how come I could hear. My grandma wanted to go visit some town named Gypsy, and my mom hollered that none of us was ever going back there."

"A town named Gypsy."

"Weird, huh? For a while I thought that meant we were Gypsies. I was still pretty young then."

"Was this town in California?"

"I guess. Though I suppose it could have been somewhere else."

"It's important, Layla. Because if we decide to follow up on this, we'll want to visit the place where your brother died."

She was starting to fidget. "Sorry. I just don't remember that much." Her tone turned defensive. "I mean, I was only a little kid and all."

Ouch.

I asked a few more questions. Layla had no idea where her real father was, his name, even if he were still alive. As far as she knew, she had no other siblings. She produced her mother and grandmother's names, along with an address in Newport Beach. Schultz was her stepfather's last name, but she drew a blank as to what her own had been before he adopted her.

"Do you have a number where I can reach you during the day?"

She recited it.

"Is that a work number?"

"Cell."

"Do you have a regular home phone, too?"

"Nope."

"Work number?"

She stood up with a look that said, "Get real."

Even perched on platforms, she was still a couple inches shorter than I, and I'm barely five-five. She was skinny as a Popsicle stick. When she slung the giant handbag over her shoulder, it nearly toppled her off balance.

"You mind if I keep this letter?"

She waved a hand. "Be my guest. Not like I'll forget what it says."

I swept her candy wrapper off the table and escorted her through the maze of cubicles. Wyatt Productions leases the second floor of a three-story renovated brewery on Main Street in Santa Monica. On warm days the ghostly smell of malt still rises off the old brick walls.

Layla opted to wait for the elevator instead of risking the stairs. Probably worried she'd fall off her shoes and break an ankle.

"I'll be in touch," I said when the elevator dinged its arrival. "After I've done some checking and discussed things with my producer."

She was already fumbling in her purse for a cigarette. As the elevator began to close, I remembered a question I'd forgotten to ask.

I thrust my hands forward to wedge the doors open. "By the way, what was your brother's name?"

That haunted look filtered back into her eyes, overshadowing the impatience for a nicotine fix. "Jake," she said in a small voice that would break your heart.

The doors closed in front of her.

CHAPTER 2

"Checking for gray hairs?"

"If I find any, you're in trouble."

"Me? You're the one about to hit the big four-oh."

"Brat."

Dane gave me a one-arm hug and grabbed his backpack. "Gotta run, Ma. Bullet's giving me a ride."

Out front an engine throbbed with the ominous rumble of a volcano about to erupt. Just to ensure the neighbors couldn't hear themselves think, the car window had been rolled down to disgorge the deafening screech of heavy metal. The horn blasted three times at the decibel level of a locomotive's.

Every dog on the block started barking.

My house is a Craftsman-style bungalow on Ashland Avenue, about half a mile from Santa Monica beach and a short walk from Wyatt Productions. I did not want neighbors organizing petitions to kick Dane and me out of the neighborhood.

"Got your homework? And tell your pal Bullet to stay under the speed limit."

Dane made a sound through his nose. "Right, Ma."

"And please, please, please remind him again to keep the noise down, okay?"

"Uh-huh." Halfway out the door, my seventeen-year-old son slammed on his brakes and peered back at me through the shaggy fringe of jet-black hair dangling in his eyes. The first sixteen and a half years of his life, that hair had been Scandinavian blond. Now it matched every item in his wardrobe. "So, hey, what about that thing Dad invited me to tonight?"

"Dane." The racket at the curb pounded like a migraine. "I thought we settled this. No staying out late on school nights, remember?"

"No, *you* settled it." His jaw shoved forward. "You're still mad 'cause Dad let me get my eyebrow pierced last week."

"One has nothing to do with the other."

"C'mon, Ma, just this once? They're gonna shoot this chase scene, and Dad said Jennifer Love Hewitt's supposed to be there."

Dane's father is Jeff Burdick. Or, as the tabloids gush, the Incredible Hunk. Yes, *that* Jeff Burdick. Star of *Caldwell,* the top-rated action series on television, featuring the ongoing adventures of gonzo-cop-turned-private-eye Stone Caldwell, who in the span of forty-one minutes each week manages to restore justice to the streets of L.A., show up the cops, and whisk the guest starlet into bed.

Our divorce was official seven months ago. A year before that I caught him and that week's guest starlet rehearsing their Method acting.

"Dane, I'm sorry. School comes first. You can watch them film some other time. On a weekend." I smothered a flare-up of resentment. Jeff knew what my rules with Dane were; until a year and a half ago they'd been *our* rules. This wasn't the first time since we'd split that he'd set me up to be the bad guy.

Dane stormed out the door, mumbling just loud enough for me to hear, "Wish I could live with Dad."

As always, the words zinged straight to my heart like a swarm of tiny spears. How on earth had we come to this? How had my sunny little blue-eyed cherub transmogrified into a moody teen who dressed like the Grim Reaper?

The Dodge roared off like a jet aircraft, restoring peace to the neighborhood. Except for the car alarm its vibrations had set off. And the chorus of still-barking dogs.

I sighed and shut the door, catching sight of my reflection in the entryway mirror. Dane's blue eyes stared back at me. Did I look like a mean old mom? Okay, how about a mean mom? Nah. Merely another failed actress. Failed wife. Failed mother. I dragged my fingers down my cheeks, pulling a basset-hound face. Cripes, kiddo, it's just a birthday.

Ten minutes later I was heading for the Mojave Desert—convertible top down, auburn hair whipping in the wind, Beach Boys harmonizing on the radio. Just kidding, except for the Beach Boys part. I drive a four-year-old Explorer, the ultimate soccer-mom-mobile, and hate getting my auburn hair mussed.

After Layla's visit yesterday, I'd scouted up a U.S. road atlas. A painstaking browse through the index had produced nary a town named Gypsy. Three named Gypsum, however: one in Kansas, one in Colorado, one in California. I opted to start with the closest one.

In a town of barely two thousand, a murdered infant would probably stick in the memories of local police. Except it turned out Gypsum, California, didn't have local police. After several phone calls I discovered law-enforcement duties were handled by the sheriff's department, headquartered twenty-five miles away in the county seat of Red Rock.

There, a very unhelpful female records clerk couldn't possibly assist me without a last name or at least a date to search for. Unfortunately, Layla's narrative had been deficient in such details. In desperation I had Lord of the Files check under Schultz. *Nada.*

Which upstanding citizen of Gypsum might remember the alleged tragedy? An Internet search came up empty for town government listings, chamber of commerce, historical society, or even a library. Eureka! A newspaper. When I called, a recording announced they were closed for the day. Question: What kind of newspaper is closed at four on a Tuesday afternoon? Answer: A very small one.

I was about to disconnect when a series of clicks assaulted my ear. "Hello? Hello? Ken Tatum. You there? Sorry, had to come back for something, took me a minute to get the door unlocked."

"Thanks for picking up. Are you the editor?"

He chuckled in a pleasant baritone. "Editor, publisher, reporter, ad salesman and janitor."

"Sounds like I'm talking to the right person, then. I'm trying to find some information about a death that may have occurred in Gypsum fourteen or fifteen years ago. A baby named Jake something. Sorry I don't have a last name. Do you recall any incident like that?"

He was silent so long I thought the line had gone dead. "Who are you?" He cleared his throat. "Why are you asking?"

Bingo.

I explained my interest, without mentioning Layla's visit or the note that had prompted it.

"You mean your show is going to do an episode about Jake?"

"Right now it's merely at the idea stage. I need to find out some more facts first." I switched to a chummier tone designed to inspire confidence-sharing. "You sound like maybe you knew Jake or his family."

"Ah, no. I don't know anything about it."

"But there *was* a local baby named Jake who died about fifteen years ago?"

"Look, I told you, I don't know anything about that. I really have to go now. I'm late for something."

"Mr. Tatum—"

I heard a click.

Well, well, well. Nothing makes an investigator drool like the scent of Someone Stonewalling. Okay, I wasn't a real investigator. But this might be my chance to prove I was more than an errand girl.

The answering machine had informed me the *Gypsum Weekly Miner* opened for business at nine o'clock tomorrow morning. Tatum must keep all the back issues stashed somewhere. What could he do, lock me out of the archives?

Maybe the paper hadn't existed back then. Still, a personal visit seemed worthwhile. If the small town I'd grown up in was any indication, it wouldn't take long to find a resident eager to fill me in on the lurid details.

Half of Wyatt Productions would be gone Wednesday, anyway. Carson Wyatt was flying to Omaha with our producer Danielle and a cameraman to tape some location shots for a segment about a real-estate mogul whose wives mysteriously kept dying off. Normally I would have tagged along to carry all Danielle's crap, run around fetching coffee, and make sure Carson's bald spot was combed over before his on-camera narrative. But Carson was on one of his budget-cutting kicks, so at the last minute I'd been dropped from the entourage.

What better excuse to ditch all the work piled on my desk and head for the high desert, hot on the trail of truth, justice, and possible career advancement?

To cover my butt, I called Mona Wednesday morning and told her I was sick.

The northbound San Diego Freeway oozed at its normal molasses flow. I controlled my blood pressure by chanting a thank-you mantra that I lived within walking distance of work. L.A. commuters waste so much time bogged down in traffic it's no wonder they convert their vehicles into mobile living rooms. While they're stuck, they can chat on the phone, watch TV, download e-mail, or eat breakfast. In the next lane, the driver of a BMW was giving herself a complete makeover in the rearview mirror.

After a sluggish crawl through Sepulveda Pass, traffic cleared. Finally, a sign directed Gypsum-bound travelers to a long, desolate stretch of two-lane highway.

From road to both horizons, stubbly clumps of army-green vegetation dotted the sand-and-gravel landscape, bearding distant low-lying mountains with five o'clock shadow. An occasional yellow-flowered shrub relieved the drab two-tone color scheme. Spiky yucca plants jabbed Tinkertoy arms toward the cloudless sky, and every so often a desiccated tumbleweed blew across the road.

About ten miles in I passed a settlement of decrepit mobile homes hunkered in a circle like covered wagons, shaded by only a thicket of satellite dishes and a few dead trees some hopeful soul had planted. A faded hand-painted sign next to the turnoff read "Desert Acres." Appropriate.

The arrow-straight asphalt dipped gently up and down, up and down across the terrain. I didn't have to worry about passing any slowpokes. No fastpokes loomed in my rearview mirror, either. Every four or five minutes a vehicle whooshed by in the opposite direction. Half the trickle consisted of big rigs towing pairs of gleaming silver tankers. Each time sunlight ricocheted off one, it hit my retinas like a flashbulb explosion.

Even out here in the middle of nowhere, campaign signs for next month's election sprouted from the rocky soil. Going after the scorpion vote, apparently. Vote Ackerman for County Supervisor! Reelect Sheriff Duane Salazar! Gwen Isaacs for School Board!

Twenty miles out the topography perked up. The road began to weave and climb through khaki-colored hills rutted with dirt bike and ATV trails. Apparently a popular weekend spot for urban road warriors to work off all that excess testosterone.

The final few miles were steep and narrow, riddled with hairpin curves. I had a hazy recollection the San Andreas Fault sheared through this part of the Mojave. Tectonic forces had patched together a crazy-quilt of multicolored rock formations, contorting them into dizzying cliffs and jutting promontories, and I had to close my eyes a couple times.

The town of Gypsum huddled in a kind of craggy amphitheater, streets laid out with no obvious relationship to right-angle geometry. The main drag boasted a three-block downtown, though really it was nothing to boast about. A third of the windows were boarded over, another third completely screened by dust, and someone needed to tip off the civic improvement association about the importance of anti-litter campaigns. Most of the buildings were one-story, probably lacking the structural support for a second one.

Hardware store . . . five-and-dime . . . shoe store . . . diner . . . video rental . . . gas station . . . another hardware store . . . aha! Newspaper office.

Street parking was head-in, and none of those fancy painted lines, either. I nosed up to the curb before it hit me: I should have parked down the block so Ken Tatum wouldn't bolt the door if he happened to glance out his relatively dust-free window. According to the dashboard clock, I was two hours and seven minutes from home.

The air was dry and surprisingly cold for a bright October day. Of course, the gale-force wind that egg-beatered my hair and blinded me with dust probably contributed to the chill factor. Unfortunately, I'd worn a skirt, and all the regulars hunched over coffee at Carmen's Café were getting a free peek at my undies.

Mustering as much dignity as possible while slapping my clothes down, I hauled open the glass door. A bell jangled overhead. Inside it was blessedly wind-free. "Be right with you," called a voice I recognized.

"Okay, thanks." The top half of the front room was painted Bargain Closeout green, the bottom covered in cheap fake-wood paneling. A desk the size of an aircraft carrier took up half the floor space, with a computer workstation angled next to it. Some kind of desktop publishing program filled the screen. A row of short metal file cabinets squatted along one wall, next to some mismatched bookcases.

The smell of ink rose from bundles of fresh-printed news-papers stacked on the cracked linoleum. I attempted to rake my hair back in place while I checked out the community bulletin board nailed inside the entrance. Church rummage sale, lost cat, Tupperware party, Lions Club meeting, bingo game. The shoe store was having a sale This Week Only. Oops, too late. The notice was dated July.

"You won't wanna miss that spaghetti feed for the volunteer fire department."

I turned to see a guy in a wheelchair propelling himself through the doorway in back. He winked. "High-school band's gonna put on its first performance of the year. They've been rehearsing *Louie Louie* all week."

"Sorry I can't make it." I pitched my voice higher than usual. "High school? In a town this size?"

"Not any more. Grade school only. High-school kids get bussed over to Red Rock."

Ken Tatum was in his early forties, short brown hair, close-trimmed beard, and mustache flecked with gray. Tan chinos with loafers, navy-blue turtleneck shirt. He rolled to a stop beside his desk. "How can I help you?" His upper body was built like a weightlifter's.

"I need to do a little research, and I was wondering if you keep back issues of the paper."

"Sure do. Don't have them on microfiche or anything,

though. C'mon, I'll show you." He spun around and headed toward the back.

"I'm not exactly sure which year I need. Somewhere between 1993 and '95." I followed him down a short hallway into a cramped storage room. This was going to be easier than I'd thought. "Where's all your printing equipment?"

"Paper's printed over in Red Rock. Guy over there can do it cheaper than I can." Rough plank shelving filled the lower portion of three walls. The shelves were stacked with covered plastic bins, each labeled with a year taped to the end. Tatum slid one out and handed it to me. "You can sit at that table. Put the bin back when you're through. And please do me a huge favor and keep the issues in order, okay?"

"Thanks." The hand-printed paper label read 1994. "Is it okay if I help myself? I may need to look at 1993 or 1995."

He shook his head. "No."

"But—"

"That's the year you want."

"But how—oh." I summoned a lopsided smile. "You recognized my voice."

"Yeah. You can stop with the Muppet imitation."

My shoulders slumped. "I was going for Marilyn Monroe."

"More like Miss Piggy."

"Okay, we even now?"

"Sure." He wheeled around to leave.

"Wait a sec." I set the bin on the round Formica table. "How come you're being so helpful all of a sudden, when yesterday you practically hung up on me?"

He rasped knuckles along his jaw. "If you're determined enough to drive all the way out here, then I can hardly stop you. You're going to dig up a bunch of gossip and speculation whether I help you or not." He shrugged. "Might as well get the facts straight."

"What if the facts aren't straight? What if this child's death didn't actually happen the way people believe?"

"C'mon, this is real life, not TV. You're wasting your time." He shook his head. "It was an awful thing, a shock to the whole community. What's the point of stirring it up after so long? It's not going to change anything."

But it might change everything for a small girl accused of a terrible crime. Who'd grown up haunted by guilt and grief, assailed by angry whispers and furtive glances and dark secrets. A girl who'd become a young woman with no one to love because she didn't love herself. Who'd thrown away her life as if it were worthless because that's how she felt: worthless. Because she thought she deserved all the bad things that happened to her.

Wow, great intro. Gotta remember to write it down.

"August," Tatum said over his shoulder as he left the room. "That's the month you're looking for."

CHAPTER 3

No infant deaths reported on any August front pages. Back to week one, and no rushing this time.

The masthead named Frank Tatum as publisher/editor back in '94. Wild guess: Ken's father. Each issue ran to twenty or so tabloid-size pages. I scanned the columns like a bit player hoping to spot my name in a movie review.

A hefty chunk of layout was devoted to display ads. A lost cause, alas, for those businesses that were now boarded-up storefronts. Carmen's Café had survived—probably serving the same blue-plate specials advertised back in '94. The shoe store was still selling footwear, but I was pretty sure the bowling alley was defunct. The movie theater was showing *Beverly Hills Cop 3* and *Revenge of the Nerds 4*. God save us from sequels. Other entertainment choices included the final week of a tent revival meeting, Casino Night at the Lions Club, and a square dance put on every Saturday by a group called the Miner Belles.

A nearby gypsum mine served as bedrock of the local economy, judging from the number of column-inches devoted to its activities, which accounted for all those trucks on the road, hauling off crushed rock to be turned into wallboard, plaster, or portland cement. It also explained the fine layer of white powder that dusted the whole town like sifted flour.

I found what I was looking for on August twenty-sixth, halfway down the left side of page three, next to the school-bus schedule. Nine-month-old Jacob Gormley, son of Mr. and Mrs.

Curtis Gormley, had died suddenly of unknown causes last Saturday. That's not a recap; that's the entire article.

Well, no one could accuse the *Miner* of sensationalizing a family's private tragedy. I checked the first week of September. The follow-up story made it to page two but was no more informative. The Fremont County district attorney had announced no charges would be filed in the death of baby Jacob. I grabbed my hair and pulled. Charges of what? Against whom?

I went back and flipped through the rest of the August issue. Jake's obituary was buried in a batch on page six. Other recently departed had all attained their Social Security years. Jake's survivors included parents Curtis and Amberlee Gormley, sister Layla Gormley, grandmother Dolores Pombo. A private family service had already been held at the True Holiness Church in Gypsum. Congregation sounded pretty sure of itself.

Seeing Layla's name in print sent a little ping of excitement through me. So far everything she'd told me had checked out. If the anonymous note writer had told the truth, this could develop into a crackerjack story.

I scratched a few notes, carefully re-stacked the newspapers, and tucked the bin back into place. Ken Tatum was gazing into cyberspace when I came out. "Find what you were looking for?" he asked.

"Uh-huh. Little shy on details, though."

He turned from his computer screen. "Well, we're not exactly the *New York Times.*"

"How about filling me in?" I dusted off the chair next to his desk and plopped myself onto it. "Or do I have to track down the biggest gossip in town? I bet Carmen across the street knows plenty."

"Got that right. Look, there's not much to tell."

I'd brought a tape recorder in my purse but decided not to push it. "How well did you know the Gormleys?"

27

"Not well." He plucked a thread on his sleeve. "Just in the sense everyone knows everyone in a town this size. Amberlee was in my class when we were kids. Through grade school, anyway."

"Then what?"

"Oh . . ." He rolled his eyes. "Her dad ran out on her and her mom. Dolores tried to hush it up. Big churchgoer and all that. She was so humiliated, she took Amberlee and moved away, then came back a few months later and told everyone her husband had died. By that time, Amberlee was so far behind in school she had to repeat fifth grade."

"Let me see if I've got these people straight." I consulted my notes. "Dolores is Amberlee's mother, so Amberlee's maiden name was Pombo?"

"Yep."

"And she was married to Curtis Gormley. And Amberlee's remarried now. Was she divorced? Widowed?"

"She and Curtis split up not long after the baby died."

"Was Curtis also Layla's father?"

"Close enough." He scratched his beard.

"Which means?"

"He raised her like she was his."

"Who's Layla's biological father, then?"

He shrugged. "Have to ask Amberlee. I never considered it any of my business."

"And you a card-carrying member of the news media. Shame on you."

Tatum grinned in spite of himself.

"Does Curtis still live in town?"

"Nope."

"Any idea where he moved to?"

"Place called Desert Acres."

I glanced up. "You mean that rundown bunch of mobile

homes just off the road?"

His eyes twinkled. "That's it."

"People actually live there?"

"People who can't afford better, yeah."

"Curtis is down on his luck these days?"

"Curtis makes his own bad luck. You want to persuade him to talk, just bring along a couple six-packs. And don't waste your money on microbrews."

"Thanks for the tip." I felt a little squeamish asking the next question. "How, uh, how did the baby die?"

Tatum gave me a sharp look. "You don't know?"

I shook my head.

"He was smothered."

I flinched. Every maternal cell in my body shrieked in dismay. "An accident? Murder?"

His gaze drifted to the computer screen. "No one was ever charged with anything."

"Could it have been crib death?"

"Not how I heard it."

"How did you hear it?" I hunched forward. "Look, I've got a source who says the sister was accused of killing him." A source. Like I was guarding the identity of Deep Throat. "Is that true?"

He shook his head. "Why don't you leave it alone?"

"Because she may have been falsely accused, that's why. And if so, the truth needs to come out."

Tatum stared. "What are you talking about?"

I'd already said too much. This guy was a reporter, after all. "Did the authorities conclude that Layla killed her brother?"

Impatient sigh. "That's what they said, yes."

"Based on what evidence?"

"Evidence?"

"What made investigators decide Layla had done it?"

Ken Tatum drummed his fingers on the wheels of his chair.

29

"Amberlee."

"The mother?"

"She caught Layla holding a pillow over his face."

The house where Jake Gormley had died stood empty. At least, I assumed the plywood nailed over the front window was a sign of vacancy and not a design choice to complement the peeling yellow paint, sagging front steps, and missing roof shingles. The architecture was basic 1960s Crackerbox, long and narrow, narrow end facing the street. One story, two or three small bedrooms, a carport tacked onto one side. Prickly-looking scrub grass had taken over whatever lawn had once graced the front.

Ken Tatum had given me the address. I walked down the driveway to the first non-barricaded window, rubbed off a circle of dust, cupped hands around my face to peer in. A bedroom, empty except for the trash strewn everywhere. Stained shag carpet, missing closet doors, couple of fist-sized craters punched in the drywall. I worked my way around the house. Other rooms I could see were in similar shape. Looked like someone had built a campfire in the middle of the kitchen floor. Cozy.

The homes on either side were of like style but better maintained, with curtains in the windows and potted cacti bracketing the front steps. Both owners had been foresighted enough to opt for vinyl siding.

I picked the house on the right, walked up and knocked. The wind carried not-too-distant sounds of the mine—trucks backing up, bulldozers shoving rocks around. My hand was poised for a second knock when I heard, "Yoo-hoo!"

A middle-aged woman stood in the driveway on the other side of the former Gormley residence, cotton-print dress whipping around her skinny legs. She made a megaphone of her hands. "They're not there."

Less than three minutes and she'd already spotted me. Just

the neighbor I wanted to talk to.

"Still up north," she called as I picked my way down the uneven sidewalk. "Usually they don't come back till after New Year's so they can spend the holidays with their kids."

"Actually, I—"

"Lord knows how much longer they can keep trucking back and forth. Down here for the winter, back up to Wisconsin soon as all the snow melts, which usually isn't till June." She hugged her bare arms around her middle. "Ned's pretty decrepit now with that arthritis and his bad heart, and Marge, bless her, is hardly any spring chicken either. Whenever I talk to her, I thank my lucky stars my boys have stayed right here, never moved someplace far off like that. My daughter, she's in L.A., but that's hardly the end of the earth, is it? 'Course, she doesn't come home to see us as much as she used to, now that she's got Tom and the kids."

I managed to slip my name in.

"Real nice to meet you. I'm Noreen Fontana." Somewhere in her fifties, short gray hair still threaded with a few dark strands. Sun, wind, and dry climate had tanned her narrow face the texture of leather. Big plastic-rimmed glasses gave her the sharp-eyed, slightly predatory look of an owl.

"You've lived here a long time, sounds like."

"Heavens, yes. Dean and me, we moved here right after we got married. He found a job out at the mine, and we bought this little house. Then the kids came along. Dean, he always promised we'd get a bigger house someday, only then he went and got killed in that mine accident. It was all I could do to support three kids."

I inserted a few sympathetic murmurs.

"This single-mom stuff they talk about now, like it's something new. Ha! That piddlin' life-insurance money sure didn't last long, lemme tell you. Had to get myself two jobs, but

31

my kids never went hungry a day in their life, no sirree. All turned out just fine, too. I told you about my daughter, she's the youngest. Justin, he's the middle one; he even graduated from college!"

Noreen's mailbox had a wooden whirligig nailed to it. The wind spun a red-and-white propeller that made a painted chicken peck its head up and down, up and down, over and over. Endlessly. A monotonous peck, peck, peck.

"But he moved back here and got a real good job out at Edwards Air Force Base," Noreen continued. "Something with computers. Married a nice gal, Brittany, from right here in town. My oldest, Travis, he was kinda sweet on her himself when they were kids, but he wound up marrying a girl from Red Rock. Allison, her name was. Poor thing. Died in a car wreck about six years ago, so Travis has to raise their little boy all by himself."

The second she paused for another breath I said, "You must remember the Gormleys, seeing how you've lived here so long."

"My, yes. 'Course, it's been ages since they lived next door. Just look at that place now!" She clicked her tongue. "Owner gave up trying to rent it years ago. Then a bunch of squatters broke in—drug addicts, by the looks of 'em. I called the sheriff soon as I noticed, but by the time the deputies showed up to roust 'em, they'd made a horrible mess."

"Were the Gormleys tenants?"

"Oh, sure. They never could have got money together to buy their own place, not with the way . . . well, they just couldn't."

"Do you know the owner's name and where I can reach him?" We'd need his permission to film inside.

"Lives in Palmdale. Why? You interested in renting the place?" She cackled.

I smiled back. "Why'd the owner have so much trouble renting it?"

"I guess nowadays this town just has more houses than it needs." She slid a furtive glance from side to side. "Plus, because of what happened." Her voice hushed. "Inside that house."

"You mean the baby who died?"

She reared back like she'd spotted a rattlesnake. "Now, how on earth do you know about that? Oh, wait. Ned and Marge must've told you, right?"

"Are you familiar with a TV show called *Cold Case Chronicles*?"

"Why, you bet. I watch all those true-crime shows. Just love 'em."

"Wonderful! I'm an associate producer with the show, and I'm here in town exploring the possibility of an episode about Jake Gormley's death."

"About Jake?" Her eyes widened. "You mean about . . . what happened?"

"About how he really died. Some questions have surfaced recently about whether his sister Layla was actually responsible."

"Questions?" Noreen nibbled a hangnail.

"Layla may have been falsely accused. Someone else might have done it."

"Who?"

I spread my hands. "We don't know. Which is why I'd like to ask you some questions, if you don't mind."

"Me? Heavens, I don't know anything."

"You knew the Gormleys, didn't you?"

"Well, yes, but—"

"What was Amberlee like?"

"Oh . . ." She studied the sky for answers. "Nice enough, I guess."

"That's kind of a lukewarm endorsement." I smiled.

Noreen thought hard. "She was pretty."

"Was she a good mother?"

Lips crimped. "I'm not one to judge."

"Come on." I produced what I hoped was a stern yet coaxing expression. "You're obviously a devoted mother yourself. How do you think Amberlee measured up?"

Noreen studied her hangnail. "Did her best, I'm sure. Considering all she had to cope with."

"Like what?"

Noreen's eyes flashed. "Like that husband of hers, for one thing."

Finally, we were getting somewhere.

"Gee, I heard he was a loving husband and father."

"That bum?" She snorted. "I don't know who you've been talking to, but they obviously didn't live next door to Curtis Gormley for five years."

This was like pull-starting my cantankerous lawnmower. Had to keep yanking the starter cord. Each time the motor would rev a little longer before conking out. If I just kept cranking, eventually it would finally catch and off she'd go.

"That's funny," I said. "The impression I had was that Curtis was a real family man, very responsible, a good neighbor. Steady. Someone you could count on."

"I never heard such . . . someone you could count on to cause trouble, maybe. The man belonged in jail. You should've heard what I had to listen to all those years, him whaling on her."

"You're saying he hit Amberlee?"

"Hit her, shoved her, dragged her around by that long hair of hers." Noreen pointed, and flabby underarm flesh quivered with indignation. "Her own mother lived right over there. You should've heard the things she told me went on! Curl your toenails, they would."

I looked around and saw another boarded-up house. "Dolores lived across the street?"

"Moved there to be close to her daughter. Only then she had

to put up with him, too."

"Did Curtis ever abuse the kids?"

Noreen moved her mouth as if tasting something bad. "Not that I ever heard of." Reluctant to admit it. "He was a no-good drunk, though. Couldn't keep a steady job if his life depended on it. And he was mean as a snake. Even got Travis sent to juvey hall once."

"Juvenile hall? Your son?"

"That horrible Curtis turned him into the sheriff! Just for borrowing some old clunker of his and taking it for a little joy ride. Boys'll be boys, won't they? Travis didn't hurt that car any. But Curtis came storming over here, threatening him. Why, I finally had to call the sheriff. Only then what happens? It's Travis who gets locked up for three days while Curtis gets off with a warning!"

"Doesn't sound fair," I murmured. "Was Curtis home when the baby died?"

The abrupt gear switch threw her. "What? Oh. Yup, he was home. 'Cause he'd gotten fired from his job, that's why. Showed up drunk as a skunk in the middle of the afternoon."

"I'll bet you heard everything that happened next door that day."

"Mmm." She gave the Gormley house a dubious glance.

"When did you first notice something was wrong?"

She lifted a bony shoulder. "Hard to say, exactly. I heard a bunch of screamin' and carryin' on, but I didn't pay it much notice. Amberlee got home right after he did, and I figured he was knockin' her around like usual. When the paramedics pulled up, I thought, boy, he must've really done a number on her this time. It was Dolores who came over and told me what happened, right after they took the poor baby away."

"Amberlee had gone somewhere that day?"

"Shopping over in Red Rock's what I remember."

"Where were the children?"

She tilted her head toward the Gormley house. "Sitter was there watching them."

"Dolores?"

"No. It was Saturday, I think. She probably had bingo that afternoon."

I stuffed all these bits and pieces into my memory. I should have taped or written them down but was afraid of spooking Noreen. "How did Layla, the little girl, usually act toward her brother?"

Noreen took off her glasses and wiped them. "Fine, far as I could see."

"Ever notice any signs she might be jealous of him?"

"Nope."

"What was your reaction when you heard she'd killed him?"

A shadow crossed her face. "Sad," she said. "I was real sad."

"Were you surprised?"

She stuck her glasses back on. "Shocked, more like."

"You must have thought about it a lot afterwards." I gave a just-between-us wink. "What do you think really happened, Noreen?"

She peered down her beaky nose at me. "I really couldn't say," she said with a sniff. "I'm not one to gossip."

CHAPTER 4

"Beat it!" yelled a voice inside the trailer. "I told you, I don't have your fuckin' money yet, okay?"

I rapped again on the screen door's pitted aluminum frame. "Mr. Gormley, my name's Harmony Magnussen. I'm not here about money."

The trailer door cracked open six inches. "Whaddaya want, then?"

"To talk. About when you lived in Gypsum."

"Huh?" He opened the door wider, brought his unshaven face up to the torn screen. "Whaddaya wanna talk about that for?"

He was a big hulk of a guy with bleary eyes, bad teeth, and breath that would stop a charging rhino. Mid-forties or thereabouts, with thinning, mud-colored hair.

"First, please let me tell you how sorry I am about Jake."

"Jake? Huh?"

Tendrils of odor wafted from the trailer to curl beneath my nose—spilled beer, week-old garbage, unwashed underwear. "I'm trying to find out more about how Jake died."

"Wha-a-a?"

I tried breathing through my mouth. "This must seem pretty bizarre, a total stranger showing up to ask questions about your son's death, but—"

He slammed the door in my face.

One lesson struggling to be an actor taught me: Might as well quit if you're not willing to be a pest. I banged on the screen again. "Mr. Gormley, I'm sorry. I realize this must be a difficult subject—"

"Am-scray!" he hollered. "I ain't talkin' to you 'bout any of that. Now get the hell outta here!"

Grief? Guilt? General orneriness?

The rest of the Desert Acres population had been eyeballing me through their filthy windows ever since I'd rousted one to inquire which mobile home was Gormley's. I scuttled past them on my way back to the Explorer.

Should have taken Ken Tatum's advice about the beer.

The Fremont County Public Safety Center was a modern two-story complex constructed from blocks of the town's fabled red rock. Jail in one wing, sheriff's department in the other. Sprinklers were showering the broad front lawn, a lush expanse the color of a pool table.

Inside, I climbed a flight of steps to the Investigations Unit, where a uniformed deputy with red hair and freckles sat manning the front desk. He looked like Opie playing dress-up.

"Hi, I'd like to speak with whoever was in charge of a case back in '94, involving a baby who died over in Gypsum. The baby's name was Gormley, Jacob Gormley."

The deputy took a bite of cheeseburger. He chewed while he studied me, as if memorizing my description for a Wanted poster. My stomach grumbled to remind me it was long past lunchtime.

Opie finally swallowed, dabbed a paper napkin across his lame attempt at a mustache. "You gotta go downstairs to the Records Unit, get the investigator's name from the case file."

The records clerk and I hadn't exactly ended yesterday's phone conversation on friendly terms. "Would it be possible for you to call and ask them to look it up?"

"Sure." He answered with his mouth full. "Soon as I finish filing all this stuff." His desk was as swamped with paperwork as mine.

Half the dozen desks behind him were occupied. Four men, a couple women, a mix of uniforms and street clothes. No one bothered to look up after I first walked in. While I stood there debating if flirting, crying, or scolding would be more effective with this kid, a beefy guy with a badge pinned to his tan uniform strode in behind me. He breezed through the thigh-high security gate like Marshal Dillon shoving into a saloon.

"Maybe one of the other deputies would remember who handled the investigation." I opted for wheedling. "A baby getting killed is the kind of case a lot of people wouldn't forget."

Marshal Dillon paused in the doorway of his glass-enclosed office.

I bit my lip, clasped my hands, hamming up the damsel-in-distress act. "Would you mind asking around, seeing if anyone here knows who handled Jacob Gormley's death?"

The cheerful gleam in Opie's eye warned me he was about to refuse.

"That was me," said Dillon. He retraced his steps and stuck out a paw. "Duane Salazar."

It took a second to realize why his name sounded familiar; I'd seen it plastered all over the county on election posters. To be more precise, reelection posters.

"Nice to meet you, Sheriff." I introduced myself.

He gripped me in a longer-than-necessary politico's handshake and gazed deep into my eyes, as if my personal concerns were his top priority. "Come on to the back; we'll talk. Get you some coffee or anything?"

And here I was beginning to think local law enforcement was uncooperative. I resisted the urge to stick out my tongue at Opie.

I declined coffee but accepted Salazar's offer of a chair. He closed his office door and settled meaty hindquarters on the edge of his desk. "How can I help you, Ms. Magnussen?" Giving himself a height advantage that forced me to gaze up from a supplicant's position.

I explained my purpose without mentioning Layla's note. Silence followed.

"Now, why on God's green earth would you be interested in that ancient history?" Salazar dragged two fingers along the edges of a flourishing gray mustache. "Not that it wasn't a tragedy, of course, but I can't think what would interest Hollywood. Whole business was pretty open-and-shut."

"You handled the investigation personally?"

"Uh-huh. Back when I was still a deputy, years before I ran for sheriff. Had to wait for old Bart Kowalski to retire before I stood a chance taking over his job."

If you counted crow's-feet like tree rings, Salazar must have been thirty, thirty-five when he'd responded to Jake Gormley's death. Hardly a greenhorn recruit who might have botched his first investigation.

"I'm interested in your impression of the case," I said. "Stuff you didn't put into the official report. Do you think the sister really did it? Or could Mom have been covering up for someone else?"

"Someone like who?"

"Well, the husband, for instance. Curtis Gormley. He had a violent temper; he was home when the baby died. Drunk, just fired from his job. Maybe Jake wouldn't stop crying, and Curtis snapped. Then Amberlee tried to protect him by pointing the finger at Layla, knowing the legal consequences for a five-year-old weren't likely to be severe."

Salazar lifted bushy eyebrows. "You think a mother would lie to protect the man who'd just killed her child?"

Odd question for a cop with at least twenty years' experience under his belt. Twenty years of witnessing all the unspeakable behavior human beings inflict on each other.

"Women trapped in abusive marriages frequently do stupid things to protect their abusers," I pointed out. "They've often been brainwashed into complete dependence—emotional, psychological, financial. Who's going to support the family if Hubby gets hauled off to jail?" I shook my head. "This isn't anything you don't already know."

Salazar grazed a palm over his crew cut. "All I can tell you is what the mother said. She came into the bedroom and saw the girl standing on a chair, holding a pillow over her baby brother's face."

I winced. "Did you believe her? Did anyone else back her up? Was there any forensic evidence that contradicted her story? What did the autopsy show?"

"Whoa, whoa, whoa." He patted the air with his big hands. "Where'd you get this idea there was something wrong with the investigation?"

"I'm not saying anything was wrong with it," I said, backtracking quickly. Salazar wouldn't appreciate any rumored shortcomings with past cases surfacing just before Election Day.

"You must have suspected who really did it," I continued. "You can probably tell when people are lying, even if you can't prove it. What did your cop instincts say?" When all else fails, try flattery.

"Look, the little girl as much as confessed."

I pretended not to be startled. "What do you mean?"

"When I got there, the kid was half-hysterical. Kept saying things like 'I'm sorry' and 'I didn't want him to die' over and over."

"As if it had been an accident?"

"Yeah." Eyes like ball bearings.

41

"Did you ask her straight out if she'd put the pillow over his face?"

"I told you; she was hysterical. No way to get a straight answer out of her."

"What about later?"

"There was no later. I was satisfied; the coroner was satisfied; the D.A. was satisfied. We had an eyewitness who saw her do it, and no way to prove otherwise. Long as Mom stuck to her story, that was it. Case closed. What are you gonna do with a five-year-old, send her to juvenile hall till she's eighteen? She'd get eaten alive there. Which is why the D.A. chose not to prosecute."

I thanked the sheriff for his time. He escorted me to the hallway, as if to make sure I left the premises. On my way out I dazzled Opie with a smile to make him think I'd successfully pumped his boss for all the information I needed.

I made a pit stop in the ladies' john, then trotted downstairs to find the Records Unit. The clerk behind the counter had the same bitchy voice as the woman who'd been so unhelpful on the phone yesterday. In person she was a dead ringer for Eleanor Harrigan, my tenth-grade English teacher, who we all called Mrs. Harridan behind her back. Excuse me, *whom* we all called.

I gave her the name and date to look up. She eyed me suspiciously over half-height glasses before disappearing into rows of floor-to-ceiling metal shelves jammed with file folders and cardboard storage boxes.

Thirty seconds later she emerged. "Sorry. The file you requested isn't there."

"You mean, it's missing?"

Her glance slipped sideways. "All I know is that it isn't on the shelf where it belongs." Not that she'd spent much time searching for it.

"Could it have been misfiled?"

That slanderous suggestion earned me the evil eye.

"Did someone check it out? You must have a system to record who borrows stuff."

She wasn't very good at lying. "I'm sorry. I can't help you."

I didn't believe either claim. Then a lawyer type in a suit walked in, giving her an excuse to ignore me. With him, she turned into Miss Personable. After a few minutes of listening to them chat about mutual acquaintances over at the courthouse, I muttered a few impolite words and left.

I hit the fast-food strip in search of a cheeseburger, and it wasn't hard to come by. At Burger Bonanza I bought a Red Rock newspaper from the outside rack and tried not to drip ketchup on it while I ate. Lot of articles about the upcoming election—candidate profiles, analyses of local issues, accusations of skullduggery hurled by opposing sides in a typical pre-election mud-fest.

Page two contained a passing reference to the scandal involving the sheriff's department. For several seconds I forgot to chew. The tail end of the article provided details. Last summer, one of Salazar's deputies had been caught playing hanky-panky with a female inmate he was supposed to be guarding. Once this sensation hit the headlines, eight former female guests of the Fremont County Jail (accompanied by their newly hired attorneys) had come forward with similar tales, all swearing they'd been intimidated into submission.

The deputy had been suspended without pay while awaiting trial; the county faced huge embarrassing lawsuits. Very bad press for the sheriff's department, especially after an audit earlier this year had exposed additional hanky-panky—financial this time—within the department's upper ranks.

Conclusion? Sheriff Salazar was battling a tough reelection campaign. Suspicion: He'd phoned Records as soon as I left his office and ordered the clerk to "lose" the Gormley file.

What was he worried I'd see? Or was the problem what I wouldn't see? Sounded like then-Deputy Salazar hadn't exactly been a relentless bloodhound in dogged pursuit of the truth. If it turned out a little girl had been falsely accused, that someone else had gotten away with killing an infant for fourteen years, Salazar sure wouldn't want it to come out right before the election. Especially on nationwide TV.

I slurped the last straw-full of Diet Coke and wondered who else might have a copy of the case file. The coroner? Rats. In this county the sheriff also served as coroner. What about the pathologist who'd performed the autopsy? His report would have been included in the file; maybe he'd kept a copy. Trouble was, how would I get his name except from the report?

If paramedics had taken Jake to the emergency room, the hospital might have records. And I could hear the hoots of laughter when I showed up asking to see them without a subpoena.

Any other possibilities?

I called Information from my cell phone and got Noreen Fontana's number. She answered, but sounded as if she wished she hadn't.

"Do you by any chance remember the name of the Gormleys' pediatrician?" I asked.

"Pediatrician?"

"The children's doctor. All kids get sick, right? Even the healthy ones need vaccinations. Who did Amberlee take her kids to?"

"Well, that would have been Doc Atwood. But he saw adults, too, not just kids."

"Does he still have a practice in Gypsum?"

"Heavens, no. He's semi-retired now. See, there used to be a medical clinic here that was open one day a week. Doc would drive out from Red Rock, but it just got to be too much for him, bless his soul. He must be well into his seventies by now."

"Does he still have an office in Red Rock?"

"Oh, sure. A few people from here, that's who they still go to. 'Course, lot of 'em nowadays want some young doctor fresh out of medical school with all the latest theories and fancy equipment."

"What's Dr. Atwood's first name?"

"Norm. Well, Norman, I suppose." She sighed. "He sure always felt bad about that Gormley baby."

"Because he couldn't save him? Was Dr. Atwood at the house that day?"

"No, no. Wasn't one of his clinic days, so he wouldn't have been in town. That's not what I meant, anyway. I meant he always felt bad while the baby was alive."

I frowned. "Why was that?"

She paused, as if making an incredulous face at the phone. "Why, because of the baby's condition, that's why."

"Condition?"

"Yes! That whatchamacallit, spinal—no, wait, that's not right."

"The baby had something wrong with his spine?"

"Yes! Born that way, poor little thing. One of those congenial defects."

"Congenital? What was wrong?"

"I told you, his spine." She lowered her voice to ghost-story timbre. "It was partly outside, you see. That's how he came out of his mama's womb, and no way to fix it, either. Oh, it makes me shudder just to think of it."

"Spina bifida?" I repressed a shudder myself. "Jake Gormley was born with spina bifida?"

"Why, yes," Noreen answered. "Isn't that what I just said?"

45

CHAPTER 5

"The tissue around the spinal cord of the developing fetus doesn't close properly." Dr. Norman Atwood had invited me right over when I'd called his office. The shaky hands clutching his teacup might explain the absence of patients in his waiting room. "The spinal canal remains open along several vertebrae, most commonly in the lower back. So the membranes and spinal cord protrude at birth in a kind of sac. Naturally, with tissues and nerves exposed this way, the baby is at high risk of life-threatening infection."

For someone who faints at the sight of blood, I was bearing up pretty well. My son Dane's periodic childhood trips to the emergency room usually ended with me on a gurney next to his. I gulped some peppermint tea to combat my wooziness. Atwood's receptionist had brought it for us, seeming glad for something to do.

Atwood's practice occupied the front half of a nondescript ranch home in a Red Rock neighborhood that had seen better days. The doctor lived in back. His office walls displayed a framed collection of yellowing degrees and faded posters diagramming regions of human anatomy I'd have preferred to remain ignorant of. No photos of spouses, kids or dogs. A coffee mug on the corner of his desk was crammed with fancy pens advertising expensive drugs. The light perfume of rubbing alcohol hung in the air.

"How do you cure spina bifida?" I asked.

"You don't," he replied with the kindly condescension of someone born in the era before antibiotics, before heart transplants, before laser wielding surgical robots—when a minor cut could kill you and cancer was a death sentence.

"Spina bifida is a lifelong condition." Atwood's cup rattled as he set it on the saucer. "Immediately after birth, a surgeon places the spinal cord and exposed tissue back into the body, then covers the opening with muscle and skin. But the neurological damage has already been done. Partial or total paralysis below the sac, loss of bladder and bowel control, seizures, hydrocephalus, a host of other ongoing medical problems."

"How would you describe Jake Gormley's condition?"

"Well, now, I can't go into specifics." He rested one veined hand on top of the other. "Confidentiality and all. But I suppose I might say that his case was fairly typical."

Atwood could have played Dr. Marcus Welby's father, with his shock of white hair, horn-rimmed glasses, stethoscope dangling from his neck. Any minute now he'd offer me a lollipop from the pocket of his white coat.

"Hydrocephalus." I fudged the spelling. "Is that something like water on the brain?"

Atwood nodded. "In a majority of spina bifida patients, fluid accumulates in the brain. A shunt, or tube, has to be surgically inserted to drain the fluid. Usually into the abdomen."

My imagination detoured around the image. "Did Jake have a shunt?"

"Now you're asking me to be specific again." He winked. "As I say, Jake was typical. And shunts typically have a high rate of infection and malfunction. In many cases, they have to be replaced, sometimes more than once."

I made another note. "If Jake had lived, what would his life have been like?"

"One can only speculate, of course." Atwood's chair creaked as he leaned back. He tented his knobby fingers. "Jake would have needed at least braces or crutches to walk, probably a wheelchair."

"Could he have gone to school?"

"Most likely. Many spina bifida patients have normal intelligence. Jake never showed any sign of retardation that I observed, though of course he was still quite young. Oops!" He reached for his tea. "I believe our conversation is straying across that patient-privacy line."

The cup began its perilous ascent toward his mouth. "A great many spina bifida kids do have learning disabilities, however. Language and reading comprehension, trouble doing math, difficulty paying attention." Clearly the doctor enjoyed having an audience. "Many also develop social and emotional problems, including depression. They need lots of special help."

"Pretty overwhelming for the parents."

"Absolutely. A devastating misfortune."

"How did Jake's parents handle it?"

Atwood gave me a shrewd look over the rim of his cup. "Wondering whether one of them put that pillow over his face, are you?"

So much for beating around the bush. "Do you think that's a possibility?"

He furrowed his brow. "I must admit, the thought did occur to me. Not that I have one scrap of evidence."

"What did you think when you heard the mother said she saw Layla do it?"

"The little girl? Oh, she was a charmer. Bright as a button." He gazed into his tea leaves. "That always disturbed me, when she was blamed for it."

"Why is that?"

"It seemed so . . . so . . . contradictory." Atwood carefully set down his cup. "She always seemed quite attached to her baby brother. The mother—oh, I've forgotten her name now."

"Amberlee."

"That's it. She'd usually bring Layla along to the baby's appointments. Couldn't afford a sitter, I suppose. All those trips to the ER, too. Layla would keep Jake entertained in the waiting room." Atwood clicked his tongue. "Golly, he was such a cheerful little guy—amazing, when you consider what he went through. His sister played peek-a-boo with him, sang songs, got him to giggle."

Sorrow incised the lines in his face even deeper. "I suppose it's possible Layla wanted to get rid of him out of jealousy, all that attention he received because of his medical problems. I never saw any hint of it, though."

A sweet little girl who'd cajoled happy gurgles from her damaged brother, growing up damaged herself. A jaded prostitute, estranged from her family. No wonder Layla's eyes were sad.

"What about Amberlee?" I asked. "She faced a lifetime of caring for a disabled child. She already had a five-year-old and an abusive husband to cope with. The strain on her must have been enormous. Ever suspect she was reaching the end of her rope?"

"Oh, that Amberlee, she was a tough one." Atwood wagged a finger. "Have to give her credit. All she had to put up with, one crisis after another, yet she always stayed calm, always managed a gentle tone to soothe the baby." He pointed at water-stained ceiling tiles. "They say the good Lord never gives you more than you can handle, and by golly, she sure could handle it. Never saw her shed a tear, not once. A real cool customer."

"What if she was bottling all her emotions up inside, until one day they exploded?"

"Possible, I suppose." Atwood frowned. "My gosh, though. What kind of monster would put the blame on her own child?"

A desperate one, maybe.

"Do you have a copy of Jake's autopsy report?"

Atwood tugged his earlobe. "Well, now, if I did, I'm afraid I couldn't show it to you."

"You could, as a matter of fact. It's public record. But the sheriff's department seems to have misplaced their file. You wouldn't be violating any rules by showing me your copy."

"Come help me look, then." He pushed back his chair. "You've got better eyes than I do."

He led me through his living quarters to a hall closet crammed with cardboard boxes. I wrestled a few aside, found one labeled G, and lifted it down. The contents were carelessly alphabetized, and Atwood's failing vision didn't help. He was making his third pass when I edged closer and spotted the file over his shoulder. "There."

"Now, how'd I miss that?" He extracted the folder and flipped it open. "What do you know? Here's the copy they sent me, right on top." He handed me a thin plastic binder. "Want to read this back in my office?"

"Would you mind if I copied it?" I didn't have time to pore over the autopsy report right now. "If you point me toward the nearest print shop, I'll bring it right back. Promise." I made an X over my heart.

"No need." He beckoned me to follow. "My receptionist has one of those machines hooked up to her computer that does everything. Faxes, copies, vacuums the floor for all I know." He led me into a cubbyhole off the reception area that looked like a former coat closet. "I even know how to use it, long as all we're doing is making copies."

He demonstrated. I pretended to be amazed. The phone rang. He was meticulously lining up page two when the receptionist stuck her head in. "Doctor, it's Mrs. Crouse. She says the prescription you gave her isn't working."

Atwood muttered what sounded like, "Mrs. Grouse."

"I can finish the copying," I assured him.

"Be right back."

The process was a lot slower than a copy shop, but there weren't many pages. I wondered, did the receptionist call him Doctor when they were alone together? After the final page emerged, I heard him still out by her desk. "Now, tell me again, Ida, how many of those little yellow pills did you take?"

I checked my watch. No way to avoid rush hour now. Dane would be home from school pretty soon, and if I didn't arrive with dinner by six, he was liable to raid my emergency chocolate.

I slipped the original sheets back in the binder and hurried down the hallway. Jake's file lay on the cardboard box in front of the closet. I was in such a rush, I knocked the folder to the floor and a bunch of pages fell out. Really. It was an accident.

Impossible to shuffle them back into chronological order without glimpsing the gist of their contents. What a nightmare that poor child had endured during his brief time on earth! Surgery when he was only a day old; a shunt inserted at one month. Four months later, another operation for something called a tethered spinal cord, which sounded too ominous to contemplate.

I sorted through an endless procession of trips to the emergency room for infections, vomiting, seizures. Six weeks before he died, the poor kid was subjected to yet another operation when the shunt malfunctioned.

I skimmed the reports, sick at heart as well as stomach. Then I read something that made my eyes bug out.

Curtis Gormley must have come in to donate blood for his son's last surgery. Jotted on some lab work was a comment in Dr. Atwood's nearly illegible script: *Note blood types—donor cannot be patient's biological father.* A follow-up comment, different ink: *Donor became quite agitated when informed of the above.*

A withered hand shot past me and snatched the paperwork. I yelped and whirled around. Atwood glowered at me, a blue-green vein throbbing at his temple.

"Dr. Atwood, I'm so sorry. The folder fell on the floor, and everything spilled out and I was just trying to—"

"I hope you'll at least have the decency," he interrupted in a cold, quavering voice, "not to broadcast on national television that I was the old fool who let you outfox me."

"That wasn't what . . . I never meant to—"

"I think you'd better leave." Behind the glasses, his near-sighted eyes narrowed to suspicious slits. "You didn't stuff any of those confidential medical reports down your brassiere, did you?"

Face in flames, I fled before he could search me.

I suspected something wasn't kosher as soon as I stepped through my back door. No Velvet Revolver blasting from the stereo. No trail of corn chip crumbs leading from the kitchen to Dane's room. No teenage son slouched in front of the TV, size-11 feet propped on the coffee table, greeting me with, "Hey, Ma, when's dinner?"

"Dane," I yelled. "I brought food from Bombay Bistro." To alleviate a smidgen of guilt about not letting him attend his father's shoot tonight, I'd splurged. "All your favorites," I called, unloading them on the kitchen table. Chicken vindaloo, palak paneer, garlic naan. "Even mango lassi!"

Silence. Sulking, or . . . ?

I made a more thorough sweep of the house. No Dane.

Back in the kitchen I punched in his cell number. The voice mail picked up immediately, a sure sign his phone was switched off. Highly suspicious. Dane never turned off his phone, for fear of missing any babe-related calls.

I said, "Your dinner's getting cold. Please call me," and hung up. Then I gritted my teeth and dialed again.

Jeff's assistant, Connie, answered. "I need to speak with him," I said.

"May I ask who's calling, please?"

Like she didn't recognize my voice. "I need to speak to him *now*, Connie."

"Oh, Harmony, is that you?" No wonder she'd never made it as an actress. "Gee, I'm sorry, but Jeff's in the middle of a take right now."

"I'll wait." My jaw was starting to ache. "I get a thousand free weekday minutes on my calling plan."

Within ten seconds I heard the familiar sexy baritone that made schoolgirls shriek and grown women swoon. "What's up, Cream Puff?"

"Is Dane with you?" I asked. "And don't call me that."

"Dane? Sure, he's right—oh."

Picture Dane frantically waving his hands, mouthing, "I'm not here."

Jeff cleared his throat. "Yeah, he's here, Harm."

Relief mixed with anger. "And did he bother mentioning that I specifically nixed this little outing?"

"Uh, no. No, he didn't mention that."

"It's a school night, Jeff."

"Look, I'm sorry. I assumed he had your permission. But as long as he's here, why not let him hang out? We're going to be done in a couple hours. I'll drive him home. You can tuck him in bed by ten."

"What about his homework? And that's not the point. If I let him stay, I'll be rewarding him for disobeying me."

Jeff may have blown his chance at Husband of the Year, but he'd always taken his parental responsibilities to heart. Even when he had to play the villain. "I'll have Connie drive him home right now."

Great. On the way, they could compare notes about what a bitch I was.

"Thank you," I said, though it stuck in my throat like an overlooked fish bone.

I put the Indian food in the fridge, no longer hungry. Too exasperated with Dane, too edgy after my brief conversation with the man I'd once loved more than life. Would I ever be able to hear Jeff's voice without that fluttery feeling beneath my breastbone?

I grabbed an apple and poured myself a glass of wine. When Dane got home, I would inform him he was grounded for a week. Which would provoke the launch of his fail-safe missile: "Wish I could live with Dad."

Lately I'd begun to debate the agonizing question of whether that might, in fact, be best for him. My son had reached the age when the shackles of childhood were definitely starting to chafe. Crouched on the starting line of adulthood, he couldn't wait to charge headlong into all the perils and possibilities that lay ahead. Would his father be a better guide through that tricky terrain than his mother?

During the destructive earthquake of our divorce, the prospect of losing Dane had been unbearable, and Jeff had felt guilty enough not to fight me for custody. Wounded pride had goaded me to reject both alimony and my half of our community property—a stiff-necked stance that eventually drove my attorney bald. Jeff had, after all, earned all the money. Except for child support and a modest settlement that allowed me to buy this bungalow, I'd flung every penny back in his face, refusing to be indebted to him for my financial well being or anything else.

Now those prideful chickens might be coming home to roost. After Dane's next birthday, he could live wherever he pleased. Face it, most kids would choose the "fun" parent, the one with a big mansion and gobs of money, the one who threw glamorous parties with guest lists that looked like the table of contents from *People* magazine.

I tossed back a slug of wine. Why didn't kids come with instruction manuals?

I settled on the couch to organize my notes about Jake Gormley. Right away I felt ashamed of whining. I'd had it so easy compared to Jake's parents. What a tragic blow to discover the child you've awaited nine months with so much love, so much hope, so much anticipation, has been born with an unfixable defect that will cripple him forever. What a nightmare to realize your child will never lead a normal life, and from this day forward, neither will you.

Raising any child was a struggle. Under the added weight of such a crushing burden, how much would it take to push an exasperated parent over the edge?

Especially a bad-tempered, violent parent who'd recently discovered the child in question wasn't his.

CHAPTER 6

Seven months ago, when my bank balance and self-esteem had sunk about as low as they could go, Carson Wyatt had dragged me out of the quicksand. The preceding half year I'd spent scouring want ads and sending out résumés for every bottom-rung, behind-the-camera job in the entertainment industry. Unfortunately, the most recent experience listed on my résumé was nearly two decades ago. Plus, I was too old.

Ever notice how even television newscasts have started to resemble MTV? Everyone's after that precious Holy Grail, the youth demographic. Yep, the Little Rascals run Hollywood now, and most of them are skeptical that someone pushing forty can "connect with" that sought-after 18-to-34-year-old audience.

I'd been so buoyed with relief and gratitude when Carson hired me that it hadn't fazed me one bit that the producer I would be assisting was ten years my junior, that most of my co-workers hadn't even been born when *Raiders of the Lost Ark* came out. Recently, however, I'd become a tad self-conscious.

"Need longer arms, Harmony?" Danielle lobbed a smirk across the conference table.

Too vain for reading glasses, I was waging a presbyopic struggle to decipher a closely typed synopsis of the next show on the production schedule. Laughter rippled from the dozen other people around the table. I managed a good-natured smile.

Carson had flown directly from Omaha to meet with cable company execs in New York, leaving Danielle in charge of this afternoon's staff meeting. Danielle, in addition to being a pain in the butt, was a multitalented dynamo who displayed more energy than the Las Vegas Strip lit up at night. Over the course of a season, she produced, directed, and did most of the writing for twenty-two hour-long episodes.

Her low-voltage resentment of me was an ongoing mystery. I posed neither a threat to her job nor any competition in the sexual sweepstakes. Men were drawn to Danielle like mosquitoes to a bug zapper, lured perhaps by her anorexic cheekbones or the way she puckered her high-gloss lips while concentrating. Fascinated by the seductive contrast between flawless pale skin and her spiky mop of jet-black hair. Hypnotized by those sultry Cleopatra eyes, not to mention the Nile-length expanse of slender thigh exposed by her stylishly short hemlines.

Rumors had been tiptoeing around that Danielle and Carson had something going on.

She gathered her papers and stood. "Okay, you've all got next week's schedule. Ahmed? I want to review the Omaha footage. Matt, you done with that sound editing yet? C'mon, people, we're falling behind. Harmony, don't forget to pick up that maggot guy at the airport Saturday. Oh, and I notice we're almost out of sweetener in the coffee room. Anything else? Okay, then—"

Like a doofus I raised my hand. "I, um, have an idea for an episode that I'd like to float by you."

Danielle froze mid-dash. "Yes? What?"

I'd lain awake since four A.M., rehearsing my spiel. I outlined Layla's story, including what I'd learned in Gypsum yesterday, refusing to let Danielle's foot-tapping rush me. "Bottom line is, I think there's more to this case than meets the eye. Maybe this poor girl did get scapegoated. If true, we could have the material for a very gripping, very emotional episode."

As soon as these concluding words departed my mouth, Danielle was on her feet again. "Nice initiative, Harmony. But it doesn't really fit, does it? I mean, this show is about cold cases, remember? It's not called 'Closed Case Chronicles.' "

"Maybe the case shouldn't have been closed. Think of the sensational publicity, if we were the ones to solve it after all these years."

"We don't have the time or resources to play detective. Weren't you at this meeting? We're falling behind schedule as it is."

"I'd be willing to investigate on my own time."

Danielle arched severely tweezed eyebrows. "If you've got that much free time, there's plenty of extra work I'd be happy to assign you." She flapped the schedule at me and breezed from the conference room.

Ahmed Saleh, one of the camera operators, leaned over my shoulder on his way out. "I thought your proposal was excellent," he said in a low voice.

I stayed behind to clean up the paper cups and the crumbly remains of overpriced gourmet cookies I'd trotted down the street for. I felt like a third-grader who'd spent all week working hard on a book report then gotten a D from the teacher in front of the whole class.

Should I have waited until Carson was present to pitch my proposal? Maybe it was dumb, and I should be thankful he hadn't heard me make a fool of myself.

Damn, it *wasn't* a dumb idea. Too late now, though. Nothing would infuriate Danielle like hearing I'd had the nerve to go over her head and discuss it with Carson. Anyway, Carson was a big believer in delegating responsibility. He'd be extremely reluctant to overrule Danielle's decision. Especially if he was sleeping with her.

Mona intercepted me en route to my cubicle, panic written all over her face. "Can you cover me for a minute?" she pleaded.

"You guys took forever in that meeting. I gotta pee something fierce."

"Sure." I trudged to the reception desk and flopped into Mona's chair. Was this my employment destiny? Professional Handmaiden? Scurrying around to satisfy other people's needs? Yes, I was lucky to have a job. But I still craved a chance to strut my own stuff, to demonstrate I had brains and drive and creativity. To prove I had worth beyond the role of someone's mother, someone's wife, someone's assistant.

Yet here I was, stuck in a gofer position while a bunch of people who couldn't even name all four Beatles clambered over me on their way up the career ladder.

The phone interrupted my pity party. After three rings I succeeded in pushing the right button. "Wyatt Productions."

"Roy Pastorelli for Carson Wyatt, please." Female voice. In other words, a secretary channeling for her boss so he wouldn't waste seconds of his valuable time waiting for Carson to come on the line. Forcing Carson to hold for *him* instead.

"Carson's out of town," I said, as if his whereabouts were a state secret. "Can I give him a message?"

"Roy just wanted to confirm their racquetball game tomorrow. Will Carson be back in time?"

"He's due back tonight." The name didn't fully register until I started to write it down. "Roy and Carson are racquetball partners?"

"Uh-huh."

Mental gears creaked into motion. "I didn't realize they knew each other."

"They worked together years ago on *AM Los Angeles*. Remember that one? Roy directed; Carson was a reporter."

"I'll, uh, leave a reminder on Carson's desk."

"Thanks. Sounds like you know Roy?"

I pretended not to hear and hung up.

Mona came back. "What's the matter? Obscene phone call?"

I made my lips move. "Roy Pastorelli's office called to confirm his racquetball game with Carson tomorrow."

"That Pastorelli sure is anal." Mona reached across me for a message slip. "Like Carson's gonna forget when they play together every single week. I mean, *religiously,* going on like three years now. I think they both must've had heart-attack scares or something."

I made a stumbling beeline for the nearest haven of privacy and barricaded myself in a stall. Roy Pastorelli. I'd only met him a few times, though he and Jeff had been friends for fifteen years. Back when Jeff first started landing significant parts on television, he'd appeared in some silly celebrity Olympics event Roy directed.

I paced the floor tiles, somewhat limited by the narrow confines. Roy's career had eventually tanked, thanks to a voracious cocaine habit. For years he was in and out of rehab, till he supposedly kicked his addiction. By then no one wanted to hire him. But Jeff had become a huge star with clout to match. He finagled Roy the director's job for an obscure cable production of *Gulliver's Travels,* which turned out to be a surprise hit that went on to win several Emmys that year.

Roy had pledged Jeff undying gratitude for his redemption. Was he still grateful enough to push his buddy Carson into hiring Jeff's ex-wife after everyone else in show biz had turned her down?

Suspicion rose like sewage from a stopped-up drain. Paranoia? Or did something really stink? Had Jeff cashed in a favor and nudged Roy to put in a good word for me with his racquetball partner?

Jeff knew how long and hard I'd been searching for work. Well-acquainted with my finances, he would have realized I was fast approaching desperation. He also knew I'd never accept a favor from him.

But how would Jeff have known I'd applied at Wyatt Productions?

Dane could have mentioned it.

I clutched my head and groaned. I'd been so proud of getting this job, so thrilled by the validation that a total stranger considered me worth a paycheck. A minor accomplishment in the vast panorama of human endeavor, but one that had provided needed repair work to my battered self-image. Here was proof I was capable of surviving on my own, of building a new life, of forging a new identity for myself as a productive, valued member of society. I am woman; hear me roar!

Was it all meaningless? Just smoke and mirrors? Had my ex-husband pulled strings to manipulate me like a marionette?

My pathetic little triumph. Down the—

In the neighboring stall, someone flushed.

"This can't be the right street," I said.

My reluctant navigator slapped down the *Thomas Guide.* "Hey, Ma, it's the street you told me."

"It's too ritzy."

"What, this chick can't have rich parents?"

"That wasn't the impression I got. And I don't care for that term."

"Rich?"

I stopped scanning hand-painted-tile house numbers long enough to glare.

Dane and I were a block from the ocean, cruising a Newport Beach neighborhood where private security signs sprouted like crab grass. Palm trees lined both sides of the street with the ramrod posture and precision spacing of palace guards. Not the scraggly, shaggy-barked trees that littered Santa Monica sidewalks with desiccated fronds; no, these were elegantly barbered palms straight off a South Pacific travel brochure.

Layla's mother, Amberlee, supposedly lived with her second husband behind one of the ivied stone walls and iron-scrollwork gates that blocked views of the Mediterranean-style villas from prying eyes like mine. Even at five miles per hour, quick peeks up cobblestone driveways yielded little more than a flash of red-tile roof, a glimpse of second-floor balcony, and more ornamental landscaping than Disneyland. Amberlee had come a long way from Gypsum.

"Maybe the parents are like, servants."

Dane was pissed off because I'd dragged him along, not trusting him to stay put while grounded. He'd disobeyed me once this week, and I wasn't about to hand him another tempting opportunity.

"Maybe," I said.

"How come you didn't call first and ask directions?"

"I did. The number's been disconnected."

"So maybe they don't even live here anymore."

"Then maybe whoever lives at their old address can tell me where they moved to."

Dane grumbled something that sounded like "wild goose chase." He rolled down his window, admitting a gust of sea air that whipped hair into my face. I bit my tongue. We'd already fought about the radio.

The breeze wove smells of honeysuckle and newly mulched flowerbeds into the briny Pacific tang. Perhaps it was my imagination, but I thought I caught the scent of brand-new leather car upholstery as well.

Dane might be right. This evening could be a waste of time. I'd shuffled home from work in a complete funk, dejected that Danielle had vetoed my story pitch, demoralized by the humiliating hunch that Jeff had orchestrated my hiring. Even Dane finally noticed. Over microwaved Indian food, he'd asked why I was so quiet. Or, to quote more precisely, what was my problem?

Omitting the part about his father, I described how Danielle had guillotined my idea.

"So?" He wolfed the last bite of chicken vindaloo. "Do it anyway."

I was about to launch into a sarcastic lecture about how that type of attitude got people grounded, when it dawned on me: The kid was right.

Why shouldn't I go ahead and pursue Layla's story on my own? All the vibes I'd picked up so far hinted there was something about Jake Gormley's death that people didn't want to talk about. *Had* a five-year-old girl been unfairly blamed? After all these years, maybe no one else cared who killed that poor baby. But I did. And so did Layla.

I've never been one to shrug and let people get away with bad behavior. Just ask my ex-husband, or a certain casting director I once kneed in the balls—there's a reason I can't go back to acting. If I uncovered a terrible injustice, wasn't I morally obligated to try to fix it?

And if my quest also led to a great hour of television that earned big ratings as well as the admiration of my co-workers, who was I to quarrel with fate? Even if Carson Wyatt had hired me as a favor, I'd make him damn glad he did.

Streetlights beamed pale cones of light every hundred feet or so, but pools of darkness in between made reading addresses a challenge. If there'd been pedestrians, I could have rolled down the window to ask directions, but the only human in sight was a dog walker who had her hands full with half a dozen hyperactive purebreds. Jogging didn't seem to be a popular form of exercise around here, unless it was on treadmills at the health club.

"Hey, Ma. Can we get a dog?"

"No."

"Aw, man. Why not?"

"One word. Poop. I am not cleaning it up."

"I could do it."

"Right. Like you clean up your room."

"Okay, we could hire someone."

"We can't afford it. Nor can we afford dog food, vet bills, and obedience lessons."

I couldn't hear Dane's mumbles. But moving in with his father wouldn't be the magic answer this time; Jeff was horribly allergic to dogs and cats.

The street dead-ended at a stone fortification that looked like the Berlin Wall without the barbed wire. A gate of massive iron bars was set between two white-brick abutments. No house number in evidence.

"This can't be it," I said.

"Wow. Like the Playboy mansion or something."

I swung the Explorer around and pulled to the curb. "Where else can it be? This is the end of the road, right? Let me see that map book."

Dane handed me the book. Even with the dome light on, I could barely make out the tiny squiggles.

"There's an intercom over there."

"Where?"

Dane pointed to a small brass grid set into the left-hand abutment.

I climbed out and walked over. Beyond the gate barricade, closely planted rows of tall Italian cypress marched up each side of the curving driveway, screening the rest of the property. This couldn't be the right place. Feeling foolish, I pressed the button. Within seconds a gruff voice barked, "Please identify yourself."

"Uh, my name is Harmony Magnussen. I'm a television

producer." Tiny exaggeration. "I'm looking for Amberlee Schultz. Does she live here?"

Faint buzz of static. "Do you have an appointment?"

"No, er, the phone number I have doesn't work anymore. Can you please tell her it's about her daughter? I'd like to speak to her about Layla."

"Mrs. Schultz is unavailable."

"But Layla told me—"

"Mrs. Schultz does not wish to discuss her daughter. Good evening." The intercom clicked and went dead.

I pushed the button again. No response. Another poke. Same result. I conquered the urge to stand there with my finger jammed against the button until someone either answered or showed up to yell at me.

By the time I got back to the car, Dane had flown the coop. An exuberant dog pack was leaping and slobbering all over him while he crouched down to scratch their ears. He wore a big goofy grin that squeezed my heart.

The dog walker was a young woman in baggy gym shorts, a UC Irvine sweatshirt, and an Angels baseball cap. "Are these all yours?" I asked as she struggled to untangle leashes. A golden retriever bounded over and attempted to sniff my crotch.

"God, no. I walk them for people who live around here. Twice a day. Cosmo, knock it off."

"Do you know the people who live at the end of the block? The Schultzes?"

"Well, not really. Not personally, I mean. Those German shepherds of theirs aren't exactly the kind of dogs you can walk in public. But I know who they are, of course."

"You live in the neighborhood?" Good thing I hadn't tried to climb the fence.

"I wish." She armed sweat off her forehead, dislodging the

Angels cap. "I know the Schultzes because of their being famous and all."

I reached out and tugged the brim straight. "Famous? How?"

"Thanks. You know, on TV. He's got that show Sunday mornings."

"What show?"

"I don't know what it's called. Bentley, get *down*." She blew an exasperated stream of air at her bangs. "One of those programs where they sing and pray and perform miracles and ask people to send money, I guess." She shrugged. "It's not like I go to their church or anything, but everyone's heard of Reverend Dietrich Schultz."

The name rang a faint, far-off bell. "Is his wife's name Amberlee?"

The dog walker nodded.

Layla's stepfather was a famous televangelist?

Surprise slowed my reflexes. Too late. A black-and-white Great Dane propped his paws on my shoulders and happily lapped my face.

CHAPTER 7

Friday and Saturday I had to work. Carson was back, and now that I suspected he'd only hired me as a favor, our every interaction seemed fraught with hidden meaning. He probably wondered why I kept staring at him.

Dane left for the ritzy side of town Friday evening to spend the weekend at his dad's, the usual routine when Jeff wasn't away on location or off schmoozing network execs at one of their "business" meetings in Maui or Palm Springs. Saturday morning I drove to LAX and picked up the maggot guy.

Fly larvae, it turns out, can be extremely useful indicators for determining time of death. Attracted by the first whiff of putrefaction, blowflies start zooming in the minute someone croaks. They proceed to lay their eggs, munch gleefully away, and . . . nature takes its course. The larvae hatch and develop at well-established rates. Other insects like ants and beetles show up on the corpse later at predictable times. By factoring in temperature and other environmental conditions, forensic entomologists can take a bug census of the body and calculate with amazing accuracy how long ago the victim died.

The expert whom we'd flown in to interview had once proved to a Tennessee jury's satisfaction that the murder in question had taken place a day earlier than the prosecution claimed—a day the defendant had spent locked in the slammer for attacking his cousin with a tire iron. The cops had little choice but to accept the revised time of death and reopen the case. Seven years later, they arrested the real killer.

The maggot guy liked to talk. You know that ashes to ashes, dust to dust stuff? By the time we rendezvoused with Danielle and Ahmed at the UCLA biology department, I'd heard in vivid detail how it all worked, and breakfast was threatening a comeback.

I got even, though. We filmed him against a backdrop of glass display cases filled with skewered specimens of all his little insect pals.

Sunday morning I rose bright and early to go to church, something I'd rarely done since the days my dad used to drag me out of bed and down the street to St. Paul's Lutheran. One of four Lutheran churches in the Minnesota town where Pop raised me after my mother abandoned us for the Summer of Love. We're talking a town of seven hundred people.

I'd Googled Dietrich Schultz and received a gazillion hits, but the first few pretty much covered the high points. The good reverend headed the flock at Church of the Holy Shepherd in Costa Mesa, an Orange County city just north of Newport Beach. His Sunday-morning service was broadcast on a week-delayed basis, edited to fit a one-hour slot called *The Glory Gathering*. Singing, praying, miracles, operators standing by to accept your donations—pretty much what the dog walker had described.

Schultz had hit the big time about ten years ago, after a nationwide cable channel picked up his local show. His biography before then seemed a little sketchy. Born in 1955, he was the only child of German parents who'd emigrated to Argentina right after World War II. Somehow they'd wound up in Texas, where their son was born, grew up, went to college. And along the way, found religion.

From what I could piece together, Schultz had begun his

career on the revival circuit, preaching to enthusiastic crowds for a week or two, then folding his tent and moving on to the next town. His followers must have been generous with the collection plate; twelve years ago he'd broken ground for construction of a permanent church.

By then he was married to Amberlee, "a devout single mother chosen by God to be Reverend Schultz's loving helpmate." They'd met when Amberlee attended services Schultz was conducting at temporary quarters in nearby Santa Ana. A local radio station had started broadcasting his sermons, and once the permanent church was completed, Schultz graduated to television.

His official web site provided my first view of Amberlee. Layla's mom was a knockout: waist-length blond hair, emerald-green eyes, a Julia Roberts smile of perfectly capped teeth. Same high cheekbones, same delicate chin as her daughter, though Amberlee's face was softer and fuller, reflecting the glow of good heath (or perhaps inner radiance). She must have been my age but looked ten years younger. At least, her computerized image did.

Reverend Schultz himself was blessed with deep-set dark eyes, rugged features, a full head of distinguished silver hair. The expression in all his head shots appeared stern yet forgiving. Despite a blocky jaw that dragged his face a bit out of proportion, it was clear the camera loved him. Probably a mutual sentiment.

I had to click through quite a few links before I came across any mention of Layla. Evidently Schultz used to trot her out every week on his TV show, mostly for a group hug and audience wave during the grand finale. One big happy family, including Amberlee and Grandma Dolores. The word *daughter* never appeared without *adopted* in front of it. Well, fair was fair. When

I'd talked with Layla, she'd never said *father* without *step* in front of it.

The most recent picture I found of her was from a three-year-old TV appearance. Her hair then was drab brown, her weight about twenty pounds closer to the heavy end of the scale. Pancake makeup didn't quite conceal a sprinkling of acne. Behind the standard adolescent sulk, I recognized the pain in her eyes.

I finished my coffee and stale bagel and headed for Costa Mesa around nine. Sunday morning is one of the few time slots that don't qualify as rush hour on the San Diego Freeway, so the trip took less than an hour. It wasn't hard to find the church, not with its ten-story glass-and-chrome campanile that resembled the control tower at nearby John Wayne Airport. Come in, God. You're cleared for landing.

An efficient tag team of clean-cut youths in navy blazers directed me to one of the few remaining parking spots. Attending the actual service wasn't part of my plan, but now I had twenty minutes to kill before Reverend and Mrs. Schultz emerged through the imposing oak-and-brass doors to greet the departing congregation. Perhaps I'd receive a warmer greeting if I appeared to be one of the congregation.

The church soared heavenward on dazzling wings of steel and white marble. I put on my sunglasses to look at it. A flashy kaleidoscope of stained-glass panels girded the exterior walls in somewhat kitschy contrast to the stark modern architecture. Frank Lloyd Wright meets Liberace.

I crossed the sea of parked vehicles and entered the rose garden, where a cloying wave of perfume nearly knocked me off my feet. Swaying feather palms flickered shadows across the curvy slate pathways that funneled churchgoers toward the main entrance. Several tourists were snapping pictures of topiary biblical figures, while some kid tried to catch a pigeon. The tranquil gurgle of fountains made me wish I hadn't drunk all that coffee.

Majestic marble steps leading up to the church entrance reminded me of the Lincoln Memorial. I huffed and puffed my way to the top only to find a security squad stationed in front of closed doors and a No Admittance sign. All wore blazers and microphone headsets, appearing deep in conversation with invisible speakers.

"The service is being taped for broadcast." A young blond gentleman with a crew cut stepped forward to explain. "No one's allowed in after it starts. But you can watch on wide-screen TV. Just walk down there, around the building to your right."

I followed the sound of organ music to a side entrance that opened into a small auditorium. Several dozen other latecomers were scattered among rows of plush theater seats, gazes riveted to a gigantic screen. Hymn lyrics crawled across the bottom, sans bouncing ball, so those inclined could sing along. I slipped into an aisle seat in back.

The hymn was a peppy one, closer to Christian-rock radio than *Beautiful Saviour*. The camera was positioned for a wide-angle shot of the congregation. Most were on their feet singing, bopping a little in time to the music. No one needed hymn books. Swags of red velvet in the background, glittering crystal chandeliers, gold-plated chalices.

Close-up of Schultz, arms thrust in the air, mouth moving, satin vestment draped around his elbows.

Pull back to show acolytes gathered around him at the altar. Backdrop of potted palms, a twelve-foot white cross, and more floral arrangements than the Kentucky Derby.

Cut to the choir, resplendent in silver robes, then to a thirty-piece orchestra in full concert dress.

Zoom out to the congregation again. A few rascals sneaking sideways glances toward the camera as it slowly panned right. Hey, Mom, I'm on TV!

Heaven meets Hollywood. The sanctuary must have seated a thousand people, skewed toward the AARP side of fifty, all but a handful white. Amberlee sat in the front pew, hands clasped over her heart, an aura of beatific adoration shining on her face. A beam of light illuminated her from above, creating a subtle halo effect around her shimmering blond tresses.

Following the hymn, Schultz beckoned her up on stage. They held hands while he led the closing prayer. Amberlee's sherry-colored designer dress was a clone of one I'd worn to the Emmys four years ago. The reverend then invited all those who'd been healed during today's service to come forward. A straggling procession of unfortunates limped, shuffled, and in one case, was bodily carried from the wings. I hated to imagine their physical condition *before* Schultz had worked miracles on them.

Once it looked like they were winding up for the big finish, I left in search of the john. Those security guys were having a nerve-racking effect on my bladder. Pastors back in Minnesota hadn't needed bodyguards. What if the Schultzes didn't even stand out front afterwards? Pastor Johnson and his wife always shook hands with everyone after the service, thanked them for coming, warned them to drive carefully—especially if the roads were icy.

On the other hand, Pastor Johnson hadn't been a media celebrity and head of a multimillion-dollar business empire. Maybe security would focus primarily on Schultz, and I could sidle up to Amberlee while they were busy moving along crackpots.

By the time I made my way back to the entrance, the huge doors were open and people were filing slowly out, cordoned into an orderly line by the men in blazers. Schultz and Amberlee held court at the top of the steps, smiling and shaking hands like the bride and groom in a receiving line. Hallelujah!

I did an end run behind security and edged into the slow-moving procession, ignoring dirty looks from people too well-mannered to protest. One inch, then another. And another. When I finally got to Schultz, he flashed his teeth, gripped my hand in his, and gazed straight through me. "God's blessings on you, my dear." Next.

I rotated Amberlee a little sideways as I grasped her hand. "My name's Harmony Magnussen," I said quickly. "I'd like to speak with you about Layla."

Amberlee's smile froze. Her pupils expanded like dots on big exclamation points.

"Layla came to see me," I babbled. "She seems troubled by something that happened in her past, and I was hoping—"

A large security person stepped forward and clamped his paw on my arm with enough force to dislodge my hold on Amberlee, whose brittle smile disintegrated. As she yanked back her hand, a slip of paper fluttered to the ground. Schultz glanced our way.

"Thank you for moving along," Security Guy growled, "so others have a chance to see Mrs. Schultz." Nice of him to thank me, when brute strength left me no choice. Whoever'd tailored his three-piece suit must have done a double take at the chest and shoulder measurements.

I barely had time to wonder why he wasn't wearing a blazer like the others before he hustled me down the first several steps. Momentum kept me going. When I looked back, he was stroking his short dark beard, stony eyes fixed on me from above, unreadable as a block of granite. Amberlee was busy smiling and shaking hands again.

Part of the deal with my job was that if I had to work Saturday I got Monday off, unless an episode currently in production went into a deadline crunch. This particular Monday I was good to go, which I did. First stop, Red Rock.

The digital display on the bank clock across the street read 10:07 when I arrived at the Public Safety Building. Temperature: sixteen degrees Celsius. I turned into the parking lot before I could learn what that translated to in Fahrenheit. Judging by the overcast sky and scraps of litter blowing along the street, something chilly.

I pulled into a spot as far from the building as possible. Then I donned a floppy straw gardening hat, an old pair of black-rimmed glasses, and a fake arm cast. The hat and glasses came from a thrift store, which is where they'd be returning once I was done with them. The cast came from a costume place on Pico. This will never work, I warned myself. Again.

The hat blew off my head before I made it halfway across the parking lot. I made a lucky grab, hurried into the building, and stumbled to the ladies' room. The reason for stumbling was that the glasses had once belonged to someone quite nearsighted, so my world was now a big blur. I stuffed my hair under the hat again, making sure no one was around to see me use my broken arm.

The ladies' room was only a couple doors down from Records and appeared to offer the best strategic position. I slipped out to make a brief recon of the hallway, taking particular note of the way doors opened and closed. Good. Just as I remembered. Next, I ran up and down a flight of steps to make myself out of breath.

Back in the ladies' room, two women were chatting to each other between adjoining stalls. I ducked into a third and waited until they finished washing hands, primping hair, and comparing weekend dates. By the time they left, I wasn't out of breath anymore, so I jogged in place for a minute, then made my call.

Back home I'd programmed the number into speed dial,

anticipating that jittery fingers might have trouble entering a long string of digits. Over the pulse hammering in my ears I heard it ring. Once. Twice. Thr—

"Records Unit."

I was panting hard, more from nervousness now. "This is your neighbor," I blurted. "Your house is on fire! If you get here quick, I think you can still save some stuff."

"What? Who—"

"Hurry!" I gasped, then punched the End Call button.

I dropped the phone into my shoulder bag and stepped into the hallway. No way to predict whether she'd turn left or right, but even if she came straight toward me, recognition seemed unlikely. She was bound to be in a huge rush. At most, she might notice the hat, cast, and glasses. This, at least, was my optimistic theory.

I was twenty feet away when she came barreling out of Records and bolted past me without a second glance, or even a first. Her panic-stricken expression kindled a flash of guilt, which I tried to snuff out by reminding myself she (might have) lied to me and (possibly) conspired in a cover-up.

The doors in the Public Safety Building were equipped with hissing closer mechanisms that dragged the door shut automatically. Also, rather slowly. Even if the stunned Records clerk retained enough sense of duty to set the lock before she sped to her blazing house, how likely was she to wait around for the door to shut itself?

I had to reach it first.

The second she flew past, I picked up my pace, speed-walking the last few yards. My outstretched palms slammed against the door just before it clicked shut. Whew!

Once inside, I checked. She'd locked it. I left it that way and darted around the counter to the same aisle she'd disappeared into last Wednesday when I'd requested the Gormley file. Of course, if she'd hidden it on Sheriff Salazar's orders, she might not have put it back yet.

The records were a hodgepodge of file folders, cardboard storage boxes, and those vertical boxes libraries keep old magazines in. At first I had trouble reading the labels. Duh! I snatched off the glasses. Armed with the correct date and a knowledge of the alphabet, I located the shelf where the Gormley file should be. Eureka!

I lifted the lid and checked the documents on top to make sure the files hadn't been switched with some other case. The phone rang, nearly stopping my heart. I was not cut out for this.

I scooped the contents of the box into the gargantuan shoulder bag I'd brought for this purpose. Hey, these were public records, and I was a member of the public, therefore entitled to a look-see. Not my fault the only way I could get it was by breaking and entering.

The phone finally stopped ringing. I scurried back up the aisle and around the counter. Just as I reached for the doorknob, it moved. As if somebody outside were jiggling it. My heart sproinged to my throat.

The clerk back already? One of her fellow county employees, armed with a key?

I heard two knocks. Okay, this was good, meant they couldn't get in. Unless some helpful soul came along and unlocked the door for them.

Above the knob was a pebbled glass panel, the kind that transmits little beyond light and shadow. Like the shadow of someone slinking around in search of a hiding place. I tried not to move. Fortunately, I was paralyzed with fright. In preparation for this unpleasant eventuality I'd concocted a story to explain my presence, but for the life of me I couldn't remember what it was.

More knocking, this time the old shave-and-a-haircut rhythm. A flesh-colored oval loomed outside the pebbled rectangle like a pale sea creature rising from murky depths. I shut my eyes. If I couldn't see them, they couldn't see me.

Behind my eyelids, I counted to a hundred. It took forever. When I opened my eyes, the face was gone. Hopefully along with the rest of the person.

Okay, can't keep standing here like the Statue of Liberty. A vision of those nearby jail cells jump-started me. I grasped the doorknob and started to crack the door open.

No, stupid! If you act like you're sneaking, people will know you're up to no good. And put those dumb glasses back on.

I took a deep breath, squared my shoulders, and marched out as if I belonged there. During the endless journey down the hall I braced for someone to holler, "You there! Wait! What's in that shoulder bag?"

No one did. I strolled out of the building and crossed the parking lot. After several shaky attempts to stab the key into the ignition, I succeeded. I only made it a couple of blocks, though, before I had to pull over to calm down.

What a rush! The danger, the fear, the exhilaration of success! Harmony Magnussen, Miss Play-by-the-Rules who feels guilty trying to use an expired pizza coupon, pulling off a heist!

I was sweating like a marathon runner, heart slamming against my rib cage. The adrenaline raging through my bloodstream felt like an illegal drug.

Know the weird part?

I kind of liked it.

CHAPTER 8

Patricia Bettencourt was a registered nurse in the cardiac ward of Red Rock Community Hospital. Fourteen years ago she'd been one of the paramedics summoned by the 9-1-1 call to the scene of Jake Gormley's death. She appeared less than thrilled that I'd tracked her down.

"Things are kind of busy around here." She made a vague gesture that encompassed the nurses' station, the patient rooms, an old guy wheeling his IV stand down the corridor, a glimpse of scrawny butt peeking through the gap in his hospital gown. "I'm afraid I don't have time to talk."

In fact, the ward seemed rather peaceful. No lit-up call buttons pushed by cranky patients, no urgent "Code Blue" bleating from the PA, no crash carts racing down the hallway, accompanied by the muffled thunder of thick-soled shoes.

"What time's your next break?" I asked.

Bettencourt hesitated. "Not for a couple hours."

Liar.

I smiled. "I'll be sitting around the corner in the waiting area. Catching up on *Reader's Digest.*"

I didn't have to wait long. Had barely started "Laughter, the Best Medicine" when she showed up.

"Let's talk in the cafeteria." She heaved a put-upon sigh. "It's more private down there."

Bettencourt was mid-to-late thirties, sturdily built, dark blond hair tied back in a ponytail. She wore a hibiscus-print smock top with a stethoscope around her neck. On her wrist was a clunky man's watch that looked safe to wear deep-sea diving.

Fourteen years ago her last name wasn't Bettencourt, but someone at the firehouse where she'd been stationed figured out which ex-paramedic I must be looking for. "You mean Pat? Pat Denny. She got married. Went back to school and got her nursing license, works over at the hospital now."

I bought Bettencourt a cup of coffee. We sat at the table farthest from the register, though judging by all the red-rimmed eyes and worried expressions, other patrons were too wrapped up in their own woes to bother eavesdropping.

"Thanks for helping me out with this." I opened one of the reports from Jake's file. If there was anything in the stuff I'd snitched that the sheriff didn't want me to read, I couldn't figure out what. "You and your partner were the first emergency personnel on the scene, is that correct?"

She nodded, sipped, made a face.

"I'd like to speak with your partner, too, if possible. Randy Metzger. Any idea where I can find him?"

"Baghdad? Mosul? He's in the National Guard."

"Oh. Well, I guess I can cross him off my list, then."

She didn't look amused.

"What was the situation at the Gormley house when you arrived that afternoon?"

She rolled her eyes. "Total chaos. What'd you expect? Their baby had just died."

I made my own face at the coffee. "Could you be a little more specific? Who was in the house? What were they doing? How were they acting?"

"We didn't have time to notice. We rushed straight back to the bedroom where the baby was. I started CPR, though that was really just for show. For the family's sake. That poor little guy was gone long before we got there."

"How long?"

She swatted an invisible gnat. "You'd have to check the medical examiner's report."

"I did. But he didn't get there for another hour. He couldn't be very precise." I leaned forward so no one else could hear. "You're a medical professional; you've seen lots of people die. How long do you think the baby was dead before you got there?"

She worked her thumbnail into a chip in the cup handle. "An hour, maybe a little longer. But that's just a guess."

"And it took you how long to drive out to Gypsum once you got the 9-1-1 call?"

"Probably thirty minutes or so." She glanced at her big solid watch, as if to demonstrate her need to get back.

"So the baby died maybe a half hour before the 9-1-1 call came in?"

"I didn't say that. I don't know." She raised her hands like this was a stickup. "Look, I was young and inexperienced then. If you're trying to prove some theory, don't rely on my opinion."

"I'm not trying to prove anything, just get an accurate picture. When you first saw him, what was your impression about how he died?"

"That wasn't my job, to determine cause of death."

"No, but you must have wondered. Your training, your experience, your instincts would have given you at least some idea."

She stared at her coffee cup and slowly shook her head.

"Okay." Frustrated, I dropped it. "The crime-scene report mentions a small amount of blood on the bedspread in the parents' room. Didn't match the baby's. Any idea what that was from?"

"No. I don't know anything about it. The sheriff—well, back then, he was a deputy—handled the crime-scene investigation. I was never in the parents' room. Just the baby's."

"His sister shared that room with him, didn't she?"

"Beats me. Wait, I think there was a child's bed in there. Besides the crib, I mean."

In fact, that's where the pillow had come from. "What was the sister's behavior while you were there?"

"Would you mind telling me the point of all this?" Bettencourt slapped both palms on the table. "The little girl couldn't stop crying, all right? She was freaked out. Who wouldn't be, with Mom shrieking, 'Why'd you do it? Why'd you do it?' every thirty seconds? Meantime, Dad's staggering around loaded to the gills, blabbering incoherently, while Grandma takes turns praying at the top of her lungs, then screaming at us to make the baby wake up. Sweet Jesus!" Bettencourt dug her fingers into the sides of her skull. "It was so awful."

Silence stretched out. Despite their own personal dramas, several people glanced our way. "Who do you think killed the baby?" I asked quietly.

Bettencourt lifted her head to gaze past my shoulder. Light reflecting off the window turned her eyes opaque.

"Look," she said in a low voice. "My husband's a deputy sheriff."

Comprehension dawned. "Salazar called you, right? To warn you I might come around asking questions. Did he tell you not to cooperate?"

Her lips welded shut.

I started gathering papers and stuffing them into my bag. "The little girl, Layla. Jake's sister. She grew up believing she killed her brother. It's ruined her life."

Bettencourt's eyelids twitched.

"Do you think she did it?" I asked.

"That's what my husband's boss concluded."

"Bullshit." I stood up. "Salazar doesn't think so, either. That's why he's afraid I'll uncover the truth, right before he's up for reelection. Won't make him look too good, will it, if the real killer's gotten away with it all these years? But hey, nobody to contradict what the mother claims she saw, right? Just an hysterical five-year-old. So, fine, make her the scapegoat. Even if it destroys her life."

I carted my coffee to the dirty-dish bin, then walked out of the cafeteria. Bettencourt caught up with me at the nearest exit.

"For whatever it's worth, I don't believe she did it."

I turned.

Her eyes focused directly on mine for the first time. "The little girl was so upset. The way she kept trying to look at her brother, to touch him . . ." Bettencourt swallowed. "I've had kids of my own since then. Usually, when they've done something wrong, they're anxious to get away, to avoid the whole thing. It makes them feel bad, to see the consequences of what they've done."

I nodded.

"That little girl—Layla—wasn't acting the way kids do when they've been caught red-handed." Bettencourt blinked rapidly. "She just didn't act . . . guilty."

"Did you send her a note recently?"

"A note? No. Why would I do that?"

"What do you think really happened that day?"

She caught her lower lip with her teeth. "I've always suspected the father smothered the baby. Then the mother covered up for him."

"He ain't in there."

I glanced around. Across from Curtis Gormley's trailer, a lanky, long-haired character in tank top and jeans sat cross-legged on the ground, shaded by the green fiberglass awning tacked onto the side of his mobile home. His arms should have been covered with goose bumps, but the tattoos made it hard to tell. He was hunched over a disassembled chain saw, a small tin of oil in his hand and a two-gallon plastic gasoline container near one of his filthy bare feet. It didn't seem the safest place in the world to smoke, but that wasn't stopping him.

"Bang on his door all you want, ain't gonna do no good."

"You know where he is?" Probably hiding in the shower, hoping I'd go away. "I'm not a bill collector or anything."

"Huh. Mighta went over to Victorville. This guy Glenn, lives next door—" he pointed with a screwdriver "—I heard him talkin' last night 'bout this construction gig he's got. Told Curtis they might be hirin'. Curtis sounded like he was gonna go check it out."

Damn! Now that I'd read the complete case file, I had some more questions for Curtis Gormley. Not that he'd answered any of my previous ones.

"Could you do me a favor?" I dug out a business card and wrote my cell-phone number on the back. "When Curtis gets home, would you please give this to him? Tell him it's important for us to talk."

Chain Saw took the card with grimy fingers, moved his lips around his cigarette while he read it. The stiff breeze snatched his secondhand smoke and blew it in my face. "This for real, man? You work for that TV show? Hey, me an' the old lady watch it all the time."

"Great!" I bared my teeth in a large smile while I backpedaled in the direction of my car. "Gosh. Well, we certainly do appreciate our loyal viewers."

"Whatcha wanna talk to Curtis for?"

"I need him to help me with some research."

"Research?" Sly amusement creased his face. He stubbed out his cigarette and donated the butt to a nearby collection. "Better try the library instead, lady. That dumbshit couldn't research his way out of a paper bag. Prob'ly can't even spell research.

Prob'ly can't even spell TV."

At that moment, I backed into a humanoid object and let out some variation of "Eek!"

The humanoid in question turned out to be Curtis Gormley. Ignoring me, he glared over the grocery sacks in his arms. "Asshole."

"Where's your truck, man? That piece a shit break down again?"

"Fuck you."

"Mr. Gormley," I interrupted before his antagonist could rev up the chain saw, "I'm so glad to bump into you. We didn't really get a chance to talk the other day, and I was hoping—"

"I got nothin' to say." He shouldered past me in a gust of beer fumes. Liquor-store, not grocery sacks, judging by their contents. Six-packs of whatever was on sale that week, with some beef jerky and corn nuts thrown in for nutrition. Meat and vegetables, two of the basic food groups.

"Hey, man, you're gonna be on TV! This lady's from that show, *Cold Case Chronicles.*" Chain Saw tugged a crumpled pack of Camels from his jeans and winked. "You musta killed somebody once and got away with it, huh Curtis?"

Beneath his sweatshirt hood, Gormley's unhealthy complexion paled to a sickroom pallor. He dumped one of the sacks on his front step while he fumbled for keys.

"Mr. Gormley, your friend's pulling your leg. That's not why I'm here at all. I just need you to help with some background information."

He wrenched open the door, grabbed the other sack and scrambled inside.

"If you'll just hear me out—"

The cheap metal door slammed in my face. Déjà vu all over again.

"Must have stage fright or somethin'." Chain Saw grinned.

I circled around to the opposite side of the trailer and pounded on a window. "Mr. Gormley, I'd sure like to hear your side of the story before we go on the air with this."

He yanked the faded tie-dye curtains closed.

"Curtis, I talked to Amberlee." Technically, true. "She's making some nasty accusations." Technically, not true.

The curtain flicked a little.

"I'd really like to be fair about this, Curtis. Give you a chance to tell your side about what happened to Jake. Otherwise, our show's going to make you look pretty guilty."

"Wasn't me!" he hollered. "The kid did it. Layla!"

"That's not what Amberlee says." And she hadn't. Not to me, anyway.

Thudding footsteps. A gunshot noise made me jump, but it was only the screen door flying open. Curtis stalked around the trailer. "She told you I killed that kid?" Jabbing a thumb at his chest, bloodshot eyes squinting in disbelief.

"Are you saying you dispute her version of events?"

"Fuck dispute. That bitch is lying through her goddamn teeth."

I shrugged. "Unless you're willing to tell your side, that's all we have to go on. Her version of events."

"Version? What version? What'd she say?"

"Well, I can't quote her exactly." Since she'd refused to speak to me. "Hadn't you just been fired from your job that afternoon?"

"Yeah? So what? Look, the guy took my pickax, okay? Didn't even ask to borrow it. I hate it when people pull that shit. I lost my temper, all right? It's his own fault he got hurt. And I didn't mean to bust his damn nose. That was an accident."

"Okay. So you were probably still angry when you got home, right? Even after stopping for a few beers along the way." I took a prudent step backward. "Rumor has it you also got pretty angry when you found out Jake wasn't yours."

"She told you about that?" Outrage corroded his voice like a rusty pipe.

I donned an expression I hoped would pass for sympathy. "It does seem pretty unfair, getting stuck raising someone else's kid. Especially when he had all those physical problems."

Curtis considered this. From all signs, a Herculean effort. "Yeah, that sucked, all right. There I was, all psyched about having a kid of my own—a boy, even. Only then he turns out to be defective." He hawked a gob of spit into the dirt. "How was I supposed to play catch with some crip in a wheelchair? Or take him four-wheelin'? Or teach him how to shoot?" He scratched two-day-old whiskers. "Well, maybe he still coulda learned to shoot." He bunched his fists. "Then, like that ain't bad enough, I find out Amberlee's been screwing around on me."

"You must have been furious."

"Hell, you can say that again." Slowly grinding mental gears went clunk. "Wait a sec, though. That don't prove I killed the kid!"

Curious, isn't it, how some people equate the absence of legal proof with the absence of guilt? *The jury said I didn't do it, therefore I didn't.*

"Why were there bloodstains on your bed that day?"

"Huh?" His jaw sagged. "I don't know nothin' 'bout that. Maybe I had a nosebleed or something."

"Okay." I plucked out strands of hair the wind had blown into my mouth. "Now, this doesn't prove anything either, but another thing that might make some people suspicious is your, uh, record of violence."

"Record? I ain't got no record. Just that thing in Phoenix, but they dropped the assault charge."

"Didn't the cops have to come out to your house more than

once on domestic violence calls?"

"That's a buncha crap," he said, then mumbled, "Nosy neighbors."

"You're saying you never hit Amberlee?"

He kicked a clump of weeds with the scuffed toe of his work boot. "Aw, man, that don't count. We always made up, didn't we? And one thing I for sure never did was hit those kids. Even though neither of 'em was mine."

"That's pretty commendable. By the way, do you know who Layla's biological father was?"

"Some trucker Amberlee hooked up with in a bar over in Red Rock." Curtis dragged a sweatshirt sleeve under his nose. "She comes to me all cryin', 'I'm pregnant and he's long gone. What am I gonna do?' " He mimicked her with a prissy whine. "I says, 'I'll marry you, that way your kid'll have a daddy.' " The harsh lines around his mouth softened. "That Amberlee, she sure was a looker. Every guy in town wanted into her pants. I couldn't believe it when she married me."

The magic of true love. "I'll bet you were a good dad to Layla."

"Told ya I never hit her, didn't I?" He pushed a hand through his scraggly hair. "Yeah, she was a cute little bugger. Smart, too. I used to watch *Sesame Street* with her. She knew all the numbers and letters, a whole bunch of words too."

"You think she killed Jake?"

Curtis's sentimental journey crashed to a halt. "Amberlee saw Layla holdin' that pillow over Jake's face." His expression hardened to cement.

"You believe her?"

"No reason not to."

"Did you send Layla a note last month?"

Alarm crumbled the cement. "No way, man. I'd never do that."

"You don't keep in touch with her?"

He shook his head like a wet dog. "Nope. Never. I ain't had no contact with either of 'em, I swear. Not since her and Amberlee moved to Victorville."

Victorville? "When did they move?"

"About a week after, uh, you know." Despite the cold desert wind, sweat sheened his broad forehead.

"After Jake died?"

He nodded. "Look, I gotta go."

"Thank you for your time." I bird-dogged him around the trailer. "Listen, are you going to be home this week? I'd like to come back with a cameraman, get all this information on tape." Already I was assessing different angles, figuring the best location to shoot. Normally we interview people indoors, but the trailer would be dark and cramped. Not enough room to set up lights. Besides, I was afraid no crew member would set foot inside once they got a whiff of Curtis's housekeeping.

He stopped so fast I almost ran into him. "What camera? You didn't say nothin' 'bout no camera."

"Well, in order to present your side of—"

"Nuh-uh. No way." He backed toward the door as if an alien had sprouted from my chest.

"Curtis, you've been really helpful, but we can't use this material unless we can show who it comes from."

"Don't use it!" he yelled. "It's . . . it's . . . shit, whaddaya call it? Off the record."

"But people will think you—"

"Let 'em think what they want! I ain't talking about none of that no more! Now quit buggin' me!"

The slam of the door was very loud.

I didn't get it. Most people will say or do anything to be on TV. Just watch daytime television. Why was Curtis so dead-set against it? What had him so panicked?

Behind me, a chain saw revved to life. No doubt about it, Curtis Gormley was scared. And it wasn't stage fright.

CHAPTER 9

Every small town in America has one. The diner where everyone gathers for midmorning coffee, gossip, maybe a cinnamon roll or piece of pie. Local businesspeople meet there for lunch. The majority of folks eat supper at home, but the place will be hopping Sunday around noon, when all the churchgoers show up for roast beef or fried chicken dinner with gravy and mashed potatoes, canned peas, a slice of that pie for dessert.

Most likely this socio-gastronomic hot spot presides over Main Street, where customers can observe all the comings and goings through checked curtains framing the front windows. In the town where I'd grown up, the diner was called Irene's. In Gypsum, it was Carmen's.

I walked in about one-thirty, late for lunch, early for afternoon coffee break. Plenty of empty booths, but I chose a stool at the counter so I could chat up the stout dark-haired woman behind it.

"You're the TV lady," she said, drying a glass with a white towel.

I raised my eyebrows. "Efficient grapevine you've got around here."

"We use those new fiber-optic cables." Her sepia eyes twinkled. She set the glass on a shelf and handed me a coffee-stained menu. "I've got a couple of chicken tamales left from the lunch special. Homemade. Pretty good, if I say so myself."

"Sold."

"Rice and beans?"

Heck, I was famished. "Please."

"Be right back." She hoisted a bin of used dishes from under the counter and used her ample hip to nudge open the door to the kitchen.

Its return swing ushered in a flushed young woman juggling four plates of food. She blew damp bangs off her forehead and gave me a shy smile. "Carmen'll bring those tamales in a sec. Get you something to drink?"

"Not unless you've got another hand somewhere."

The smile broadened, revealing crooked eyeteeth. After she'd delivered the food to a booth of men in dusty overalls, she fished me a Diet Coke from a big red-and-white cooler at the far end of the counter.

Carmen reappeared. "Thanks, Marisa." She set the tamales in front of me. "You wanna take your break now, before things get busy again?"

"Sure." Marisa untied her apron and disappeared into the back.

"Is all this your children's artwork?" I indicated the framed finger paintings, construction-paper collages, and crayon drawings displayed around the café.

"Children?" Carmen had a gold bicuspid that winked when she smiled. "Aren't you nice. No, those are my grandkids' masterpieces."

"You must be very proud of them." The first bite of tamale made me blink. "These are fabulous. Any more back there I can take home for dinner?"

Looking pleased, she snapped her fingers. "Sorry. All out." Her long hair was threaded with gray, anchored back from her face by jeweled combs. Embroidery circled the neck of her short-sleeved peasant blouse. She wore an apron over a long, loose skirt printed with tropical birds. Below the hem, white socks and running shoes.

"Harmony Magnussen." I held out my hand.

"Carmen Benitez." Rings adorned nearly every finger—silver, turquoise, opal, tiger's-eye. Somebody else must wash the dishes.

"So, Harmony Magnussen." She propped a dimpled elbow on the counter. "What's this I hear about you coming around, stirring things up, getting people all curious?"

I swallowed some rice. "I'm supposed to ask you the questions."

She tipped back her head and laughed.

"C'mon, you probably know everybody's secrets," I said. "I'll bet there's not much goes on in this town you don't know about."

"Oh, now she's trying to butter me up." Wagging a finger. "You're right, though. I tell Kenny Tatum he should pay me—I'm his ace reporter!"

"I saw your restaurant ad while I was searching his archives." I paused before shoveling in more food. "How did people react, when they heard Layla Gormley had killed her little brother?"

Carmen's mouth puckered as if she'd bit into a lemon. "That's the trouble with you TV people. What kind of dumb question is that? They thought it was terrible, of course! How else would they react?"

"You're right," I said through a mouthful of beans. "That was a dumb question. I guess what I meant was, did people believe it?"

"Amberlee saw her do it." Exaggerated shrug. "So she said."

"You sound skeptical."

"Skeptical, schmeptical. Who can say? I wasn't there. Neither were you."

"I notice people in Gypsum call her Amberlee, with the accent on the first syllable. But on TV, they pronounce it Amber *Lee*."

"Sounds fancier, doesn't it? You watch that show—what's it called?—*Glory Gathering?*"

"I watched it once."

"Truckload of cow manure, huh? Oops, sorry. You're eating." She crossed her arms. "It just makes me mad, all those poor sick people thinking that guy can cure them. If all it takes is prayer, why can't they pray for themselves? You trying to tell me God won't listen to them, but he'll listen to some holier-than-thou smarty-pants who thinks he's got some kind of direct dial-up connection to the Almighty?"

"I take it you're not a fan."

She flicked her fingers in disdain. "I saw him in person once, before he got famous. Not impressed then, not impressed now. Who cares how big a church he's got or how many people fawn all over him, or how much he can afford to pay for a haircut? It's what's inside a person that counts. God knows that. You can't fool God with a bunch of high-priced window dressing."

"But if people really believe he has the power to cure them, maybe it helps," I said, playing devil's advocate. "After all, the mind is a powerful healer."

Carmen snorted. "You should make a commercial for him."

"No thanks. I have enough trouble trying to produce reality television." I swung around on my stool while she cleared plates from the quartet by the window. "Did you know Amberlee?"

"Sure," she replied. The question prompted elbow jostling from the workmen, a muffled comment, snickers. "Hey, be nice," Carmen scolded.

Across the street, a charcoal-gray minivan pulled up in front of the *Weekly Miner* office. Ken Tatum lowered a collapsible wheelchair out the driver's side. Eventually, he maneuvered himself into it via a demonstration of upper-arm strength both inspiring and painful to watch. The van had to be equipped with hand controls.

"Poor guy." Carmen noticed the direction of my gaze. She clattered dishes into the bin. "I know you're not supposed to feel sorry for people like that, but I can't help it. Senior year in high school, Kenny was high scorer on the basketball team."

"You were in his class?"

"My little brother, Manuel, was on the same team. My parents made me go to some of his basketball games. Manuel, he mostly sat on the bench. Kenny, though, he was a star."

"What happened?"

"Accident." She removed the plate I'd all but licked clean. "Happened maybe ten years ago. Though usually when I guess, it turns out to be longer. The brakes went out on his car, right outside town. You know that steep winding section?"

I winced. "Oh, boy."

"That's where it happened. Tough luck, huh? Except it was a miracle he wasn't killed, so maybe he was lucky. You want dessert?"

"No, thanks." I waited while she stepped to the register to trade good-natured gibes with the four men paying their bill. "What was that about?" I asked, after the bell over the door signaled their exit. "Earlier, when I mentioned Amberlee."

"Those guys, you mean?" Dismissive wave. "Don't pay them any attention. They're just jealous." She wiped up the scattered detritus of their meal. "Every guy in town had a crush on Amberlee, one time or another, but she wouldn't give most of them the time of day. Now she's a famous TV star. So they make fun of her. Stupid machismo, that's all it is."

"What was your opinion of her?"

The gold tooth winked. "Do I get to be on TV if I tell you?"

I laughed. "You might. So far you're the only person who'll agree to talk to me on camera."

"Ooh, I'd have to get my hair done first." Her smile faded. "Wanna know the truth? I always felt sorry for Amberlee."

"Why?"

"Oh, lots of reasons. Her daddy died when she was young. After that, her momma had to work, so Amberlee got left alone most of the time. Except on Sundays, when Mrs. Pombo would drag her to one of those really long services." Carmen's upper lip curled. "Those ministers at True Holiness Church sure like to hear themselves talk. Poor Amberlee would have to sit for hours and hours while most other kids were free to run around and goof off."

"Doesn't sound like much fun."

"No. After she grew up, she got pregnant and had to marry Curtis. He didn't treat her right, that guy." Carmen clicked her tongue. "The baby girl turned out fine, a real sweetie, but Amberlee's second baby had a terrible birth defect, and later on, the way he died . . ." She shook her head. "Oh, that lady has lived through some tough times."

"Has she ever come back to Gypsum since she moved away?"

"No. I don't think she was very happy here. You know how she seemed to me? Restless. Always had this faraway look in her eye, like she was searching for something."

"Fame and fortune?"

"Could be. Or Prince Charming. Or a nice little house with a white picket fence, someplace with flowers and trees, where the dust doesn't blow in your eyes all day and mine machinery doesn't keep you awake at night." Carmen was getting a faraway look herself.

"She certainly got her wish."

"I hope so. Hope she's found her happy ending."

"What about her ex-husband?"

The bell announced customers. "Need menus?" Carmen called.

"Just having coffee," the senior of two women replied as they settled into a booth.

Marisa emerged from the kitchen, tying on her apron. "I'll get it, Carmen."

"Thanks. Remember, Gloria drinks decaf."

"I remember."

Carmen leaned a hip against the counter. "Now, what were we talking about?"

"Amberlee's ex-husband."

"Curtis? Oh, he's not so bad."

"Other than drinking too much and beating up his wife?"

She pulled back in surprise. "Well. I see you've been talking to people."

"The man himself, for once. Also Curtis and Amberlee's neighbor."

"Noreen, I'll bet."

"Uh-huh."

"She's always had it in for Curtis, ever since he pressed charges so Travis had to spend a few nights in jail for joyriding."

"That's Noreen's son, right?"

Carmen nodded. "Me, I thought Travis got what he deserved. That car was Curtis's pride and joy, some old Mustang he'd got from a junkyard and restored real nice. All scratched up by the time Travis got through with it."

She began sponging the already spotless counter, as if it went against her nature just to stand there and jabber. "Travis did finally straighten out. Went back and got his GED, started working at the gas station, learned how to fix cars. Even saved enough money to open his own little repair business. But back when he was a teenager, look out! Here comes trouble." She winked. "Isn't that right, Marisa?"

Down the counter the waitress was refilling sugar dispensers, though her concentration appeared more focused on our conversation. "Boy, that's for sure." She giggled.

"Marisa was friends with Travis's little sister, Sherri."

"Is she the one who lives in L.A.?"

Marisa nodded. "Hollywood, actually." Her eyes widened. "You're from Hollywood, aren't you? Maybe you know her. Sherri Stern, she works at the police station?"

"A cop?"

"No, no. She does paperwork and stuff."

"Civilian clerk?"

"I guess." Marisa brightened. "But sometimes she gets to fingerprint the criminals when it's real busy!"

"I'm afraid I don't know her."

"Oh." Wistfulness shone in her eyes like spotlights at a movie premiere. "Hollywood. Sherri's so lucky."

Clearly Marisa had never been there. Pimps, drug dealers, and assorted street crazies weren't nearly as glamorous as they sounded.

"Do you remember when the baby next door to Sherri died?" I asked.

"Sure," she said, still gazing at the topless sugar dispenser in her hand as if it were an Oscar. "That was like, a huge deal. Everybody remembers it."

"How old were you?"

"We were away at Girl Scout camp when it happened, which was summer before seventh grade, so I guess like, twelve?"

"Did you know the baby's sister, Layla?"

"The girl who did it? Not really. I mean, she was just a little kid. But Sherri and I used to watch her on TV, after her mom married that minister." Marisa exhaled an envious sigh. "That would be so cool, being on television," she hinted.

Carmen pretended to snap a towel at her. "Back to work, Vanna. Those ladies need refills."

Marisa hoisted both coffee pots and floated off in a trance.

I pulled the crime-scene report from my shoulder bag, trying not to smudge greasy fingerprints on it. "I need to locate the babysitter who was there the day Jake died. Do you know somebody named—" I held the page at arm's length "—Brittany Kimball?"

"Brittany?" Carmen turned from the blackboard, where she'd been erasing lunch specials. "She was there that day?"

"She left a little while before Amberlee discovered the baby was dead."

Rings glinted as Carmen drummed fingernails on the chrome counter edge. "You don't think Brittany had anything to do with that, do you?"

"The chief investigator didn't think so."

"That doesn't answer my question."

I spread my hands. "I don't think one way or the other. How can I, when I haven't even talked to her?"

"You go easy on that girl."

"How about if I leave my rubber hose with you for safekeeping?"

Carmen fought back a smile. "I'm going to tell you where she lives, only because someone else will if I don't. But don't you go upsetting her. She's . . . fragile."

"How so?"

Carmen hesitated. "Find out for yourself. She lives on West Fremont. Go two blocks down the street, take a right, then left when you hit Fremont. Number 122. She got married, though. Her last name's Fontana."

"Fontana? As in Noreen?"

"She's married to Noreen's younger boy, Justin."

"Small world."

Carmen shrugged. "Small town."

The sign by the register declared "We Accept Cash, Cash, or Cash." I paid the bill in cash. Then I asked for a receipt. From Carmen's reaction, this marked a unique event in the café's history. Renegade associate producers weren't entitled to an expense account, but maybe I could deduct six bucks off my tax return.

I waved goodbye to Marisa, thanked Carmen for a delicious meal.

"Don't you pull any of that Geraldo stuff on Brittany," she warned as the bell jangled above my head.

After I turned onto Fremont, my cell phone broke into the Lone Ranger theme. Apparently, my son the comedian had reprogrammed the ringtone again. I pulled to the curb before I answered. Safety first. Even though Gypsum streets offered plenty of clearance for distracted one-hand swerving.

"Harmony Magnussen?" The booming yet intimate voice of a stage actor. Familiar in an out-of-context way, as if from an old commercial.

"That's me."

I braced myself for a pitch from the latest financial telemarketer my credit-card company had sold my number to.

"This is the Reverend Dietrich Schultz," the booming yet intimate voice announced. "I understand you wish to speak with my wife."

CHAPTER 10

Brittany and Justin Fontana lived on the right side of the tracks. At least, one assumed the part of town farthest from the mine was considered most desirable. When I climbed out of the Explorer to walk up their circular driveway, the sound of large trucks backing up to loading chutes was barely audible.

The house sprawled like a hacienda—beige stucco walls, red-tile roof, vast arched windows. The drapes were closed, even though the desert sun was shrouded by pearl-gray overcast. I shuddered, less from cold than at the size of the water bill required to keep the broad front lawn lush as a golf course. Other landscaping fell more into the drought-resistant category, with visual results that bespoke a professional gardener. Either that, or one of the Fontanas had way more patience for endless weeding, clipping and mulching than I did.

In lieu of a front-door peephole, a small, hinged window of rippled glass was set into the dark oak planks. Vertical wrought-iron rods spanned the opening to prevent overeager salesmen from reaching inside to grab occupants by the collar. When a woman close to my age finally unlatched the spy window to see who'd rung her doorbell twice, the bars made her look like a prisoner.

"Is Brittany Fontana home?" Brittany had been fifteen when she'd baby-sat Jake and Layla for the last time, which would make her twenty-nine now.

The woman peering through the bars said, "That's me."

I explained who I was.

"Oh, no," she said. "I don't want to be on TV."

"No problem," I said, presenting both palms for inspection. "See? No cameras. May I ask you a few questions?"

"I don't think . . . I'd better not—"

"Layla said to be sure and say hi to you." The lie sprang off my tongue so easily I almost whirled around to see who had said it.

"She did?" A feeble ray of sunlight broke through the anxiety clouding Brittany's eyes. "Gosh, I never thought she'd remember me."

My conscience dealt me a swift kick in the rear. "It would help a lot if Layla could understand what really happened. Her mother won't tell her much. I hate to say this, but Layla's been pretty messed up by her brother's death."

"Oh, God. Oh, no." Muffled between her fingers. "Please. You'd better come in."

Brittany was barefoot, a stick figure in a jade blouse and black harem pants that drooped like clothes from a hanger. She led me across a vast tiled foyer as if balancing a book on her head. Dull brown hair was woven into a French braid, which fell between her prominent shoulder blades straight as a plumb line. Briefly I considered hiring her to give Dane posture lessons.

Navajo rugs hung from the foyer walls. Once, while Jeff was on location near Santa Fe, we'd spent an entire afternoon with a very patient rug merchant, arguing over which one to purchase. To my amateur eye, these looked like the real McCoy.

In the living room sat a Sony widescreen that would have completely overpowered the average American den, yet fit unobtrusively into this acre or so of polished oak flooring. I'd interrupted a rerun of *Mork and Mindy,* one of the episodes with Jonathan Winters. In addition to a pair of tweed Barcaloungers angled in front of the TV, the leather couch and matching loveseat also reclined. Wall decor consisted of several Thomas Kinkade prints—idealized visions of fairy-tale cottages and stone country bridges.

"Please, sit down."

A crocheted afghan and body-sized dent on the loveseat suggested where Brittany had been curled up. I sat on the end of the couch and resisted the urge to lean back and put my feet up. The end table near my elbow displayed about a dozen framed family photos, the kind relatives send you at Christmas. Several were face down, as if someone had bumped the table and knocked them over.

"Would you like something to drink?" she asked. "Tea? A soda? Something, uh, stronger?"

Her gaze slid to the coffee table, a massive cross-section of glazed walnut burl. On it sat a Chinese lacquer tray holding a half-full pitcher of orange juice, a bucket of melting ice, and a crystal decanter with the stopper resting beside it. Within easy reach of the loveseat, an empty tumbler smudged with fingerprints rested halfway off a coaster.

"Thank you, no. I just had lunch."

The tracery of fine lines around her mouth constricted in disappointment. The decanter contained colorless liquid. It, too, was half full. Or, perhaps more significantly, half empty.

Brittany plucked the remote from the coffee table. Instead of switching off the TV, she lowered its volume a couple notches so as not to miss any good laughs during our conversation.

She brought her feet up to sit in a semi-lotus position. Her toenails were painted glossy pink, like the inside of a seashell. "You said Layla was messed up." She tugged the afghan over her lap and played with the fringe. "What exactly did you mean?"

"Unhappy. Confused. She's grown up feeling ashamed and

guilty for something she has no memory of." I decided not to reveal her career choice, though I wasn't sure whom I was protecting. "She's estranged from her family. It's like she's lost her emotional moorings. She seems to make choices that guarantee bad things will happen to her." I shook my head. "Maybe deep down inside, she's convinced bad is what she deserves."

"That poor kid." Brittany's voice trembled. "I always wondered . . ." She started to reach for her glass, then yanked back her hand. The diamond on her wedding ring set was the size of a cocktail onion. "Does she need money?"

"That's not really the problem. What she needs is information."

Brittany held her spine ramrod straight, as if her life was one long struggle against gravity. "I'm not sure I can help much with . . . with information."

"How often did you baby-sit Layla and Jake?"

"Not very."

I could see how pretty she'd once been, with gold-flecked brown eyes, cover-girl cheekbones, a full-lipped mouth. Only now her eyes were a road map of red veins, her cheeks sunken hollows, her mouth bracketed by premature age lines. Shriveled, somehow. As if all the joy had been sucked out of her.

"Amberlee couldn't really afford to pay for baby-sitting," she continued. "Usually she got her mom to watch the kids, but for some reason Mrs. Pombo couldn't do it that afternoon. It was Saturday, I remember. Amberlee called one of my friends first, but Jen wouldn't do it for what she offered to pay." Brittany swallowed with a dry click. "Jen suggested she call me, and I . . . I told Amberlee I'd do it for half my regular rate."

"Why did Amberlee need a baby-sitter that afternoon?"

"She wanted to go grocery shopping over in Red Rock."

Brittany had a deliberate, precise way of speaking. The brief pause at the start of each sentence created a time-lag effect, like the way some overseas phone calls sound. Or like someone making a conscious effort not to slur her speech.

"We used to have a little store in Gypsum, but the prices were kind of high. Most people went out of town if they needed more than a few items. Amberlee sounded desperate. She said they didn't have hardly any food in the house. Plus, they were out of disposable diapers." Tears blurred Brittany's eyes. "Horrible, isn't it? The way it turned out, she didn't need them after all."

On TV, the audience was laughing hysterically at Robin Williams. Brittany dabbed her eyes with a corner of the afghan. Her skin, stretched taut over sharp facial bones, had the wan, bleached-out texture of someone whose mother refused to let her play outside during a lengthy bout of mono.

"How long did you baby-sit before Amberlee came home?"

"I got there about two." Brittany sniffled. "Amberlee said she'd be gone at least three hours, but it was barely four o'clock when she got back. Anyway, Curtis got home right before she did." Her hand edged toward the glass, jerked back. "We weren't expecting him."

"He was supposed to be at work, you mean?"

"Yes. But he got fired for starting a fight."

"What happened when he got home?"

"Well, he was in a pretty nasty mood. Drunk, too." Quick glance at the decanter. "Yelling, kicking things. People used to gossip about how he got rough with Amberlee. I knew I shouldn't leave the kids alone with him, but he scared me. Luckily, Amberlee drove up right as I came out the front door."

"How did she react when you told her about Curtis?"

"I didn't have time. She rushed past like she didn't even see me. I wondered if she'd already heard about him getting fired, because she looked pretty upset. I decided to get the money from her later, but of course I never did." As if I'd accused her of something, Brittany exclaimed, "How could I, after what happened?"

I've got a news flash for people who insist you can't smell vodka fumes. "Who do you think killed Jake?" I asked.

"I don't know!"

"You don't think Layla did it?"

Longer hesitation than usual. "No," Brittany said through stiff lips. "I never believed that."

"Why not?"

"Because . . . she loved her brother."

"Maybe she was jealous."

"You should have seen her with him! She was so good, so patient and sweet. Singing him songs, rubbing his head, begging to hold him. Amberlee said I should try and get him to take a nap; he was so cranky that day. I had to practically drag Layla out of the room so he would go to sleep." Tears leaked down Brittany's face. "She wanted to keep playing with him. She called him her baby doll."

I reached over to cover Brittany's hand. It felt like she'd dipped it in the ice bucket. "While you were baby-sitting, what was Layla doing? After you took her out of Jake's room."

Brittany wiped her eyes with the back of her other hand. "Watching cartoons, mostly. In the living room."

"Was she upset when she couldn't play with her brother?"

For the first time, the faintest trace of a smile. "Not when she found out *Scooby-Doo* was on."

"Did anything unusual happen while you were there?"

"No." She pulled back her hand.

"Did you send Layla a note recently?"

"A note?" Brow furrow. "I don't even know where—"

A mechanical sound rumbled through the walls. I hadn't

thought Brittany's spine could get any straighter, but I was wrong.

"That's my husband, Justin."

Sounded like the garage door opening. Apparently Brittany hadn't expected him home from work so soon. She clutched fistfuls of afghan. "Please, can you say you're selling something?"

"I don't think that'll work."

"But—"

"I've been asking questions around town, so he's probably heard about me already. His mother is one of the people I spoke to."

Brittany's shoulders slumped. On her, it amounted to half an inch.

In another part of the house, a door opened and shut. Brittany seemed to retreat inside herself, eyes sliding out of focus as if absorbed by some distant inner vision. Footsteps echoed louder on the foyer tile.

The guy who entered the living room was thirty, max. Short, spiky black hair, deep-set eyes, narrow face with sharp, foxy features. His nose veered slightly off-center, giving him a somewhat jaunty demeanor that was enhanced by the leather bomber jacket finger-hooked over his shoulder.

"Well, well, well. I see we've got company!" He navigated around the recliners and tipped up Brittany's chin to brand a kiss on her mouth. She sat motionless, back ramrod straight, hands folded in her lap. Her husband made the same noise I do when biting into a Godiva chocolate. In this case, it wasn't very appetizing.

"Hi, I'm Justin Fontana." He stuck out a hand. The sleeves of his pinstriped shirt were rolled up, tie dangling loosely from the unbuttoned collar.

We shook. He let me run through my entire spiel, even though he probably knew who I was already.

"Sure, I remember when that neighbor kid died." He sucked air through his teeth. "What a tragedy, huh? Uh-oh, what happened here, hon?" He reached over to right the fallen pictures on the end table. "We have another earthquake? Maybe we need to get new frames so these don't keep falling over."

He showed me the picture in his hand. "This is my big brother, Travis. Good-looking guy, huh? People used to say he got the looks, I got the brains. Here's another one of him. Poor guy lost his wife a few years ago. Car wreck. This is their boy, Zack. My nephew. Cute little guy, isn't he? He's pretty special to us, since we don't have any kids of our own. Isn't that right, Britt?"

She nodded in marionette fashion.

"It's kind of dark in here. You forget to open the curtains, hon?" He crossed the room and whipped back the drapes with a magician's flourish. Brittany avoided my eye. Floor-to-ceiling glass revealed an unspoiled view of rugged desert terrain, low mountains huddled against the horizon.

Justin settled himself on the loveseat and dropped an arm around his wife. "What's this, Happy Hour?" Arching his brows like he hadn't noticed before. "Good idea, but we need some more glasses, don't we? Is this yours, Ms. Magnussen?"

"I don't care for anything, thank you."

Brittany lunged for the tumbler. "I'll get some glasses from the kitchen," she mumbled.

Justin caught her wrist before she could escape. "Hold on there, hon. Don't make a special trip for me, long as our guest won't join us."

"I don't mind—"

"Hand me that remote, would you? You just snuggle right here next to me and take a load off your gorgeous feet. I know, I know, you've only got that part-time bookkeeping job and we don't have any kids yet, but it's still a lot of work running a house." He switched off the TV "Now, let's hear what you two ladies have been talking about."

Neither of us uttered a peep. Me, out of amazement.

"Come on, now. What is this, some big secret? What's to tell, anyway? Brittany'd already left the house before little what's-her-name killed her brother."

"Layla," Brittany spoke up. "And she didn't kill him."

Surprise, anger, amusement shuffled across Justin's face in rapid succession. "Oh? And just how do you know that," he teased, "when you weren't even there?"

"I just . . . never thought she did, that's all." The spunk rushed out of her like air from a deflating balloon.

"Face it, hon." He patted her knee. "Sometimes the least likely people do awful things no one would have believed they were capable of." He sent me a·wink. "What other thoughts have you been sharing with Ms. Magnussen, hon?"

"Nothing. Just stuff about Curtis and Amberlee."

"How about you, Mr. Fontana?" I wriggled from the couch depths to perch on its edge, knees glued together like Grandma Magnussen taught me. "You lived right next door," I said. "Were you home when it happened?"

"Me? No. I worked at Wrigley's Hardware back then, Saturdays and after school. Had to hear about all the commotion from the customers."

"How old were you?"

"Same age as Britt." He squeezed her shoulders. "How old were we back then, hon?"

"Fifteen."

I practically had to read her lips.

"Fifteen," Justin repeated. "Hard to believe we've been together that long, isn't it?" Another squeeze. "High-school sweethearts, like in the movies. Got married right after graduation, so Britt could come with me when I went off to college."

"I understand you work at Edwards Air Force Base."

"Yup, that's right. Computer database manager. Mom must've been bragging about me, huh?"

"Are you in the military?"

"Civilian contractor." He crossed an ankle over the opposite knee. "Joining up means all that moving around, one faraway place after another. Britt and I like it right here in Gypsum, don't we, hon?"

If he called her hon one more time, I might have to smash the decanter over his head. "Quite a commute from here to Edwards. What is it, forty-five minutes?" I lifted my eyebrows. "You must get up before dawn, if you're home from work by three." Not his usual habit, Brittany's ambushed reaction had seemed to imply. Was it mere coincidence he'd interrupted our conversation?

Brittany peeked sideways at him. Justin forced up the corners of his mouth. "Matter of fact, I was talking to my mom on the phone, and she happened to mention a strange car in our driveway." He chuckled. "Call me a worrywart, but I decided I'd better come home and make sure everything was all right." He crushed a kiss against Brittany's temple. "Guess I just can't help being overprotective where you're concerned—"

I braced for it . . .

"—hon."

I sprang to my feet. "It's been a pleasure meeting both of you. Thanks so much for your help."

Justin unclamped his arm from Brittany and stood up. "Hey, now you're being polite. I doubt either Britt or I said anything helpful, did we?"

"Too early to tell. You never know what might turn out to be important later."

He stroked his chin and frowned. "Pardon my saying so, but this TV business seems like a big waste of time. I mean, after all

these years, how can you possibly prove little what's-her-name
didn't hold a pillow over her brother's face?"

"Maybe I can't," I said. "But I'm sure going to try."

CHAPTER 11

"Wow. Looks like a clothes factory blew up."

Dane's comment reflected an accurate description of my bedroom. One of the few material legacies of my marriage was a ridiculously extensive wardrobe. Two-thirds of it swooned across my bed like passed-out coeds at a frat party.

"I can't figure out what to wear tonight."

"Oh," Dane said. "I thought maybe you were getting ready for a yard sale."

"Not a bad idea." I held up an Armani number for visual critique. Too stylish? Not stylish enough? What did one wear to interview the wife of a famous televangelist?

Though it sounded as if their plan was to interview me. That, at least, was the impression Dietrich Schultz had conveyed during our brief conversation yesterday. Date, time, place, be there promptly or forget it. Slipping Amberlee my cell phone number on Sunday had paid off, even if her husband was the one who'd picked my note off the ground and called.

In the end, I selected a tailored charcoal-gray suit with a high button-up collar that made me look like a Puritan.

"Remember," I told Dane, "no going anywhere. That means you do not set foot outside this house unless it's on fire. I should be home by ten."

He sat hypnotized over the controls of the latest *Tekken*, which he'd brought home from his weekend at Jeff's.

"Yo, King of the Iron Fist! Have you finished your homework?"

He responded with an ambiguous grunt, which I chose to interpret as, "Yes, and I promise not to sneak out while you're gone this evening. Love ya, Ma. Drive safely."

The sounds of Armageddon accompanied me out the door.

Earlier today I'd consumed several hours at work making notes on the Jake project, stashing them out of sight whenever someone walked into my office. Aside from all the tasks I was actually getting paid for, I'd charted a timeline and committed every "fact" or "clue" to a separate index card. Might work in mystery novels, but if these exercises produced any revelations, they failed to jump out at me.

So I diagrammed the whole mess into a convoluted sprawl of rectangles, which I then attempted to connect via lines, arrows, or dotted trails, many signposted with question marks. Sadly, a lot of rectangles still floated in isolation like icebergs adrift in the North Atlantic.

Further abusing company time and resources, I also ran all the investigation reports through the copier, then stole stamps from Mona's desk so I could anonymously mail the original file back to the Fremont County records clerk.

Tuesday evening, traffic was light—in other words, moving forward—on the southbound 405 until an accident near the Garden Grove Freeway halted me and ten thousand other drivers amid a sea of red brake lights. The trick when you get stuck like this is to locate the emergency flashers up ahead, guesstimate the distance, then factor in your current velocity (which may equal zero). The solution to this equation determines whether or not it's worth bailing out onto surface streets.

I wasn't very familiar with this part of Orange County, so I grabbed the map book and paged through it, easy when the car wasn't moving. The best bet appeared to be getting off at Bolsa

Chica, then taking Warner over to Pacific Coast Highway. Problem was, I'd just passed an exit. And at this glacial crawl, reaching the next off ramp was going to take a while.

I checked the dashboard clock. Still plenty of time before my appointment with Amberlee. I'd left home early, in case I encountered traffic.

Another glance at the clock. One minute had passed, and I'd crept forward maybe ten feet. Still almost a mile to the exit. I drummed my fingers on the steering wheel. Claustrophobia closed in around me. So many cars, none of them moving. I was trapped.

If I had a mantra, I could have chanted it. As an alternative relaxation technique, I tried to focus on something else. Like yesterday's trip to Gypsum. Plenty of food for thought there. Starting with Brittany Fontana.

Why would a seemingly intelligent, potentially attractive young woman with no apparent money woes pass the afternoon zoned out in front of the TV, guzzling screwdrivers?

Of course, if I were married to her husband, I'd probably spend all day drinking too. What else might Brittany be trying to blot out with the closed curtains, the mindless television, and booze?

Heavy drinking hadn't damaged too many memory cells. She seemed to have a clear recall of details about the day Jake Gormley died. Was there something she was trying to forget?

The baby was cranky, she'd said. Brittany had been young, inexperienced, maybe a little resentful about earning only half her usual baby-sitting fee. Had she covered Jake with a pillow out of sheer frustration, to muffle the maddening sound of his screams when he wouldn't stop crying?

Maybe she hadn't even realized he was dead. When Curtis arrived home unexpectedly, Brittany had left in a hurry, without checking on the baby. What if Layla then scampered back to the

113

room to play with him? If Amberlee had walked in right as Layla was lifting the pillow off her brother, no wonder she'd jumped to the obvious, horrifying conclusion.

I could already hear Carson's dramatic voice-over: "How many fifteen-year-olds would have the courage to step forward and say, 'I did it,' especially when the person unfairly accused was a child too young to be tried and sent to prison? So Brittany kept quiet and let Layla take the blame.

"Although she'd gotten away with the killing, Brittany's conscience wouldn't let her off so easily. Guilt ate away at her soul year after year, trapping her in a brittle shell of misery. Locked in her own private prison of self-torment, she turned to the only illusion of escape she could find: the bottle."

Nice theory. What would make it even nicer would be some facts to back it up.

At long last I reached Bolsa Chica and sped off the freeway with a stream of other cars, like water spurting from a leaky pipe. I pulled up to the polished brass intercom one minute late.

I identified myself to the invisible speaker with the same twinge of embarrassment I experience in fast-food drive-through lanes. Seconds later, tall iron gates swung inward at stately speed. For some reason I pictured the Big Bad Wolf opening his jaws. Maybe because the gold-tipped pikes along top reminded me of fangs.

As I drove into the tunnel of Italian cypress, I could almost hear the gates lock shut behind me with an ominous clang.

The cypresses ushered me around a curve that opened into a million-dollar ocean view. More accurately, considering current real-estate prices, several millions. The lights of Newport Harbor sparkled below like jewels tossed against the velvet black Pacific. Farther out, a handful of lone ships chugged toward port at San Pedro or Long Beach. Stationary beacons dotted near the coastline marked offshore oil rigs. Farther out to sea, infinitesimally darker, loomed the rugged silhouette of Catalina Island. The Schultz—home? mansion? palazzo?—had been constructed a prudent distance back from the bluff to avoid landslide zones. Picture Tara airlifted to the Italian Riviera. Ionic columns, second-floor balconies, scrolled brackets beneath the eaves of a low-pitched ceramic-tile roof. Tall Palladian windows divided into small panes seemed an odd choice for a house with such a spectacular view. The main entrance was recessed behind an arch flanked by pilasters. All this clearly visible, thanks to a bank of spotlights concealed in the shrubbery that lit up the facade like Disneyland.

Several asphalt tributaries branched off the driveway, presumably leading to the garage, guesthouse, and other structures deemed unworthy of nighttime illumination. A discreet sign next to one pointed: Deliveries.

I parked as close to the front as I could, which still meant a fifty-yard hike along a flagstone path set into the perfectly groomed emerald lawn. My left foot had just descended from my Explorer when a pair of barking German shepherds came racing out of nowhere. I yanked my foot back inside before they could start gnawing on it.

Obviously, these dogs had never watched *Rin Tin Tin*. Why is it you never have tranquilizers and hamburger when you need them? I cracked open the window and was about to drive them off by playing one of Dane's CDs at high volume when a large barrel-chested man in a suit strode through the spotlights and across the flagstones.

"Klaus! Hilda! Down!"

At his signal, the two snarling brutes instantly quit scratching my car door and dropped into submissive, motionless postures, front paws extended like sphinxes. Somehow, this was even scarier.

When my rescuer stepped closer to give me the all-clear signal, I recognized the bearded security guard who'd hustled me away from Amberlee last Sunday. Reluctantly, I stuck my foot out again.

"Don't worry, they're well trained."

I gave the dogs a wide berth. Ears erect, hackles raised, only their eyeballs moved, tracking me like an unsuspecting rabbit. Either Klaus or Hilda emitted a steady growl.

"I'm Davis Litvak," the security guard said, sounding about as friendly as the dogs. "Follow me, please."

I climbed semicircular front steps that were impossible to span in one stride, forcing me to mince my steps to cross them in two.

Litvak stood aside and waved me through the front door, a massive slab of teak with a fanlight above it. My sensible heels echoed like metal taps against the marble floor as we crossed the entry hall. Without time to snoop, I could only snatch brief glimpses of adjoining rooms. Crystal chandeliers, gilt-framed oil paintings, Aubusson rugs, long mahogany dining table with silver candelabra, overstuffed furniture upholstered in cream-colored fabric. The entry hall was open to the second floor, which was partially screened by a white wooden balustrade. A broad burgundy-carpeted staircase curved gracefully upward. The air smelled of lemon furniture polish and the sickly sweet narcissus fragrance of cut flowers past their prime.

Litvak led me down a side hall, through the door of what appeared to be the Reverend's study. Schultz rose from behind a mahogany desk. His satin robes had been replaced by a fir-green cashmere turtleneck and dress slacks.

"Ms. Magnussen, welcome." He drew off gold-rimmed reading glasses. "It was a pleasure meeting you last Sunday. I hope you enjoyed the service."

"Very much, thanks." If he remembered our two-second

encounter, I was Princess Anastasia. "I appreciate you and your wife taking time to speak with me." Meaningful emphasis on wife, of whom there was nary a sign.

"Oh, we always do our best to help out our friends in the news media." He came around the desk, shook my hand, flashed his perfect white teeth. "You're a television reporter, is that correct? Local or network?"

"Actually, I'm a producer. With *Cold Case Chronicles*. On nationwide cable. Our show deals with mysterious deaths that go unsolved for years."

Frown lines materialized around his mouth. On TV his bland good looks made him appear more youthful than his early fifties, even with silver hair. In person, he looked closer to his real age. Then again, who doesn't?

"I'm afraid I'm a bit confused." He stroked his prominent chin like a bad actor trying to convey deep thought. "I understood you wished to discuss our daughter, Layla."

"I do."

Both of us turned at the sound of a muffled disturbance. Litvak stood barring the doorway, his back to us, head lowered while he muttered to someone. After some muted discussion, he stepped aside to reveal Amberlee.

She tossed her long platinum mane like a high-strung filly. Once confident of our full attention, she flipped on the smile-switch and breezed forward. "Hello, I'm Layla's mother."

Behind her, Litvak crossed his tree-trunk arms and glowered. Schultz made a faint sound. "Amberlee, I thought we—"

"So nice to meet you." Her malachite eyes glimmered as we shook hands. She'd dressed for the occasion in a twin sweater set and matching skirt the color of orange sherbet. "Please, won't you sit down?" She sank gracefully onto an antique brocade sofa that had probably punished many a Victorian tush. "I'll have Elena bring us some tea." She patted a spot next to

117

her until I obeyed. "Now, then. You say you've actually seen Layla recently?"

I shifted, trying to get comfy. "That's right."

Amberlee twisted a strand of pearls around her finger and bit her lip gloss. "How is she, poor thing?" A small beauty mark trembled near her mouth.

"Layla seems fine," I answered untruthfully. "Except she's troubled by the tragedy in your family's past."

Amberlee gripped my arm like a blood-pressure monitor. "It is tragic, isn't it?" Her voice dropped to a theatrical hush. "Such a beautiful girl. Such a terrible, terrible waste."

"Oh." I blinked. "Yes, very sad. But what I'm referring to is—"

"Her father and I are simply devastated by it." She fluttered a hand in Schultz's direction. "We've prayed and prayed for guidance, but in the end, it's all part of God's plan, isn't it?"

Schultz cleared his throat. "Amberlee, it seems she's not—"

"And who are we to question His infinite wisdom and mercy? We simply have to accept, to keep praying it's His will to bring our dear Layla home someday. To show her the error of her ways. To let her know our hearts are full of forgiveness." Amberlee clasped her hands in a beseeching pose. "Maybe if you put all that in your report, Layla will hear it and come back to us."

Her eyes sparkled prettily with moisture. Despite the pious demeanor, she managed to radiate a halo of earthy sensuality as irresistible as catnip. No wonder all those tomcats in Gypsum had the hots for her.

"When was the last time you saw your daughter?" I asked.

"Well, the police stopped bringing her home after she turned eighteen." Her sentence climaxed in a tearful squeak.

Schultz squeezed onto the other end of the sofa and wrapped an arm around her. Amberlee pressed her face into his chest and wept behind a gossamer curtain of blond hair.

"Ms. Magnussen," he said, patting Amberlee's shoulder, "I'm afraid my wife is too upset to continue. Davis will show you to the door."

That wiped the scowl off Litvak's puss. As he unfolded his arms and started toward me, I took a deep breath and touched her wrist. "Amberlee." Emphasis on the first syllable, the way they said it back home. "Layla needs to know how Jake really died."

The room froze in a tableau of suspended animation. Then Amberlee flung up her head, whipping Schultz's face with her hair. "What did you say?" Her cheeks blotched scarlet. "I thought you were doing an exposé about her being a hooker!"

"Amber*lee*." Schultz gave her a not-so-gentle shake. "That's enough now. You mustn't get yourself all worked up. Davis, would you please escort our guest to her car?"

"What do you mean, how Jake really died?" Amberlee gawked at me, her flush spreading like spilled tomato juice. "Layla killed him, of course. I saw her, but it was too late."

"If you'll come with me, please." Litvak clamped a hand on my arm.

Amberlee grabbed the other one, as if teaming up to rip me apart. "Did she tell you something different? Is that it? Because she was barely out of diapers, you know. She can't even remember what happened."

"Are you sure you weren't mistaken?" I plunged ahead, desperate to salvage what little I could before my interview swirled down the drain. "Is it possible Jake was already dead when you saw—"

"That's enough!" Litvak hauled me up on my toes. "Mrs. Schultz, as your attorney, I strongly advise you not to say anything more."

Attorney?

Amberlee shot him a daggered look. She opened her mouth,

glanced at Schultz, snapped it shut.

"Please take your hand off me," I said pleasantly to Litvak. "Or I'll be forced to tell the *National Enquirer* I was assaulted in Reverend Schultz's home while he and his wife stood by and watched."

Litvak complied, as if my temperature had suddenly skyrocketed to broiler range, which wasn't far from the truth.

"If you care at all about your daughter," I said to Amberlee, "think about what this has done to her."

Then I spun on my heel and marched out, startling an unfortunate maid in the process. Litvak trailed me at a safe distance. Five seconds after I slammed the front door, I heard it open again. Felt his dark, steely gaze drilling between my shoulder blades, watching me all the way to my car, making sure I didn't sneak around back and try to break in through the French doors.

I was mad enough now to take on the dogs, but they'd vanished. Along with my best chance to uncover the truth about Jake Gormley's death.

CHAPTER 12

The neighbors on either side of my house, obviously people with too much time on their hands, turned every holiday into a competition to see who could put up the most ostentatious yard display. With Halloween only a couple weeks off, my house was under siege from leering skeletons, gore-dripping corpses, ghosts floating through oleander trees. Cobwebs festooned the bougainvillea, as a mechanical Frankenstein rose from a bird-of-paradise plant to utter a menacing *bwa-ha-ha* before sinking back into the foliage. The other neighbor had rigged a witch on a broomstick to circle around and around a jacaranda tree, treating passersby to endless lunatic cackling.

The decorations matched my mood. During the drive home from Newport Beach, I'd progressed from anger through dismay and on to self-recrimination. Final stop, depression. I'd just blown my one shot at coaxing answers from the person most likely to know how Jake really died.

Curious how the Schultzes had been willing to talk, as long as they thought my intent was to broadcast something like "The Reverend's Secret Shame: Stepdaughter's Slide into Sin." But the moment I brought up Jake, they hit the mute button. Something about his death they were desperate to hide? Or simple panic when the interview didn't go according to script?

Amberlee hadn't been following her lines, either, judging by the facial acrobatics of her husband and their attorney. Was Schultz even aware Amberlee had had another child? He must be, even though Layla claimed the subject of Jake had been strictly verboten while she was growing up. Amberlee and her mother couldn't possibly have tried to conceal such an enormous secret, could they? What would be the point?

No, Schultz had to know. When I'd mentioned the name, neither he nor Litvak had asked the magic question: "Who's Jake?"

Funny, isn't it, how lawyers hovering in the background always make clients seem less innocent?

I bounced over the bone-jarring concrete hump at the foot of my driveway. Decades ago the city of Santa Monica had planted ficus trees along the curbs in this part of town. The trees were attractive, fast growing, hardy enough to thrive in an urban environment with little or no TLC. Boy, did they thrive. Over the years, shallow roots grew to the size of giant octopus tentacles, spreading outward like some mutant sea monster, pushing up sections of sidewalk, undermining streets, snaking their way inside sewer pipes to wreak havoc with residential plumbing.

And who got stuck with the bills? Homeowners. Who were also legally liable if someone tripped over an uplifted chunk of sidewalk in front of their property. I had to get my driveway fixed. Soon as I had an extra thousand bucks.

The garage, like our house, dated from World War I and had never been retrofitted with an automatic opener. I'd fallen into the lazy habit of leaving the car near the kitchen door. When I parked and got out, I could see a jet taking off from LAX, five miles down the coast. The briny dampness of sea air filled my lungs. Cold tonight. Whatever happened to Indian summer?

Inside the house, Nirvana was wailing at maximum volume. Yelling "I'm home" was useless. Dane wouldn't have heard a 747 drive up. I made straight for the living room and the stereo controls, then pulled up short. Sniffed telltale fumes. Dane had company. So unexpected, it took me a moment to place her.

Dane bounded off the couch to turn down the music. "Hey, Ma." He head-flicked bangs out of his eyes, which darted randomly between guilt, sheepishness, and defiance. "Guess you know Leilani, huh?"

Layla was draped over one end of the couch, gold platform sandals kicked off, skirt hiked up near the top of her thighs. No, on closer inspection, it was actually tugged down. She was wearing a see-through blouse over a skimpy camisole, along with my favorite blue sweater.

She wiggled fingers at me, the ones not holding a cigarette. "Hi." She'd had a perm since I'd last seen her. A ponytail sprouted from the top of her head in a cascading fountain of peroxide curls.

"Well." I caught my breath. "This is a surprise."

A half-empty Bud Light bottle sat on the coffee table, next to a saucer of butts and ash. Two points for Dane. No beer in front of him. Plus, he'd slipped a coaster beneath hers. Also on the table: a couple of bowls, two spoons, and an empty pint container of Ben and Jerry's Cherry Garcia.

Spread open amid the debris was one of the family photo albums Jeff and I had divvied up as divorce spoils. This seemed a very un-Dane-like activity for entertaining young female guests. Nirvana must have been Layla's choice, too, since Dane now scornfully relegated them to the Oldies category.

He was eyeing me like a new bomb-squad recruit contemplating his first solo assignment. I carefully lowered myself into my grandmother's antique rocking chair.

Two questions were forefront in my mind. "How did you find my address?" I asked Layla. And, could Woolite get the smell of smoke out of that sweater?

"I stopped by that production place where you work. Only they told me you'd already left."

"When was this?"

"Today. 'Round five." She tapped an inch of ash onto the saucer. Part of an expensive set my aunt had given Jeff and me for a wedding gift. "It's been like, a week, since I told you about the letter and all. I was wondering if you'd found out anything."

"And someone at Wyatt Productions told you where I live?"

She fanned her cigarette through the air. "No, no. Hey. No. I didn't bother asking, even. But when I was walking back to the bus stop, I saw you headed up the hill. So I followed."

"You . . . followed me?"

"Tried to, anyway." She shook her head. "Man, you're really in shape for your age! I could barely keep up on that big hill between here and the ocean. I was huffing and puffing so hard, thought I'd never catch you. Luckily, I saw which house you went into. Only then my girlfriend called. She was like, having a major crisis, and I couldn't tell her I was busy, you know? So I walked down to Lincoln, hung out at Mickey D's for a while, trying to talk her off the ledge." She sidled Dane a coy glance. "By the time I got back, you weren't here."

"I told Leilani you'd gone to talk to her mom," Dane added helpfully.

"And then—" She smacked her bare thigh. "He told me who his dad was. I was like, omigod, I can't believe Jeff Burdick is your father! So he said, here, I can prove it." She tapped the photo album. "You know, I used to be on TV myself once, some dumb church program. *Caldwell* is, like, absolutely one of my all-time favorites. Really. I mean, it's like karma or something, meeting Jeff Burdick's son."

"Lucky it happened to come up in the conversation." I lifted an eyebrow at Dane, whose usual policy with social encounters was to play down any connection to his famous father.

Layla slowly rotated her head to stare openmouthed at me. "And you! You slept with the man, for God's sake! I'll bet he was totally fantastic in the sack wasn't he? Come on, 'fess up."

Dane and I both reddened. "Getting back to your letter," I said. "I still haven't found out who sent it, but I have learned some information about your past. The town where you once lived is called Gypsum."

"Not Gypsy? Well, close."

"It's out in the desert, the other side of Edwards Air Force Base. I spoke to your old neighbor, Noreen. Mrs. Fontana."

Layla shrugged. "Can't say it rings a bell."

"How about Brittany Kimball?"

"Who?"

"She used to baby-sit you. In fact, she was there the afternoon Jake died."

Layla's eyes narrowed. "You think maybe she could have done it, not me?"

"It's a little early to accuse anyone. Do you remember Curtis Gormley? Your stepfather?"

"My what?"

"Your mother's first husband. He raised you from the time you were born until they split up, after Jake died."

Blank stare.

"He told me he used to watch *Sesame Street* with you."

Something flickered deep in those green eyes. As if hypnotized, Layla lifted her beer in slow motion. Just before it touched her lips, she pulled back the bottle, sniffed the opening, frowned in puzzlement. Then her eyes misted with tears. "Daddy," she said in a tiny voice.

"So you do remember him." I felt absurdly pleased.

"Oh. My. God." She set down the beer with the reverence due a holy relic. "This is like, so weird. I just flashed on him all of a sudden, right out of nowhere. He used to toss me up in the air and catch me. Sometimes he'd pretend he was gonna drop me, and I'd scream so loud Mom would get mad at both of us."

Her smile faded. "Why'd you call him my stepfather?"

This could get tricky. "Curtis married your mother shortly before you were born, but it seems someone else was your biological father."

"Who?"

"No idea." *Some trucker Amberlee hooked up with in a bar.* "Nobody I spoke to knew."

"Lemme see if I got this straight." She stubbed out her cigarette. "Mom shacked up with some guy who skipped town when he knocked her up? And afterwards, my dad married her?"

"I, uh, guess that about sums it up."

"Wow." Layla shook her head. "Is that cool, or what?" Admiration spread across her face like sunrise. "How many guys would have the decency to step up to the plate like that, huh? Raise some other dude's bastard like their own. Boy." Her eyes shone. "It's like he's . . . he's some kind of . . . of hero."

Not quite the term I'd have applied to bad-tempered, beer-swilling, thickheaded Curtis Gormley, but I didn't plan to disillusion her.

She crossed one leg over the other, providing Dane a tantalizing glimpse of flesh from the far end of the couch. "So," she said, bouncing her foot. "You happen to run into my grandma while you were down there at the old Heavenly Homestead?"

"No. Just your mother and stepfather. And a lawyer named Litvak."

"That creep?" Her nostrils flared as if assailed by something foul. "He still around?"

"Has he been your parents' attorney a while?"

"Like, since forever. He was some pet project of Dietrich's, back when he was in prison."

"Dietrich was in prison?"

"No, no, Litvak. Guy's got ex-con written all over him, doesn't he? Even dressed up in those monkey suits he wears.

126

One time I was like, spying on him outside his window? When he took off his shirt, he had these prison tattoos all over his arms. Scary."

"Litvak lives at your parents' estate?"

"Far 's I know. In one of the guesthouses. He uses the front part for an office. Supposedly he found salvation in the slammer, after listening to one of Dietrich's boring sermons on the radio." Layla rolled her eyes. "He wrote Dietrich some letter, then Dietrich wrote back, blah, blah, blah. Daddy Dearest hired him to be a bodyguard or something when he got out of the joint, then sent him to law school. Now, when Dietrich says jump, Litvak says how high?"

"What was he in prison for?"

"Beats me. We weren't exactly best buds, you know? Jerk was always on my case about why I didn't act right, how come I was always getting in trouble and embarrassing His Holy Highness. I think it was Litvak's idea to send me away to that boarding school, till I got kicked out."

She swallowed some beer, twirled a coil of hair. "You didn't see Grandma, huh? She was pretty cool. Used to slip me a few bucks if I was hard up. Basically, though, she's got to do what Mom and Dietrich tell her, or . . ." Layla catapulted a thumb over her shoulder. "Out on her butt."

Dane guffawed. "C'mon. They wouldn't kick out your *grandma.*"

"In two seconds." She snapped her fingers. "Just like they did to me."

I cleared my throat. "Your mother seems to really miss you. She sounds anxious for you to come home."

"Oh, sure. That's probably how come the time before last when I got arrested, they told the cops to stop bringing me back, then slammed the door in my face."

"You've been arrested more than once?" Dane sounded impressed.

"Sure. Just happened again Labor Day weekend." She shrugged. "No big deal. My, um, agent bailed me out pretty quick. I've been getting arrested since I was fifteen, when I started running away. Cops would bring me home. Everybody'd holler at me. Then I'd run away again. It's a lot easier now that they don't drag me all the way back to Orange County." She reached for the purse at her feet. "Okay if I use your bathroom?"

"Down the hall, second door on the right."

She scuffed on her sandals. The moment she'd clomped out of the room, Dane seized the nearest patchwork pillow and clutched it to his chest like a shield. "Don't start, Ma."

"You know the rules." I cranked my voice down to simmer. "No smoking in the house. No underage drinking. And what is she doing with my sweater?"

"She told me she was twenty-one! And what was I supposed to do, let her freeze?"

"You're not supposed to let strangers in the house."

"Oh, come on. You think she could've overpowered me?"

"Dane, she's not your typical teenager. She's very . . . troubled."

"Look, she didn't offer me any freebies, if that's what you're all freaked out about."

I banished the image with a shudder. "She's got a criminal record. She could be casing the house for one of her cohorts to rob later."

"Cohorts?" He snorted. "Ma, even the writers on Dad's show don't use bogus terms like that."

I pointed down the hall. "She could have drugs in that purse. You know what would happen if the police burst in and found them? Not only would you go to jail, but we could lose this house."

"For cryin' out loud, why would the cops bust in here in the first place? And why are you getting on my case? She's your friend."

"She's not my friend. She's a work-related acquaintance."

Dane flipped the pillow aside. "Weren't you saying the other day how you felt sorry for her? How terrible it was that she'd gotten totally screwed up thinking she killed her brother? That people shouldn't be judgmental, considering all the emotional crap she had to deal with growing up?"

Ouch. Hoisted with my own petard. I picked up the pillow and sat beside him. "You're right, I did say all that, and I appreciate that you were paying attention."

"Jeez, sometimes you treat me like a retarded four-year-old."

I nudged his ribs. "Cut me some slack, huh? I know you're almost an adult. But I've been worrying about you for seventeen years. You can't expect me to quit cold turkey."

"Yeah, yeah." He studied his hands and sighed. "You think . . ." The metal hoop through his eyebrow glinted. "You think she'd go to the prom with me?"

I gasped.

Behind that maddening shag of black hair, his blue eyes twinkled. "God, you're so easy."

I hit him with the pillow. "Brat."

We were still slugging it out when Layla reappeared. Her smile flickered uncertainly, as if she couldn't decide whether it was our laughter or the blows that were real. "My dad and I used to pillow fight," she said. "At least, I'm pretty sure I remember."

Then a bleak wind seemed to sweep the wistful happiness from her eyes, ushering in the sorrow I'd seen before. Sorrow for what she'd lost. For what she'd never had. For what she believed she'd done.

"Come on." I brushed hair out of my face. "I'll give you a

129

ride home."

Dane stood at the same time. "I'll come, too."

"Homework?"

He slumped like I'd mortally wounded him. "Okay, okay."

On the way back to Hollywood, I sketched Layla the outlines of what I'd learned so far. "Don't get your hopes up," I warned. "We may never know how Jake really died."

She stared out the window at passing neon. The glass reflected someone whose hopes hadn't been up for a long time.

"Not my business," I said, "but have you ever considered counseling? To help you deal with all this stuff in your past?"

"Forget it." She blew a raspberry. "I'm fed up with shrinks. I got enough of that whole scene while I was growing up."

"You've seen therapists before?"

"Sure. Mom and Dietrich kept it hush-hush, of course. Wouldn't want the press getting wind their kid might be wacko, right? Hell, every time I'd screw up, they'd send me to a new one, then start praying to Jesus that this time I'd finally straighten up and fly right. Guess I disappointed them, huh?"

"A good therapist can be really helpful, Layla. Maybe if you chose one yourself."

"Look, I don't need to have my head examined, okay? All that talk-about-your-feelings bullshit. I'm doing just fine on my own."

Time to back off. For now. I drove her through a Taco Bell on La Brea, at least winning my argument that Cherry Garcia ice cream didn't constitute dinner. But Layla scored the final point by refusing to give me directions to her apartment. Despite the chilly night and a flurry of maternal-style protests, she insisted on hopping out near the corner of Sunset and Highland. She turned to wave, then tottered down the sidewalk, vanishing into the desultory flow of sightseers and street people.

I hadn't uttered a peep about my sweater. What the heck. I

probably would have wound up selling it for fifty cents at a yard sale someday.

As I was circumnavigating the block to head back toward La Brea, a wailing crescendo alerted me to flashing lights rapidly filling my rearview mirror. I pulled over to let a police car race by. The Hollywood station on Wilcox was less than half a mile away. Once the threat of a ticket had passed, my knees went mushy with relief.

Several scofflaws whizzed by in the cruiser's wake before I could ease back into traffic. Once I headed west again, the road map of "clues" I'd diagrammed this afternoon unfolded itself inside my head.

I was braked at a red light, waiting to turn left, when one of those question-mark connections sideswiped me.

Soon as I could, I pulled over again. This time to make a phone call.

Chapter 13

Shortly after midnight the theme from *Star Wars* woke me from a sound sleep. Someone had been playing with my cell phone again. My first thought was *Emergency,* and my heart lurched into overdrive.

By the time I fought my way out of the covers, groped through the dark for my purse, and located the answer button, I was gasping for breath. "Hello?"

"Miss Magnussen? Amberlee Schultz. I wanted to let you know that I watched your show tonight and found it very interesting. Goodness, I didn't wake you up, did I? I thought you TV people never went to bed before dawn."

Yeah, me and Conan O'Brien. "No, no, I'm glad you called. I felt our last conversation was sort of, ah, cut short."

"We didn't even get to have our tea, did we? Oh, I do hope you'll accept my apologies. My husband tends to be a teensy bit overprotective sometimes. God bless him. He can't stand to see me cry! Men are so funny that way, aren't they?"

Glare from the bedside lamp made me squint. "I certainly didn't mean to upset you."

"Heavens, it was such a shock, that's all! I mean, there I was, under the impression you'd come to discuss Layla, when out of the blue you started talking about my precious little Jake, and I . . . I . . ." Her tone dropped into ghost-story hush. "Chills ran up my spine."

"I'm very sorry for any misunderstanding." I scrambled for

my notebook, shoulder-clamping the phone to my ear. Not easy, the way cell phones have shrunk to the size of postage stamps. "Of course, this is partly about Layla. About how the tragedy of her brother's death has affected her."

I heard a tongue click. "Really, now," Amberlee said. "How could it possibly affect her when she was too young to remember? I should think your viewers would want to hear how it's affected me! After all, I was Jake's mother. How do you think I felt, walking into that bedroom and seeing my four-year-old daughter holding a pillow over my baby's face?"

Four? Try five. "I can't even imagine."

"No one can." She hauled in a quavery breath. "Then to cradle his cold, lifeless body in my arms—"

"His body was already cold when you picked him up?"

"Well, no." She sounded miffed at my interruption. "No, of course not. It's just a figure of speech. Because I could tell he was dead."

I scribbled rapidly. "Did you try to revive him?"

"You mean, like mouth-to-mouth? Sweet Jesus, no, I was far too traumatized. Besides, I wouldn't have had the faintest idea what to do. It's not like I was a nurse or anything."

"Jake had lots of medical problems, didn't he?" I leaned back against the headboard, notebook propped on my knees. "It's a shame no one ever showed you how to do infant CPR."

"A shame? It's practically criminal!" Theatrical sigh. "I guess all those doctors were too busy to waste any of their valuable time teaching a young mother something that could have saved her poor baby's life someday."

I produced a sympathetic cluck. "I suppose Curtis didn't know CPR, either."

Pause. "Curtis?"

"We spoke the other day. He was generous enough to share his side of the story with me."

The sharp intake of breath nearly sucked me into the phone. "You mean he . . . but he swore he'd never . . ." Sputtering ensued. "Don't you dare believe one word that man says!"

"He seemed pretty convincing to me."

"Miss Magnussen, I don't believe in speaking ill of other people. 'Judge not, lest ye be judged,' as it says in the Bible. I'm afraid, however, you leave me no choice. Curtis Gormley is a drunk and a liar!"

"Did he kill Jake?" I asked.

"What?" A clatter, like phone hitting marble. "He most certainly did not. Why, that would make me a liar, wouldn't it? I saw Layla do it. Do you have any idea the enormous amount of anguish that causes me? How much I've suffered all these years, haunted by that horrifying image?"

"Must be a nightmare." I stifled a yawn. "Still, it would be perfectly understandable if you did cover up for Curtis. After all, he was your husband. Father to your surviving child. You were financially and emotionally dependent on him. What would you and Layla have done if he got sent to prison?" I dangled the bait. "Pointing the finger at Layla, at someone too young to face serious legal consequences, would have been a very smart move. Who could blame you?"

"I told you, it was Layla who held that pillow over my baby's face," Amberlee said, refusing to bite. "I saw her. Besides, why on earth would Curtis want to kill Jake?"

"Maybe he lost his temper. He was drunk, angry about being fired. He might have resented Jake for being a financial burden or for all the attention he received because of his illness. Plus, I heard Curtis really hit the ceiling when he discovered Jake wasn't his."

Amberlee emitted a strangled squawk, took a moment to recover. "Who," she demanded through clenched teeth, "have you been talking to?"

"Lots of people," I said cheerfully. "Everyone's been very helpful."

Our connection developed substantial hissing. "Your program didn't strike me as one of those tabloid shows," she said after a minute. "I presume you are interested in the truth?"

"Absolutely."

"Well, I'm the one person on earth who can tell it to you."

"I'd be happy to drive back to your—"

"No, no. Reverend Schultz would be extremely unhappy if he knew I intended to subject myself to such a painful trip into the past. Can you meet me tomorrow at the Queen Mary? The boat? You know, in Long Beach? Tell them at the entrance you're there for a meeting with Dolores Pombo."

"Your mother?"

"Yes. Whatever you do, don't mention my name. I'll reserve one of the conference rooms. Meet me there at two P.M."

"Two P.M. Thursday?"

"No, tomorrow? Oh, look at that, I guess it's tomorrow already. Two o'clock today. Wednesday. And don't come lugging one of those monster video cameras. Bring a hand-held, so you look like a tourist and not a TV reporter."

Mentally I zoomed in on my cluttered desk at Wyatt Productions. The long list of interviews I was behind on scheduling. The computer Inbox flooded with all those viewer e-mails it was my job to wade through. The budget figures for the Omaha episode, which I'd promised to have for Danielle by five. If I skipped out at one to meet Amberlee in Long Beach, I'd never make it.

"See you today at two," I told her.

It took me an hour to fall back asleep.

Worry Number One: I was risking my job by pursuing this story on my own.

Worry Number Two: Why was Amberlee willing to talk on

camera, when her husband was dead set against it? She hadn't dreamt up this cloak-and-dagger rendezvous aboard the Queen Mary on the spur of the moment. She had to have planned it before calling, before I'd hinted that others were offering up their own versions of Jake's death, perhaps tarnishing her sterling image in the process. Had the Schultzes changed tactics? Decided that tossing me an interview bone might make me go away? Was it Amberlee's goal to throw me off track by lying?

Worry Number Three: Global warming. Once I get started, I can't stop.

At six forty-seven, the phone rang again. I bleated noise into it.

"Harmony? Mark Ellison. I didn't wake you, did I?"

Naturally, I denied it. Why is this everyone's automatic re-action, when the truth is so obvious?

"Don't you know better than to lie to a cop?" he teased. "My apologies. But you left a message to call no matter what time."

"Next time I say that? Ignore me."

"Come on, the last thing you need is more beauty sleep. You get any more beautiful, you'll cause pileups on the freeway."

"Only if drivers catch sight of me first thing in the morning and panic."

Mark was the West L.A. homicide detective whose name appeared each week as police consultant during the closing credits of *Caldwell*. His main function was to be the big spoilsport who kept the show's writers from straying too far from reality. On occasion he came up with a clever plot twist, never complaining when it was promptly stolen. His consultant's salary helped support an ex-wife and two kids in college.

Mark and Jeff had hit it off after they met during the series pilot, the friendship soon expanding to include me. Over the show's seven seasons, Mark had lost a little hair, gained a little weight around the gun belt, but would no doubt elicit regretful sighs at his twenty-fifth reunion from all the girls who'd ignored him in history class. I'd always suspected Mark had a teensy crush on me. Okay, understatement. Call it woman's intuition, but I knew. Jeff always seemed oblivious.

Mark had called twice since my divorce, brief how-ya-doin' conversations during which more seemed unsaid than spoken. So far he hadn't pushed, hadn't made any move to test the longtime safety screen of semi-flirtatious banter nailed between us. I wanted to keep it that way.

Last night was the first time I'd initiated contact. I hated to take advantage of whatever soft spot Mark might have for me, but I needed help. Which didn't make me feel less guilty.

"I found the arrest record you're looking for," he said. "Schultz, Layla, aka Leilani. She was picked up Sunday night of Labor Day weekend, near Grauman's Chinese."

The theater hadn't officially been called that since Mann's bought it thirty years ago. "Then she would have been booked at the Hollywood station?"

"Uh-huh. Monday being a holiday, she had to cool her heels in lockup until her pimp could bail her out Tuesday morning."

"Did you find out if there's a civilian clerk named Sherri Stern who works at Hollywood Division?"

"Sheryl Stern. Currently working swing shift. Last month she was on graveyard."

"Mark, thanks. I really, really appreciate this. I, um, hope you didn't have to break any rules."

"Anything for you, schweetheart."

"That is possibly the worst Bogart imitation I have ever heard."

He chuckled. "Want to tell me what this is all about?"

Fade-in: The bar across the street from the studio, where the *Caldwell* cast and crew hung out. Mark and Jeff, hunched over a couple beers.

137

Hey, get this. Your ex called me the other night to ask a favor. You'll never guess what she's up to.

Scene ends with a jovial round of har-hars about how cute it was, me playing private eye.

So cute that Jeff might mention it to his pal Roy Pastorelli, who might pass it on to his racquetball buddy Carson Wyatt, who might wonder why his lowly associate producer was running around claiming to be the producer of a *Cold Case Chronicles* episode that his second-in-command—and alleged secret lover—Danielle had already put the kibosh on.

"Not now," I told Mark. "Maybe later."

"Story of my life," he said with a sigh.

The Queen Mary's last voyage took place in 1967 when the aging cruise ship was auctioned off to the highest bidder and set sail for her new home in Long Beach, California. She'd struggled through stormy financial seas ever since, weathering a succession of different operators, aborted renovations, temporary closures, and economic downturns, never quite surfacing as the tourism treasure chest the city fathers had envisioned when they'd plunked down three and a half million for her.

I'd bribed my co-worker Ahmed Saleh, one of the camera operators—sorry, cinematographers—to tape my interview with Amberlee. The bribe involved my ex-husband's autograph.

After Danielle had shot down my story idea in front of everyone, Ahmed had been the only person to praise all the work I'd done. In my book, that alone qualified him for this assignment, never mind the fact he'd graduated first in his UCLA film-school class three years ago. He was reliable, hard-working, unflappable in the midst of chaos. Quiet by nature, polite to the point of chivalry. Best of all, he knew how to keep his mouth shut.

At the southern end of the Long Beach freeway, I followed

the Queen Mary signs to the parking lot. Ahmed managed to grab his camera case from the back seat and rush around to open my door before I'd even stuck the keys in my purse. He was only a few inches taller than me, wiry and welterweight, with close-cropped dark hair and a toothbrush mustache he probably thought made him look older. No matter what the weather, he always dressed the same: pullover sweater, dress shirt and tie, impeccably polished black shoes. According to workplace scuttlebutt, years ago his parents had betrothed him to a girl still patiently waiting for him back in Cairo.

A stiff offshore breeze made a mess of my hair as we crossed the parking lot, lashing us with fumes of fuel oil and decayed sea life. Seagulls wheeled and squawked above sailboats tacking along the harbor channel. Against the brilliant blue-sky backdrop, a string of flags fluttered from the bow of the Queen Mary to the top of her mainmast.

"Impressive," was Ahmed's comment. He studied the colossal black hull, the white superstructure, the three large red-and-black smokestack funnels. "Why is there a Russian submarine parked next to it?"

"Um . . . replacement for the Spruce Goose?"

"The Howard Hughes plane?"

"It used to be housed in that big white dome. Wasn't enough of a tourist draw, so they hauled it up someplace in Oregon. You've never been here before?"

"No."

"You and plenty others, I guess. The Queen Mary's always been sort of a white elephant."

"Sorry?"

"Something not very profitable that takes a lot of money to run." We passed a poky collection of souvenir shops and ice cream parlors trying to pass itself off as an old English village. Visitors were outnumbered by a flock of pigeons squabbling over spilled French fries.

Access to the Queen Mary was via a tall structure housing elevators and a ticket booth, connected to different decks by walkways. Though the sign read Hotel Queen Mary, the ship's renovated interior also included shops, restaurants, and convention facilities. Tourists could explore limited areas on a variety of guided and self-guided tours.

We rode the elevator up to the reception desk. I'd forgotten to go over our cover story, but Ahmed didn't blink when I announced we were there to meet with Dolores Pombo.

Armed with a map of the Promenade Deck, we crossed over the water into the ship. "Wow," Ahmed said, gazing around at the lavish Art Deco interior. "Looks like the Titanic."

"I'm almost certain you just committed a horrendous breach of maritime etiquette," I said. "Come on, the map shows the Regent Room down this way."

The woman who answered my knock sported a peach cloud of permed hair. Mid-sixties, encased in a bold floral-print dress that clung a tad snugly and emphasized the bulging contours of her midsection. She wore orthopedic shoes and too much lipstick. Her ankles were swollen.

"We're, ah, here to see Dolores Pombo?"

"You're lookin' at her, toots. You must be the TV hotshot." She raked Ahmed with a suspicious glance as we entered.

"Miss Magnussen, how wonderful to see you again." Amberlee sailed forward from her pose by the window and extended a perfectly manicured hand.

"This is Ahmed Saleh. He'll be operating the camera."

"Delighted to meet you." She batted her eyelashes with a coy head tilt, probably a Pavlovian reaction triggered by the presence of male chromosomes. "Mother, wouldn't you like to stroll around the ship as long as we're here? I noticed some interesting shops when we came in."

"Already seen the ship, remember? That convention you dragged me to three years ago. Those snake handlers or whatever they were."

"Oh, Mother, they were not snake handlers! They were decent, God-fearing religious folk who were absolutely thrilled to meet Dietrich in person and hear one of his inspiring speeches."

Dolores rolled her eyes.

"Really, though. Wouldn't you rather go shopping or something? This is bound to be awfully boring for you."

"Heck, wouldn't miss this for the world." Dolores dragged a chair from several dozen arranged in rows, and plopped herself down with a thud.

"Fine." Amberlee looked like she was about to stomp her foot. She turned back to us. "Now, then, I thought the best place to film me would be in front of that nice picture over there."

An oil painting of a river landscape dominated one end of the room. Ahmed frowned. "It will not work."

"Of course it will!"

"That tree will look like it is sticking out of your head."

"Well, just shoot me from a different angle, why don't you?"

He shook his head. "The biggest problem is that the background will be too distracting. People will be looking at the painting, instead of your beautiful face."

"Oh."

"Much better to have a simple background. This is a very attractive room—see the high ceiling, the old-fashioned light fixtures, the wood-paneled walls? They appear to me to be original. Very classy, very elegant. Like you. So." He shoved a dozen chairs aside, placing one in front of a now-vacant stretch of hardwood veneer. "If you will please sit here, then I will test the lighting. We want to make sure everyone can see you properly."

Amberlee walked over and sat, docile as a lamb.

While Ahmed unloaded his gear and set up the collapsible tripod, I moved some more chairs out of the way. One of my usual jobs on location was substitute makeup artist and hairdresser, but Amberlee had expertly taken care of these chores herself. Champagne hair shimmered down her spine like a shampoo ad, not a strand out of place.

Ahmed handed me the miniature lavaliere microphone. "Can you please clip this on the lovely lady? About six to eight inches below her mouth, please."

Amberlee's outfit resembled what a female ax-murderer's attorney might have counseled his client to wear in court—prim long-sleeved navy dress, white peter-pan collar, delicate gold cross hanging from a slender chain. I had to get a little up-close-and-personal to conceal the body-pack transmitter for the mic, but she seemed accustomed to it.

At last all was ready. Lights, camera—

Before the tape started rolling, I dug out the list of questions I'd prepared for Amberlee.

CHAPTER 14

"People always say, 'Amberlee, with your looks and personality, why on earth don't you get your own TV show?' You know, something especially for women, that would come on right after *The Glory Gathering.* Call me old-fashioned, I guess. The truth is, merely standing in my husband's shadow fills me with all the joy and satisfaction I could possibly dream of. What in heaven's name would I do with my own television program?" Modest shrug. "Though I suppose I could offer advice for a happy marriage, and discuss raising children, or invite celebrity guests to talk about how important God is in their lives. Sort of like a religious Oprah. Only white, of course. Maybe I'd even offer beauty tips. It's certainly no sin to make the most of what the Good Lord's given us, is it? Take you, for instance. I'd be more than happy to share the name of my hair stylist. Oops! Sorry. Well, you can just edit that part out."

Along with ninety-five percent of everything else she'd said.

The format for *Cold Case Chronicles* kept the interviewer off screen, editing out questions later, so in the final cut the subject appeared to be narrating a story instead of undergoing interrogation. Amberlee had a politician's knack for taking any question and twisting it into one she wanted to answer. Pinning her down was like trying to stab a housefly with a toothpick.

Example: "How long was it after you arrived home that afternoon before you went into the children's room?"

"Oh, dear." Heavy sigh. "I've so often thought, what if I'd

Karin Hofland

only gone in there a few minutes sooner? What if Curtis hadn't beat up that poor man and gotten himself fired that day? What if he hadn't stopped off in a bar on the way home and gotten drunk? What if he hadn't started taking everything out on me the minute I walked in the door? Why, that man could try the patience of a saint, and I've certainly never claimed to be a saint. 'Pride goeth before a fall,' as it says in the Good Book. But I guess God had bigger plans for me, and that's why he brought Dietrich and me together. Ever since I first saw him, captivating the crowd at that revival meeting, I knew we were destined to be soul mates. Now, there's a man who should be nominated for sainthood! All the good works he's done, all the people he's helped cure. Why I remember one time, this poor woman with no legs came to our Sunday service, and . . ."

Ahmed, monitoring the audio through headphones, remained stoic throughout. Dolores Pombo sat off to one side, knees sagging apart, facial reactions suggesting she wished she'd gone shopping after all.

The only new nugget to be mined from the interview came near the end, while Amberlee was once again singing her husband's praises. "And to those who might be skeptical that Dietrich can actually perform miracles, I always remind them of Layla, how he restored her ability to speak."

Whoa. "Layla couldn't speak?"

"Why, not for a whole entire year after she killed her baby brother!" Amberlee arched finely plucked brows in dismay. "At first she couldn't stop saying she was sorry, she was sorry, over and over. Then all of a sudden, boom! That was it. Wouldn't utter another peep no matter how much I begged her. As if God had struck her dumb as punishment for what she'd done."

"Did you take her to a doctor?"

"Oh, they couldn't do anything." Impatient hand flick. "No one could help me, not until I married Dietrich and he gener-

144

ously offered to share his power of healing. All of a sudden Layla could speak again! It was a miracle."

Interesting. Not that it shed any more light on Jake's death. I lobbed Amberlee a couple more questions to dodge, then wound up the interview. In all that footage there must be something we could salvage, even if it was just a few clips to give viewers a visual of Jake's mother. Most of Amberlee's rhapsodizing bore little relevance to the case. The truth, which she'd promised to reveal, seemed as elusive as ever.

"Well, this was worth missing my soaps for." Dolores shoved herself upright on arthritic joints, grabbed a lobster-red fanny pack, and strapped it around her waist. "Think I'll step outside for some fresh air."

Ahmed passed me the cassette tape with a shrug. He was touchy about his camera equipment, so I didn't offer to help stow it.

Amberlee donned a pair of designer sunglasses. "When do you think this episode will air?"

Around the Twelfth of Never, I thought.

Ahmed and I were retracing our route off the ship when I spotted Dolores propped against a deck rail, puffing smoke rings and watching the breeze snatch them away. "Wait here," I said. "Might as well take a shot at Mom."

"Personally, it is the other one I would shoot."

Dolores eyed my approach as if suspicious I might invite her to a Tupperware party.

"Mrs. Pombo, I'd like to thank you so much for taking the time to accompany your daughter today."

"Yeah?" She barked a cough of laughter. "Not much to thank me for, is there? Sounded like Amberlee gave you diddly squat. Unless for some reason your viewers find it fascinating to hear all about Dietrich and his magic powers."

I smiled. "You don't believe in miracles?"

"Miracle, schmiracle. Too bad he didn't fix my grandson's spina bifida long as he was curing all those people, huh? Bunch of hogwash, you ask me. Church I was raised in, same one I raised Amberlee in, we didn't truck with those Holy-Roller types. Speaking in tongues, pretending they could cure cancer . . . bah! But the minute Amberlee clapped eyes on Reverend Dietrich Schultz, she had to have him." Dolores pulled a face. "He's a looker, I'll give you that. Not to mention rich as a Rockefeller."

I leaned an elbow on the railing. "Is it true Layla didn't talk for a year after Jake died?"

"Yep." She took a hit of tobacco. "Wouldn't say a word, poor kid. Amberlee 'bout had a fit. I imagine Layla started talking again just so Dietrich'd shut up and quit prayin' over her." Dolores blew a slipstream of smoke through her nose. "Hear tell you've seen her recently."

"Last night, as a matter of fact."

"She still workin' the streets?"

" 'Fraid so."

Dolores shook her head. "She got a raw deal, that kid." Then, cigarette clamped between her lips, she zipped open the fanny pack, scrounged around, pushed two crumpled twenties and a single at me. "Here. That's all I got left of the spending money they dole out each week. Next time you see Layla, give her this, all right?"

I hesitated. "I think she needs a different kind of help than money."

"You think I don't know that? Cripes, I watched her grow up, remember? Give it to her anyway. Tell her to call me sometime."

I took the bills. "You lived across the street from Amberlee and Curtis, didn't you?"

"Done your research, I see."

"How did you happen to be at their house when Jake was

found dead?"

"Why? Think I mighta had something to do with it?"

"I think there are some pieces that don't fit. Maybe you can help me put the whole picture together."

Onshore below us, a family of four was trudging in the direction of the parking lot. Dad pushed the toddler in a fold-up stroller with two silver-foil balloons tied to one handle. A girl about kindergarten age clung to Mom with one hand, an ice cream cone with the other. A pair of Mickey Mouse ears perched lopsidedly on her head.

Dolores positioned both forearms on the rail as if to track their progress. "I'd just got back from bingo that afternoon. Happened to glance out the curtains." Her profile displayed a sharp boundary between face powder and the pale crepe paper of her neck. "Here comes Curtis, stumbling in their front door, tanked to the gills. Not an unusual sight, mind you, except normally he'd be at work. One of the gals at bingo, her niece was a clerk out at the mine. She'd told me earlier about him getting canned."

Below us, the toddler began to shriek and kick his little sneakers. Meltdown approaching.

"Amberlee's car was gone." Pink scalp showed through her thinning fluff of orange hair. "Then pretty soon the babysitter came scooting out like Curtis had chased her off. Oh, great, I thought. Now the kids are alone with that drunken fool. But right away Amberlee drove up. She tore inside before I could warn her, so I went running over to even the odds a little."

Dolores raised the dwindling cigarette stub to her mouth. "Curtis could be mean as a snake when he got loaded. Probably in a foul temper anyway, 'cause of losing his job. I figured if he started using his fists on Amberlee, at least I could grab a frying pan and whack him."

One of the balloons broke free from the stroller. The mother dropped the girl's hand to lunge for it, but the mammoth diaper bag hooked over her shoulder weighted her down. Wind snatched the balloon out of reach, sent it soaring toward the polished blue sky above the harbor. The kindergartener joined her sibling in a chorus of wails.

"Where was Layla when you arrived at their house?" I asked.

Dolores lifted a shoulder. "No idea. Not in the living room, anyway. Curtis was there, sprawled on the couch with beer spilled all over his shirt. When I came in, Amberlee was reading him the riot act."

"What about?"

"Take your pick." She ticked off possibilities on her fingers. "Getting fired, getting drunk, getting beer on the couch. Amberlee was really letting him have it. Guess she figured he was so plastered, she could duck if he started swinging."

"Did he?"

"Nah. Amberlee stomped out of the room." We watched the exhausted mother drag the howling girl toward the parking lot, Dad and stroller bringing up the rear. "I tried to talk sense into Curtis, told him his behavior was a sin, that he owed it to his family to straighten up and fly right."

Down below, the mother-daughter tug of war suffered a casualty when the Mickey Mouse ears tumbled off. As the girl made a desperate grab, the ice cream slithered off her cone to land on the pavement.

Dolores's mouth crimped. "Curtis got a funny look on his face, then stuck his fingers in his ears and started singing some idiot song. I was about to grab his beer and pour it down the sink when Amberlee started screaming."

On cue, so did the little girl.

"What did you do then?"

"Ran fast as I could back to the kids' room, what else?" The makeup line quivered along her jaw. "First person I noticed was

Layla, huddled up against the wall, tears streamin' down her face, yanking her hair. Then Amberlee, carryin' on fit to beat the band. 'Jake's dead,' she cried. 'Layla killed him.' Sweet Jesus, my veins just filled with ice water." Dolores shuddered. " 'Let me see him,' I said. 'Maybe he's just unconscious.' She had him clutched to her chest so tight, no wonder he couldn't breathe."

"Where was Curtis?"

"Right behind me." Dolores cleared her throat and sniffed. "Guess Amberlee was screaming so loud, he could hear even with fingers stuffed in his ears."

I laid a consoling hand on her arm. "Did the baby feel cold?"

"Don't know." She flipped her cigarette butt over the railing to join countless others in the murky water below. "Amberlee wouldn't let anyone else touch him."

Something Dolores had said bothered me. Problem was, I couldn't pinpoint what. If only the camera had been running on her.

I dropped Ahmed off at the Starbucks near Wyatt Productions so he wouldn't have to lie about accompanying me on my unauthorized excursion during company time. If anyone from work spotted us, they'd simply assume we were involved in a different kind of hanky-panky.

I called Dane to warn him dinner would be late, then took Olympic over to La Brea, thus avoiding freeway rush hour. Not that slogging along Westside surface streets at five o'clock was much of an improvement.

L.A.P.D. Hollywood Division resembled a windowless brick elementary school, except for all the bail bondsmen across the street. I found Sherri Stern mopping up vomit just inside the glass door to the rear parking lot.

"If only your friend Marisa could see you now," I said.

Sherri's dark frizzy hair was tied back in a ponytail. She

giggled. "Yeah, maybe she'd get over all that Hollywood glamour stuff." Then it registered that a complete stranger had made the remark. She peered at me closely, stuck the mop in the bucket and squeegeed sweat from beneath her bangs with the back of a rubber glove. "You know Marisa?" she asked, confusion denting her brow.

"We met the other day in Gypsum, when I had lunch at Carmen's."

Hazel eyes expanded to handcuff diameter. "That explains it. You're the TV reporter, right?"

"Producer." I introduced myself.

"Pardon me if I don't shake hands." She wrinkled her pert nose, angled her heart-shaped chin at the brown tile floor. "Some DUI just puked all over the place. Hope they revoke his license. Bad enough when I gotta clean up my kids' barf."

Noreen Fontana's youngest was in her mid-twenties. Not the classical definition of pretty, even cute, but her freckled face and quick-start smile made her instantly appealing. She wore a plastic smock to protect her clothes.

"Yeah, Mom phoned me last week, all wound up because someone was doing a TV show about poor Jake."

"You remember him?"

She bobbed her head. "Not that we saw him much. He was sick an awful lot. And even though I was twelve, Mom never let me baby-sit. She was afraid something might go wrong and I'd get blamed."

"Do you remember the sister?"

"Layla? Sure. In fact, I was just saying to Mom, what a co-incidence! Hardly a month goes by after I see her, when somebody comes around asking about her family's tragedy."

I felt the satisfied jolt of that third slot-machine cherry dropping into place. "You've seen Layla recently?"

"Last month." Sherri's expression sobered. "I hardly

recognized her, though."

"I'm amazed you recognized her at all, considering she moved away when she was five."

"I used to watch her and Amberlee every week on that church show. Heck, half of Gypsum did." She plucked a "Caution - Wet Floor" sign from a stack someone had dumped nearby. "Last few years Layla hasn't been on the show, but she hasn't changed all that much. Except she's gotten awful skinny. Her hair's a totally different color. Plus, her face just has that hard look, you know. The look . . . um, some people get."

"I already know she was picked up for prostitution."

"Okay. Even though it's public record, I didn't feel I should say anything. I mean, we used to be neighbors and all." Sherri bit her lip. "Looked to me like she's had a pretty rough life."

"Did you speak to her?"

"No." She began spacing yellow Caution signs around the perimeter of the mopped area. "Layla looked kind of familiar when they brought her in to Booking, but I couldn't place her right off. After they took her back to a cell, I checked the booking sheet. She was using a different first name, I forget what, one of those hooker-type names. And of course, I knew her as Layla *Gormley,* so even when I saw the last name Schultz, it took a minute for it to click." Sherri swirled her mop through the polluted bucket. "I was hardly going to go back and say hi, though. Probably just embarrass her."

I edged out of spatter range. "You must have been surprised to see her."

"Boy, I'll say! Mom happened to be visiting us for Labor Day weekend, and as soon as I got home I said, 'You'll never guess who I saw.' And she couldn't."

"Did you see Layla again, before she got bailed out?"

"No. I had the rest of the weekend off for the holiday. She was gone next time I came to work."

"Any second thoughts about not talking to her?"

"What do you mean?" She slapped the mop onto the stinky residue.

"Maybe you wished you'd said something. Just a friendly hello, even. Whenever someone catches me off guard, later on I always think of things I should have said."

"Well, I didn't." Clutching the mop handle in front of her with both hands.

"You didn't mail Layla a note?"

"A note?" Wariness crept into her voice. "No. Why would I do that?"

"To make her feel better, maybe."

"About what?"

"To let her know, for example, that not everyone blames her for what happened to Jake."

Sherri began swabbing the vomit zone with renewed vigor. "No. I didn't send her any note."

"You could have gotten her address, right? From the booking sheet?"

"I didn't." Eyes on the floor.

"Did someone else ask you to get Layla's address?"

"No."

Someone had, though. Someone Sherri had told about seeing Layla. Someone who used to worry her daughter might get unfairly blamed if something bad happened to Jake. Someone who'd known Layla back then and apparently felt sorry for the way her life had turned out.

YOUR NOT THE ONE WHO KILLED HIM.

What made her so sure?

CHAPTER 15

Thursday morning the Santa Ana winds blew into town, gusting hot dry air through mountain passes, raising the temperature eighteen degrees, and turning a small Malibu brush fire into a neighborhood-threatening blaze that made all the local morning news shows. Weeks of unusually cool weather had lulled Southlanders into the wistful delusion we might escape the disastrous fire season that flared up every fall, inevitable as the start of the school year.

Walking to work I sniffed the tang of burning chaparral, mixed with the grimy metallic scent of all the inland smog now blowing toward the coast. An 1893 tourist brochure for the Santa Monica Pavilion Restaurant had encouraged visitors to "enjoy the beautiful sea scenery and inhale the appetizing ozone." Either ozone implied something different back then, or city boosters had peculiar ideas about its health benefits.

I rounded the corner of Main and was startled to see two police cars angled to the curb in front of the brick building that housed Wyatt Productions. Never a good way to start your work day. A pair of uniformed officers book-ended the entrance. My heart sped up, along with my feet.

"What happened?" I asked the older cop, crossing my fingers the trouble was on either the first or third floor.

"Break-in." He shifted a toothpick to the other side of his mouth. "Some TV outfit."

Once I convinced them of my employee status, I raced

upstairs to find a crime-scene technician dusting the outer doors for prints. A circle the size of a dessert plate had been neatly sawed out of the glass at doorknob level. "Is this where they got in?"

"What gave it away?" The technician didn't bother to look up. "You people need to upgrade your security system. An amateur could defeat this setup."

"Was whoever broke in an amateur?"

"Looks like he knew enough to wear gloves."

Who didn't these days?

Behind the reception desk, Carson slumped in Mona's chair and delivered weary answers to a man with a hound-dog face and an off-the-rack suit. Could have been either a plainclothes detective or an insurance adjuster. He was transcribing Carson's words like he'd heard them all before.

I scurried past to avoid interrupting. Carson lifted his frayed eyebrows to acknowledge me. Normally he was a spiffy dresser, so the gray sweats and rumpled, unshaven look indicated the emergency call had caught him still asleep. Thinning hair was mashed around his bald spot like a wheat field after a tornado.

The cubicles I passed were all deserted, though moving heads floated here and there above the partitions. I zeroed in on the closest one, which belonged to a sound guy named Matt. "What happened?"

"Some asshole broke into the tape library. Totally trashed the place, man."

"What for?"

"Who the hell knows?" He dragged fingers through the invisible hair on his shaved scalp. "Place looks like the Big One just hit. Shelves knocked over, everything tossed around on the floor. It'll take hours to tell what might be missing."

I freed his arm and hurried toward the room where all the show's videotapes were stored and catalogued. Yellow police tape festooned the doorway in a halfhearted barricade. Inside, a female crime tech was dusting for prints under the watchful eye of the tape librarian. Alicia's glum expression conveyed aware-ness that her job description was about to include cleaning up the black snowfall of fingerprint powder.

A uniformed officer herded me into the conference room, where a majority of the staff stood around and anxiously chewed the cardboard rims of their latte to-go cups. Danielle had a cell phone pressed to each ear and looked mad enough to spit carpet tacks. Mona's eyes were slightly swollen, outlined in pink as if dry winds had stirred up allergies.

"Can't believe all the cops around here," a video editor was muttering to our makeup artist. "Shit, when my apartment got burgled a couple years back, nobody even bothered showing up till the next day."

Ahmed sat back in the corner, spooning yogurt from a container. I flopped down next to him at the conference table. "What's the story?"

He swallowed, then pointed his plastic spoon. "When Mona came to work this morning, she found a hole in the front door."

"Mona got here before anyone else? That's a first."

He allowed a small smile. "I believe she and her live-in gentle-man friend had some sort of argument. She called the police—"

"On her boyfriend?"

"No, no, when she saw the hole in the door. Then she called Mr. Wyatt. The policemen came very fast. Have you seen the tape library?"

"Yes."

Ahmed frowned. "This is very bad. It will take many hours to restore everything to its proper place."

Carson entered the room ahead of the suit guy, panned his gaze around, pointed in our direction.

My pulse kicked up a notch.

"Ms. Magnussen? Mr. Saleh? Detective Amos, Santa Monica Police Department. Would the two of you mind stepping outside, please?"

My worst nightmare, hauled off to the principal's office in front of the whole class. "What's wrong?" I asked at a pitch audible only to dogs. I cleared my throat and tried again.

"I have a few questions, that's all."

Ahmed stood. "Is there a problem, Detective?"

"If you'll both come with me, I'm sure—"

"Whoever broke in made a big mess of both your offices," Carson said. "Like the tape library."

"Oh, no."

Detective Amos glared at Carson as if he'd caught him spray-painting the chief's home address all over bathroom walls at the county lockup. "Yours were the only two cubicles that appear to have been disturbed," Amos said, switching the accusatory spotlight to us. "I'm hoping you might have some idea why."

A sick feeling began to gurgle in the pit of my stomach. Everyone in the room stood watching us. As I rose unsteadily to my feet, Ahmed's troubled glance intersected mine.

Co-workers melted aside like the UCLA defense as Carson escorted me around the table, hand hovering protectively at my elbow. Ahmed and Detective Amos followed. When we left the conference room, so did everyone else.

My cubicle was closest. By the time our little posse arrived, my stomach was in full churn. If intruders had wrecked the tape library out of sheer vandalism, what would have drawn them to Ahmed's office and my office?

Unless they were after a specific tape their destructive search of the library had failed to produce. A tape they had reason to believe might be stashed in either Ahmed's office or mine.

Because only Ahmed and I had been involved in the taping.

I blinked in disbelief at the shambles. Drawers yanked out,

shelves swept clear of contents, files strewn across the carpet. One folder had fallen open to reveal a copy of my pitifully short resume, which I had a gloomy hunch I might be updating soon.

All for nothing. The thieves hadn't found what they were looking for. Which I knew for a fact, because—

My glance jerked back to the resume. To the address typed at the top.

With the ominous roar of an approaching avalanche, dread hurtled toward me. I whirled and seized Ahmed's arm. "You have to drive me home."

"Ms. Magnussen," the detective said. "I realize you're upset, but I have some questions before I let you—"

"My son is home asleep." I locked my desperate gaze on Ahmed. "They could have gotten my address—"

"I will take you."

Everyone probably stared as Ahmed and I fled the scene like a pair of guilty suspects. I didn't notice.

First period had been cancelled for a teachers' meeting, and Dane wasn't one to pass up an opportunity to sleep in. Before leaving for work, I'd reset his alarm and moved the clock across the room, so he'd have to drag himself out of bed to switch it off. Despite a drowsy promise from beneath the covers, I intended to call home later to make sure he hadn't fallen back asleep. But what if—?

Fear nearly made me throw up.

Ahmed drove like a madman. The five-block journey took forever. I flung open the passenger door before his Toyota had even screeched to a stop in the driveway. Though my hands were shaking badly, I managed to stab the key into the lock on the first try. Ahmed hurried up behind, murmuring something about caution, but I was already through the doorway.

A cry of "Dane!" lodged in my chest. The living room was a war zone—furniture upended, drawers flipped over and emptied, every volume in the bookcase clawed open and dumped on the floor like a flock of dead birds.

Someone emitted the terrified shriek of a trapped animal. I was halfway across the room before I realized it was me. Dodging the obstacle course of debris, I flew through the house. When I hurled myself into Dane's bedroom, it was empty. "Dane," I howled.

Ahmed appeared in the doorway, chest heaving, letter opener clutched in his fist like a dagger. "I do not think he is here, Harmony."

Oh, God. Where, then?

I made a frantic circuit of the house, wrenching open closet doors, peering under beds, calling his name over and over. No sign of blood, but how could I determine if there'd been a struggle when every room in the house looked like someone had been dragged from it kicking and screaming?

I heard Ahmed on the kitchen phone, asking for Detective Amos.

Dane's phone! I stumbled back to the front door where I'd dropped my purse. Snatched up my cell. Jabbed the Auto Dial button.

Somewhere, Dane's phone was ringing. I didn't hear it in the house. *Please, please, please . . .*

"Yo."

My heart lurched to my throat. "Dane?" I squeaked.

"That you, Ma? I'm up, I'm up. Promise."

"What? Where?"

"Boy, what a lousy connection. Where, is that what you said? I'm in the kitchen, just finishing breakfast. My ride'll be here in five minutes, and yes, I put all last night's homework in my backpack already."

He sounded way too nonchalant for a person with kidnappers listening in over his shoulder.

Sacrificial Lamb

"That's funny," I wheezed, doubling back to make sure Ahmed didn't have company. "I'm standing in the kitchen right now and I don't see you."

Silence. Then, "You're home?"

"Yup." Relief joined the flow of adrenaline gushing through my system. "But you're not."

"Oh." Muffled noise, like he'd covered the phone. "Well, actually, I am eating breakfast. At Denny's. With Bullet. He, uh, picked me up early."

By prior arrangement, no doubt. Dane had probably whipped off the covers the second he heard the door close behind me. The headbanger music that served as sound track for his morning ablutions must have repelled any intruders until after he drove off with Bullet.

"Did you suffer some kind of memory lapse? About being grounded?"

"Ma, you said that was after school!"

"I believe this still violates the spirit of our agreement." I sagged back against the fridge. "And by the way, I love you very, very much."

"Huh?" No doubt screwing up his face. "Uh, yeah. Ditto."

"You didn't happen to notice any strangers lurking outside the house when you left, did you?"

"Uh, no. Why?"

"I'll explain later. Can you go to your father's house after school today? I'll pick you up in time for dinner."

"Sure thing. See ya." Cheerful again. After all, Jeff hadn't grounded him.

"See ya." I hung up.

Ahmed had finished his conversation as well. "Detective Amos is coming over," he said. "What are you going to tell him?"

"The truth." I righted the nearest dining-room chair and col-

159

lapsed into it. "Ahmed, I'm so sorry about your office . . ." Head slap. "What about *your* house?"

"The police are on their way to check my apartment." He made a small shooing motion. "It is a minor inconvenience, nothing more."

"I feel awful about getting you involved. I had no idea something like this would happen. I'm going to tell Carson I tricked you into filming that interview."

With a frown, Ahmed lowered himself onto another chair. "That is not necessary. We are a team, are we not?"

"I never got the go-ahead for this story. In fact, Danielle flat-out told me to drop it."

He picked up the letter opener, tapped the table in a slow, measured rhythm. "In my opinion, this case would make an excellent episode. If you will please forgive such presumption, I think you are a very talented, very smart lady." He brushed his mustache with a knuckle. "Perhaps in light of what has just occurred, Mr. Wyatt will allow you to pursue the story officially."

"More likely he'll fire me."

"Then he would be a fool, and I do not believe Mr. Wyatt is a fool. I would consider it an honor to continue working with you on this project."

Tears prickled my eyelids. To hold them back, I shifted subjects. "You were there yesterday. What on earth did Amberlee say during the interview that could have prompted someone to come after the tape?"

Ahmed lifted a shoulder. "I heard nothing that seemed of any significance. But I feel bad I did not suggest we make a copy of the tape right away."

"I meant to do it this morning. Never mind. They would have stolen the copy, too."

"It is a shame we cannot replay the interview."

"We can." I sidled him a conspiratorial smile and pointed toward the front door. "The tape is still in my purse."

CHAPTER 16

I didn't tell Detective Amos I still had the tape. It defied every law-abiding bone in my body, but I was afraid he would confiscate it. When questioned, Ahmed and I played dumb about what the thieves could have been after. Swell. Now I'd corrupted him enough to lie to police.

The intruder had slid most of the glass louvers from the old-fashioned bathroom window above my tub. One of the cops scolded me and said I really should replace this tempting criminal access route. I nodded dutifully. Yep, soon as I got my first unemployment check.

By noon the police had packed up and trooped over to Ahmed's apartment, which had also been broken into. I dillydallied, torn between tackling the cleanup and returning to work, which proves how much I dreaded facing Carson. With a sigh, I traipsed around to the back of the house, where my unwelcome visitor had set down the louvers. I hosed off the fingerprint powder and carefully wiggled them back into their slots. The smell of drifting smoke had thickened. I retrieved my purse, locked up, and hiked down the hill to Wyatt Productions.

I spilled everything to Carson—how I'd been investigating Jake Gormley's death on my own, the Dietrich Schultz connection, my suspicion that Amberlee's interview had led to the break-ins. Carson had gone home since this morning to shave and change into a shirt and tie. He listened in noncommittal silence, desk chair tilted back, fingers tented beneath his chin.

No visible reaction till I confessed I still had the tape.

A newshound gleam lit his eye. "Any idea if there's something incriminating on it?"

"Not that Ahmed or I heard." I shrugged. "Unless pompous self-absorbed prattle is a felony."

"Better view it again," he said. "And this time stick a copy in a safe-deposit box."

"Uh, does that mean you want me to—"

"Keep on it for a few more days. Who knows, maybe you're onto something." He let his chair spring forward. "Seems like you've rattled somebody's cage. If it turns out the sister didn't kill him, it'd be quite a story. And the connection to Schultz makes it even more intriguing."

He folded his hands on the desk like a headmaster about to deliver a stern lecture. "In the future, however, no more cowboy stuff. We're a small outfit. Money's tight. I don't have the luxury of allowing my crew to chase after every idea that captures their interest. I'm a journalist, but I'm a businessman, too. It's a tough call sometimes." He opened a desk drawer and extracted a roll of Tums. "Want one?"

My face felt hot. "No, thanks."

He thumbed one into his mouth. "Bottom line is, we have to be selective about which projects we budget time and money for."

This was my cue to protest that I'd only worked on this story during off-hours. Except yesterday I'd cut out early, and Carson knew it. I kept my mouth shut.

"As you're well aware, we're behind schedule on this Omaha episode." He gestured at paperwork piled on his desk. "Today's break-in was a major disruption, what with the police all over the place, the who-knows-how-many hours it'll take to put the library back in order. Not to mention you and Ahmed both disappearing all morning." He patted the air as if to soothe

163

ruffled feathers. "Understandable. I realize this incident is personally very upsetting. But it's also an example of why we can't get sidetracked with projects that may or may not pan out." He narrowed his eyes. "I'm taking a gamble on you, Harmony. Let's hope it pays off."

I left his office, tail between my legs but job intact. At least for now. Did Carson really believe I could solve a fourteen-year-old mystery, or had he let me off easy because his racquetball buddy owed my ex-husband a favor?

Well, I could either sit around and stew over that humiliating possibility, or get busy and prove I was up to the challenge. What the heck, I could do both.

Ahmed duped several copies of the tape. I followed Carson's advice and rented a safe-deposit box at the corner bank. Then, despite the threat posed by crumbs to video equipment, Ahmed and I holed up in the editing room with a couple of sandwiches and replayed Amberlee's interview three times, dissecting every irrelevant utterance, every self-serving observation in hopes of tweezing out even the tiniest, most obscure sliver of hidden meaning.

End result? Still no clue what the thief might have been after. By the third time through, I could mouth the monologue along with Amberlee. "Miracle, schmiracle," I muttered.

"Sorry, what did you say?"

"Just quoting Dolores Pombo." I frowned. "Wait a second. Stop the tape."

Ahmed's hand shot forward. "Did you hear something we have missed? Something she said about her husband?"

"No, something her mother said. Hang on a sec, let me try to remember." The deck of the Queen Mary. Breeze blowing, seagulls squawking, scorn dripping from her mouth like ash from her cigarette.

The flashback launched me to my feet. "Dolores said if

164

Reverend Schultz could perform miracles, why didn't he cure her grandson's spina bifida?"

"His what?"

"Jake had a serious birth defect called spina bifida."

"Oh. That is very sad, but—"

"But Amberlee didn't even meet Schultz until after Jake died, so how could he have cured him?"

Ahmed didn't exactly jump up and down yelling aha! "Maybe Mrs. Pombo forgot." He spread his hands. "Maybe she did not literally mean he could have cured Jake, she was only expressing doubt that the Reverend can perform miracles."

"Maybe." I paced like a prosecutor summing up for the jury. "But if Amberlee and Schultz did meet before Jake died, it would have been while she was still married to Curtis."

Ahmed crumpled his sandwich wrapper and dropped it neatly into the white takeout sack. Then did the same with mine. "During the interview, does she not say she saw him for the first time at a revival meeting?"

" 'I knew we were destined to be soul mates,' " I mimicked.

"What is a revival meeting?"

I explained. "The official story on their web site, though, is that they met when Amberlee joined Schultz's congregation in Orange County."

"Would those services have been revival meetings?"

"Doubtful. I think Schultz had a regular church by then, at least a temporary one. If the two of them met while Amberlee was still married to someone else, it makes sense they'd want to hide it."

Ahmed fingered his mustache. "Are you saying that is why somebody tried to steal the tape?"

"Seems like a possibility. Imagine how it would tarnish the squeaky-clean, divinely inspired version of their courtship, if any hint of adultery brushed up against it. Except . . ." I frowned. "How could the thief have known what Amberlee said during the interview? Unless . . ."

Our eyes met. The vision of Dolores Pombo wriggling through my bathroom window gave us both the giggles.

"Of course, we're assuming the thief knows what's on the tape," I said. "But not necessarily. Amberlee might know something so explosive, he couldn't risk any chance that she'd even hinted at it."

"You are assuming the thief is a man." Ahmed crossed his arms. Eighty-five degrees outside, and he was wearing a sweater. "What if it was Mrs. Schultz herself? Perhaps she said something she later regretted."

"But what? We've spent hours reviewing that tape. I think the thief learned about the interview afterward. Either he suspected Amberlee was up to something and followed her, or she couldn't resist crowing about her first starring TV role. Or maybe Dolores let it slip to someone. Someone who didn't want Amberlee talking to me."

"Ah. Her husband?"

I nodded. "If Schultz met Amberlee before she left Gypsum, maybe he knows something about Jake's death. If he's kept mum about it, letting Layla take the rap all these years, then exposure could destroy his extremely profitable career."

"A lot of ifs and maybes."

"Yeah, it'd be nice to nail down some actual facts. I'm driving out to Gypsum tomorrow. If Carson okays it, will you come along? So far I haven't convinced anyone to talk on camera, but you could shoot background scenes."

"I will have to rearrange my schedule, but that is no problem." Ahmed kneaded his temples. "It is hard to imagine Reverend Schultz breaking in to steal the tape."

"He could have sent a flunky," I said. "A flunky with criminal experience who could be trusted not to betray the Schultzes because his own fortunes are hitched to theirs."

"I am guessing from the sly look on your face that you have an idea who this flunky person might be."

"The Schultz attorney happens to be an ex-con." I gave a Cheshire-cat smile. "Seems the good Reverend showed him the light, paid his way through law school, then hired him as his right-hand man." I mimed an explosion. "If Schultz's career goes up in flames, so does Davis Litvak's."

Ahmed's eyes darkened. "A lawyer? Breaking the law?"

"I rest my case," I said.

The house Jeff and I bought after the first season of *Caldwell* perched on Adelaide Drive, overlooking Santa Monica Canyon, where long-gone seaside resorts like the North Beach Bath House, the Pavilion, and the Arcadia Hotel had once enticed Victorian-era tourists to splash in the surf—and inhale the appetizing ozone.

Flash forward to World War II and the influx of workers who'd flocked to Southern California to serve wartime industries like Santa Monica's Douglas Aircraft Company. GIs shipping out to the Pacific passed through the West Coast, the lucky ones on their way home as well. Once the war ended, a lot of returning vets and relocated workers looked around, noticed the weather, smelled opportunity, and decided to stay.

The house where Jeff now lived alone—as far as I knew—had been constructed during the postwar boom, perhaps by someone who'd salvaged fond memories of lush island plantations from the bloodshed and horror of the South Pacific. Weathered ironwood shingles, tall windows framed by slatted shutters, high ceilings with lazily rotating fans. Pink and orange bougainvillea cascaded from trellises above the hibiscus bushes.

The second-floor veranda was paradise for watching sunsets, lounging in patio chairs, sipping rum drinks adorned with small paper parasols. An Olympic-size pool shared the backyard with several species of palm, a banana tree, and the tangled buttress roots of a massive Moreton Bay fig. A towering screen of bamboo camouflaged the security fence enclosing the property. Its prodigious leaf litter consumed a major portion of the pool cleaner's time and irked the neighbors no end.

I turned up the driveway, stopped at the gate, pushed the intercom button.

Though we'd never hired live-in help, frequently Jeff's agent, his assistant Connie, or some other entourage member answered. "That you?" asked the star himself.

"Dane ready?" The day I'd packed my bags, I'd vowed that in my new life I would speak as few words to Jeff as possible.

"Why don't you just punch in the code, Harm? I haven't changed it."

"Invade your privacy? I wouldn't dream of it. Who knows what kind of embarrassing situation I might interrupt."

The speaker emitted an exasperated blat. Seconds later the lock clanked and the gate began to slide open. Two teens on bikes braked to watch me drive through. With any luck, they were not a pair of deranged fans.

I pulled around back. Jeff strolled out the kitchen door, barefoot. Above shorts that showed off his Muscle Beach legs, he wore a South Dakota State T-shirt so thin and faded from countless washings it was nearly transparent. I'd given it to him on one of our early anniversaries to commemorate how we'd first met, in a college production of *Our Town*. Simultaneously zinged with Cupid's arrow and bitten by the acting bug, we'd moved to L.A. six months later, both a semester shy of graduation.

Jeff rapped on the window. I lowered it without switching off the engine. "I wish you wouldn't be so stubborn," he said.

I slid my sunglasses down my nose two inches before pushing

them back up. "As long as we're discussing character flaws, I've got a list of yours right here. Hang on a sec while I dig it out of my purse."

"Okay, okay." He raised his palms in a backing-off gesture. His sun-streaked brown hair had grown a little shaggier since I'd last seen him a month ago. Maybe Caldwell was going undercover this week. "Boy, smell that smoke." He crinkled his rakishly asymmetric nose. "I hear they've lost three houses already in Malibu."

"Is Dane here or not?" I asked. "He's still supposed to be grounded."

Jeff flashed the boyish dimple that had converted my college-girl knees to mush. Unfortunately, my knees were almost forty years old now, but the dimple still had a similar effect. "Whoa, look at the time! Already Happy Hour. Why don't you come in for a glass of wine or something?"

"You let him go to the Promenade, didn't you?"

Jeff let his head drop back between his shoulder blades as if beseeching the heavens for patience. "No, I did not. He's inside doing his Spanish homework, as a matter of fact."

Miracle, schmiracle. A few flecks of ash danced in the air like errant snowflakes.

"Look, Dane said you sounded all freaked out on the phone this morning." He leaned tan forearms across my open window, treating me to a tantalizing whiff of familiar sweat and unfamiliar after-shave. "Is everything okay?"

"My house got broken into." So much for deciding not to tell him.

Concern laced his yummy chocolate eyes. "Jesus, are you all right? Were you home when it happened?"

An odd hiccup caught in my chest. Before I could stop myself, I'd blurted out everything—the interview, the tape, the break-in at Wyatt Productions.

"You didn't tell the cops you still have the tape?" Frowning as he massaged his neck. "Big mistake, Harm. Let the pros handle it, huh? You shouldn't be playing detective."

Shouldn't have broken my few-words-as-possible rule, either. "I'll certainly take that advice under consideration," I said. "Seeing as how it comes from one of the most famous fake detectives in the world."

"I'm worried about you. Is that a crime?"

"Do me a favor and cross me off your worry list."

"Fine. I'll worry about our son, then. What if Dane had still been home when this goon broke in? What if he'd gotten hurt or held hostage because you're running around pretending to be Miss Marple?"

Sour smile. "I see myself more as a Charlie's Angel, thanks. Besides, nothing happened to Dane. He's way more likely to get hurt racing around with Bullet and company. And if you're so concerned about his safety, how could you promise him flying lessons when he turns eighteen?"

"You're changing the subject because you know I'm right. If you won't give up this crazy idea of playing cop—"

"Did Mark Ellison say something to you?"

"Mark? About what?"

"Never mind."

Jeff shoved his square jaw forward. "If your new career is more important to you than our son's safety, maybe you should let him live with me."

"You bastard."

For a few moments, the only sound was the neighbor's leaf blower.

Jeff nodded grudgingly. "Okay, that was a low blow. But I'm serious about him moving back here."

"No wonder." I circled my hand through the air. "What a wholesome environment for an impressionable young man:

cocaine parties on the veranda, starlets cavorting naked in the swimming pool—"

"Are you nuts? None of that ever went on while you lived here, and it doesn't go on now. You think you're the only one who cares about keeping Dane away from that shit?"

I hauled searing, smoke-charged air into my lungs. Released it slowly. "No," I said.

Most of the anger dissolved from his eyes. He stuffed his hands into his pockets. As he rocked back onto his heels, I noticed Dane frozen on the step outside the kitchen door, backpack hoisted over his shoulder, grim expression chiseled onto his face like stone.

I caught my breath. Jeff wheeled around.

"Wow," said Dane, the barest sneer twitching his lips. "This is better than reality TV."

CHAPTER 17

"I do not think Mr. Curtis Gormley was very happy to see us."

I swallowed tuna salad and waved my fork at Ahmed. "What gave it away? The door slammed in our faces? The death threats? The shotgun?"

"It does not seem wise to allow such an unstable individual to own a firearm."

"Welcome to America," I said. "Land of the free, home of the NRA."

We were in the back booth at Carmen's, planning our next move over a late lunch. During the last twenty minutes, half the population of Gypsum had found some excuse to saunter down the sidewalk and check us out through the window. The café was packed, mostly with idlers using the pretext of coffee to get a closer look at us. Carmen could barely keep up, brewing pot after pot, grumbling that normally this time of day she got to rest her feet. Our waitress, Marisa, swung by every few minutes to refill our iced tea glasses and gawk at Ahmed's camera case like it was the Holy Grail. Someone had once stolen Ahmed's equipment from his car, so now his beloved Panasonic accompanied him everywhere.

Curtis's reaction to the camera had been the exact opposite of Marisa's. We'd knocked on his trailer door, armed with a token of goodwill—a six-pack of tokens, to be exact. I'd even remembered from my last visit to Desert Acres which brand of beer had filled his shopping bags. I didn't have much hope he would change his mind and agree to an interview, but sometimes persistence pays off. Or we might have lucked out and found him too drunk to remember why he didn't want to talk to us.

"Guess we'll have to drink all that beer ourselves," I said.

"Thank you, but I do not drink alcoholic beverages."

"More for me," I said.

On the drive from L.A., we'd stopped in Palmdale to pick up the key to the Gormley house and secure signed permission to film inside. Yesterday, when I'd contacted the landlord, the first words out of his mouth had been a demand for an exorbitant fee. Like a broken record, I kept repeating I wasn't Steven Spielberg, that we only paid compensation in cases where filming actually cost the owner money. Eventually he caved in with a sigh. "Maybe the house'll get famous, and I can finally find someone to rent the dump," he said, not sounding too hopeful.

It was eerie, actually setting foot in the place I'd heard so much about, had envisioned so often in my imagination. Here was the front door Brittany had hurried out that afternoon. The living room where Curtis had lain on the couch in a drunken sprawl while Amberlee yelled at him. The hallway Dolores had rushed down when she heard the screaming. The kids' bedroom, where poor little Jake had taken his last breath.

Any semi-usable furniture had been carted off ages ago. Ahmed filmed the entire interior, quite a technical challenge in the murky light filtering through boarded-over, grime-encrusted windows. I doubted we'd ever use more than one or two shots, unfortunately. Transformed by a fur coat of dust, trash-strewn floors, and droopy ceiling tiles, the house bore little resemblance to the way it had looked fourteen years ago. At least, I hoped so.

Molting wallpaper in Jake and Layla's room revealed an older layer I recognized from crime-scene photos: faded merry-go-round horses. The only other room I'd seen a picture of was Curtis and Amberlee's, where traces of blood had been found on the bedspread. That room hadn't changed much, except one or more subsequent occupants had kicked holes in the drywall and derailed the closet doors from their runners.

The house reeked of neglect, decay, despair. Dry wind whistling through the rotted eaves barely masked the ghostly echoes of former residents—shouts of anger, wails of anguish, screams of frustration. A sound like the desiccated rattling of old skeletons skittered behind the walls. Lizards? Scorpions? Maybe desert rats, the same ones who'd trailed calling cards of rodent feces over most flat surfaces. No wonder the place had sat un-rented for so long. It gave me the willies.

I shivered, though it was near eighty degrees in the café. I wore a sleeveless blouse with loose cotton slacks and was eager to toss them both in the laundry. "Know what I think?"

Mouth full of cheeseburger, Ahmed shook his head.

I squeezed more lemon into my iced tea, stirred, clinked the spoon on the glass. "I think Curtis killed him."

Ahmed patted his mouth with a napkin. "Perhaps that is why he is so camera-shy."

"He was furious about getting fired; he was drunk; he had a history of violence." I tapped my spoon to emphasize each point. "All of a sudden he's out of work with three other mouths to feed."

"You believe he is that cold-blooded?"

"I'm not saying he planned it. Planning doesn't seem Curtis's strong suit. I think the pressure just built up inside him and he exploded. Like at work."

"What happened at work?"

"He beat up a fellow mineworker. That's what got him fired. The guy borrowed a tool without asking. Curtis lost his temper. The one time I got him to talk, he said he just snapped and didn't mean to hurt him."

"I cannot believe a man would murder his own son."

"That's just it! Curtis had recently learned Jake wasn't his. And by all accounts, he wasn't exactly a good sport about it."

"Well, it would certainly explain why he refuses to speak about what happened."

"It also explains why Amberlee put the blame on Layla. She was covering up for her husband."

Ahmed clutched his skull as if the very thought pained him. "Terrible. To murder a baby." Looking distressed, he sidled out of the booth. "You will please excuse me for a moment? I need to . . ." He gave an embarrassed head tilt toward the restrooms behind me.

"Sure."

"You will be kind enough to keep an eye on my camera?"

"I'll guard it with my life."

With a reluctant parting glance, he disappeared. "Oh, please excuse me," I heard him say. A moment later Ken Tatum wheeled by. He hadn't noticed me, sitting with my back to him, but I tracked his progress out of the café and across the street to the newspaper office. Guy could really move. I snitched a French fry off Ahmed's plate. Seemed like ages ago I'd searched the *Weekly Miner* archives, uncertain whether Jake Gormley had even existed. A mere nine days, incredibly enough.

My hand froze in mid-snitch. The newspaper. Those old ads . . .

The instant Ahmed reappeared, I catapulted from the booth and grabbed his arm. "Come on. We need to check something."

"But I have not yet finished my cheeseburger!"

I whisked his plate off the table and headed for the register. "We'll get it to go."

Ken Tatum was behind his desk staring into space when Ahmed and I jangled the bell above the *Weekly Miner* entrance. He flushed when he saw us, as if his thoughts might have been of an X-rated nature. He shook hands with Ahmed and said,

"You know the way," when I requested another look at the archives.

Back in the cramped storage room, I transferred the 1994 bin from shelf to table. Ahmed watched me flip through the August issues. "Pardon me, but I believe that is the wrong date," he said. "Did Jake not die on the twenty-second?"

"The ad I'm looking for ran during the first half of August." I leafed quickly through tabloid-size pages. "There!" My finger nailed newsprint to the table. Ahmed craned his neck to study the ad. Excitement percolated through my system like the first rush of morning coffee.

"Ah, one of those revival meetings," he said. "Here in Gypsum."

"Notice who the star attraction was?"

Dark eyebrows leaped toward Ahmed's hairline. "But why is his name not in bigger print?"

"This was before he got so famous. And look! Next stop on the circuit . . . Victorville!"

Ahmed scratched his chin. "I do not understand the significance."

"According to Curtis, Amberlee took Layla and moved to Victorville about a week after Jake died."

"That is so? You think she was following him?"

"Be interesting to find out, wouldn't it?" I folded the paper and tucked it into my purse. "But now at least we have proof that Reverend Schultz led a revival meeting here in Gypsum a couple weeks before Jake died." I put the remaining issues back in the bin, back on the shelf. "Dolores said their church disapproved of such, uh, flamboyant forms of worship, but you can't tell me Amberlee would have passed up the biggest show in town. I grew up in a place like this, and believe me, whenever some new form of entertainment comes along, everyone goes."

"Excuse me, Harmony, but you have put that newspaper into

your purse."

"I don't buy the coincidence that Schultz was here and Amberlee didn't meet him, then they just happened to cross paths less than a year later. They had to have known each other while she was still married to Curtis. Come on, let's go."

Ahmed and camera case barred the door. "Let me see if I understand correctly." Troubled ridges spanned his forehead. "It is your intention to steal this newspaper?"

"Don't worry," I said. "I never rat out my accomplices."

I'd penciled Noreen Fontana near the top of my Talk-To list. Oddly enough, she hadn't joined the small assembly that milled in front of the Gormley house while we were inside filming. Soon as we'd wrapped up, I'd gone over to knock on her door. No answer. Her car was in the garage, however, stirring a buzz of speculation among watchful bystanders.

After Ahmed and I strode brazenly out of the newspaper office, we swung by her house again. The car was gone, and still no Noreen. Guess I wouldn't get to ask if she'd written that note to Layla.

I hopped back into the driver's seat, assisted by a furnace blast of wind. "Noreen might know where Amberlee and Layla moved to," I said, using the rearview mirror to finger-comb my hair. "If Amberlee left a forwarding address, maybe Noreen's hung onto it all these years."

"Why do you want Mrs. Schultz's address?"

"I thought we could drive over to Victorville, flash around the Reverend's photo, ask if anyone remembers him visiting her."

Ahmed pulled a snow-white hankie from his pocket to mop his brow. "You wish to do this now?"

The sun had turned the parked Explorer into a broiler oven. I keyed the engine so chilled air whooshed out the vents. "I know it'll be late when we get home." Today was Friday, so

Dane would be going to Jeff's after school. "But what if we can find a witness who'll swear the two of them were carrying on while Amberlee was still married to Curtis?"

"I suppose it would cause serious damage to the Reverend Schultz's reputation."

"Yes, but that's not the goal. What if Schultz knows something about Jake's death? Maybe with a little leverage, we can pry the truth out of him and Amberlee."

"By leverage, you mean—"

"Okay, okay. Blackmail."

Ahmed folded his handkerchief into a perfect square and tucked it away. "How are you going to learn this address?"

"Oh, come on," I teased, slapping the steering wheel with both hands. "Do I have to think of everything?"

His mustache twitched in amusement. "What about the electric company? Surely their records go back fourteen years."

"They won't share without a search warrant. Same goes for other utilities, or credit card companies, or magazine subscriptions."

"What about the Department of Motor Vehicles?"

"They won't give out any license or registration info. Not since an actress named Rebecca Schaeffer was murdered by a stalker who got her home address from the DMV." I adjusted a vent to blow-dry sweat off my face. "But you're on the right track with public agencies. I wonder if Amberlee was getting a welfare check."

"Would the little girl have attended school in Victorville?"

"She was five . . . yeah, Amberlee might have enrolled her in kindergarten." Wheels started spinning. "I could pretend to be Layla's mother, cook up some story about needing a copy of her records for college applications."

"And I could stand guard outside the school to warn you when I hear the police sirens."

"Thanks. I just realized schools are probably about to close for the weekend. Didn't Amberlee say she took Layla to see a doctor when she stopped talking?"

There was also a chance she'd left their forwarding address with a previous one. I pictured the steam coming out Norman Atwood's ears when he'd caught me snooping through his confidential files. "Forget the doctor."

"Property records?"

"Good, good, except back then she couldn't afford any. What other records would they have at the courthouse?"

"Births, deaths, marriages—"

"Divorces! If Amberlee was in a rush to dump Curtis so she could pursue a more promising soul mate, she probably filed for divorce right after moving to Victorville. And the final decree would include either her address or her attorney's."

"In which county is Victorville?"

"San Bernardino, I think. But she would have had to live there three months before filing." Having recently obtained a Judgment of Dissolution myself, I'd become something of a reluctant expert on California divorce law. "She probably filed here in Fremont County. Which means the first place to check is with the county clerk in Red Rock."

Shoot. The opposite direction from Victorville. Not to mention that on my previous visit to the courthouse, I'd called in a phony fire alarm and stolen public records. What if my Wanted Poster was tacked up there on a bulletin board?

"Perhaps Mr. Curtis Gormley has a copy of the divorce papers he would be willing to show us."

"Very funny." I snapped my fingers. "I'll bet his lawyer does, though."

"Who is his lawyer?"

"No idea. But somebody around here might remember."

"Perhaps a friend or relative?"

"Curtis seems kind of short on both. But I know somebody who keeps tabs on everyone in town. Somebody who knew Curtis fourteen years ago."

"Who?"

I put the car in Drive and swung a U-turn. "Hope you saved room for pie."

"Loophole."

"Beg pardon?"

Carmen was finally resting her Reeboks. She slouched on a vinyl stool with her back to the counter, flapping her stained apron to supplement the lethargic breeze from the overhead fan. "That's what we call him, Loophole." Her gold tooth glinted. "Behind his back, anyway. His name's Parker McGuire."

"He represented Curtis during the divorce?"

"He represents everybody for everything, unless you hire someone from out of town. Which people don't, since the only thing worse than a lawyer is a big-city lawyer. What do you want to talk to him for?"

"We're trying to find out Amberlee's address when she moved to Victorville."

"How come?"

"Background. Is McGuire's office nearby?"

"Now, exactly how far away do you think it could it be? Across the street, two doors past the newspaper. Upstairs. There's no sign."

"No sign? How are people supposed to find him?"

Carmen shrugged. "Anybody who'd want to hire him knows where he is."

We braved the dust storm, counted doors, climbed steps. The building looked like a good candidate for urban renewal. In lieu of government programs, a bulldozer would suffice. Scabby paint, sagging gutters, boarded-up downstairs window. McGuire appeared to be the only tenant. Hopefully, he passed his low overhead on to his clients.

He looked about as happy to see us as he would a pair of process servers. "I'm about to lock up for the weekend," he announced when I stuck my head through the doorway into the shabby interior that apparently served as reception area, office, and conference room combined. What kind of self-respecting ambulance-chaser would greet potential business with such lack of enthusiasm?

"We won't take up much of your time, promise." Ahmed creaked behind me across the warped wood floor. Thrift-store furnishings included a desk, several bookcases jammed with dusty legal volumes, a bank of dented metal file cabinets against one wall. No receptionist, no potted palms, no glossy magazines to peruse while waiting. Decor consisted of a few framed certificates hung askew above the bookcases and a water stain on the ceiling.

McGuire was fifty-something, with thinning hair the color of cardboard and the red-rimmed eyes of an allergy sufferer. He propped his elbow atop an open file cabinet while I explained what we were after. His wardrobe was perfect camouflage for his surroundings—frayed white shirt with yellowed armpits, too-wide tie with a grease spot on it, wrinkled suit trousers that looked as if he'd been ignoring that Dry Clean Only tag.

He regarded me over the rims of his Dollar Store reading glasses. "I can't reveal any information without my client's permission." The programmed, uninflected delivery of a robot.

"Heavens, no, we wouldn't dream of asking you to violate any rules." I fluffed my hair and tried to sound shocked. "The information we need is actually public record." Dazzling him with the full force of my smile. "You probably received a copy of the Gormleys' divorce decree when the final judgment was entered, right? That's all we want to see." A little Marilyn

Monroe pout. "Otherwise, we'll have to wait all the way till Monday to look it up at the courthouse." Vigorous eyelash fluttering. "I'd really, really appreciate it if you could help us out." I gave my blouse a discreet tug to lower its neckline.

McGuire shoved the file drawer shut. "Okay," he agreed. "Bound to take less time than arguing." He stepped to another cabinet and crouched to open the bottom drawer. "You learned anything new about their little boy's death?"

I didn't float my current theory that his former client might have killed him. "Do you think there's anything new to learn?"

"What are you, a cop? I ask a question; you answer with another."

"Sorry." I sensed our newfound rapport slipping away like real estate in a mudslide. "People have been very helpful."

"That I doubt." He riffled through files. "Most of them would just as soon forget it ever happened."

"Why's that?"

"It's a whole different ballgame, isn't it, when a baby gets killed? Shakes up the community, makes them uncomfortable. Takes the fun out of gossip. Also the fact another child allegedly committed the crime. People don't even have a decent villain to hiss at."

"When you say allegedly . . ."

"Don't get excited, that was just lawyer's reflex. I don't possess any special inside information that someone else did it. Here." His knees creaked like the floorboards when he stood up. "I suppose you want me to copy this."

"That would be super," I said, sounding like Gidget.

He sent me a wry look over his glasses. "I'll see if I can get this scanner to work. My copy machine died last week."

While he fiddled with cables and rebooted his antique computer, I studied the framed degrees. Not too many attorneys bother hanging their high school diplomas. "You went to

UniHi?" University High School in West Los Angeles. "How long have you lived in Gypsum?"

"Twenty-one years come February." He lined up the thin sheaf of stapled pages on the scanner. "Law firm I worked for sent me out to depose one of the mine executives for a case we were litigating. This was a week after I'd been passed over for partnership again and two days before my doctor informed me I had an ulcer. My wife was complaining she never saw me, the mortgage payments on our house in L.A. were killing us, and we'd just found out there were gangs at our kids' school."

He flipped over another sheet to copy the next. "This place may not strike most people as paradise, but it looked pretty good to me that day. Plus, the only attorney in town had dropped dead of a heart attack the month before. I took it as an omen."

"Ever miss L.A.?" I asked.

"Every time I get a craving for Thai food," he said. "Kids all went off to college and never came back, except for visits. But I've never regretted moving here."

I skimmed the divorce papers he handed me. Right away, a paragraph caught my eye. "Curtis wasn't required to pay any child support for Layla?"

"Back up," he said. "Look at the custody section."

"I thought child support was a legal obligation no matter what the custody terms."

McGuire tapped a clause. I read it. "Curtis terminated all his parental rights?"

"Against my vociferous protests, believe me." He switched off the computer. "At first he was all revved up to fight for joint custody, even if it was mainly to hassle Amberlee. Though he did express some affection for Layla."

"Were you aware Curtis wasn't her biological father?"

"Hard to keep a secret like that in a town this size." He

183

slipped the original decree back into its file. "California law, however, considers a husband the legal father of any child born to his wife during their marriage. Even with a DNA test to prove otherwise, a judge might not let him off the hook. For the protection of the child."

"But Curtis was allowed to sign away his parental responsibilities?"

"Only because Amberlee insisted on it."

Protecting Layla from a man who'd killed her other child? Or eager to shove Curtis out of the picture because she already had a new father lined up?

McGuire extracted a key ring from his pocket and started to lock file cabinets one by one.

"Did Curtis change his mind about suing for custody because it got him out of paying child support?"

Without turning, McGuire said, "Now we're trespassing into that lawyer-client privilege area."

"Sorry." I exchanged glances with Ahmed. "Listen, I realize you're limited as far as what you can say, but would you consider letting us interview you on camera?"

McGuire lowered himself behind his desk, removed his glasses, straightened both his tie and posture. As if the tape were already rolling. "Would I get to review the list of questions first?"

"Of course." I could see visions of media lawyers dancing in his head.

"I'll think about it over the weekend." He handed me a business card. "Call me next week and maybe we can set something up." Like his incredibly busy schedule might not permit an opening.

"Thanks very much for your help." I wrote down all my numbers for him. "You certainly have excellent recall of a case you handled so long ago."

He rose to shake my hand. "That case has always bothered me."

"Because the baby had recently died?"

"No." He lifted a briefcase from the floor, parked it on his desk, clicked it open. "Because of the nasty shock I got one morning when my client walked in here with the crap beaten out of him."

"Curtis?"

"Two black eyes, busted nose, maybe a broken rib or two." He glanced around as if an ethics panel might be eavesdropping. "Guess it's hardly a secret. Whole town was buzzing about it."

"From what I've heard, getting into fights is kind of his hobby."

"Yeah, but this was different." He transferred a John Grisham novel from desk drawer to briefcase. "The timing, for one thing. It happened the same day Curtis changed his mind all of a sudden and insisted on signing away his parental rights. Just like Amberlee wanted. He sat right there in that chair and wouldn't budge, no matter how much I argued with him. Which is something else that troubled me."

McGuire shut his briefcase. "Any halfway decent lawyer gets pretty good at reading people. And that poor guy was scared shitless."

CHAPTER 18

The town of Victorville had lost its main tourist attraction several years back when the Roy Rogers–Dale Evans Museum packed up and moved to Branson, Missouri—lock, stock, and Trigger. Happier Trails, I guess.

The museum's defection hadn't seemed to cripple the local economy, judging by all the strip malls and instant neighborhoods erupting across the high-desert landscape. With a population near seventy thousand and climbing, Victorville's remaining attractions included relatively clean air, relatively cheap housing prices, and relatively manageable commutes to southern California's bustling Inland Empire.

Ahmed and I hit town during rush hour, which as Los Angelenos, we barely noticed. The clerk at the gas station minimart turned out to be geography-challenged, but a customer waiting in line grabbed a napkin and drew us a map to Amberlee's former address.

The two-story apartment house was creeping up on middle age but hiding it well. Fresh paint concealed whatever cracks marred the beige stucco; light fixtures and railings gleamed; Rain Bird sprinklers *chicka-chicked* across the newly-mowed lawn. A courtyard between the two wings enclosed a fenced swimming pool surrounded by palms trees and well-barbered shrubbery.

I voted to start knocking on doors right away, but Ahmed pointed out we could save time by first determining whether any tenants from the Amberlee era still lived here.

The mailbox showed the manager in Apartment 7. We traipsed up a flight of steps and down an outside corridor to the rear left unit.

A scrawny woman in curlers and harlequin glasses opened the door a few inches as I was about to knock again. "No vacancies," she declared. "I could put you on the waiting list for twenty bucks, though."

"We're not here about an apartment," I said. The chemical fumes of a home perm wafted through the gap, along with the theme music from an *NYPD Blue* rerun. "Say, you're not by any chance a fan of TV crime shows, are you?"

Ten seconds later we were inside. Ever wonder where all those old magazines and newspapers end up after you set them curbside for recycling? By the looks of it, here. Stacked carpet to ceiling in a jaw-dropping marvel of structural engineering, towering paper walls were segregated into twine-encircled bundles that emitted the musty smell of an old garage. I couldn't understand why the floor joists didn't collapse and deposit the entire load into the downstairs neighbor's living room.

"You must enjoy reading very much," Ahmed said.

"Why, yes." She splayed a hand over her heart. "I've always been a regular bookworm."

An overfed tabby coiled itself around one of her skinny ankles. At once I was able to identify another component of that chemical odor: cat pee.

She hoisted the animal into her arms, where it proceeded to nibble on food crumbs clinging to the bodice of her paisley housecoat. "I'm Viola Purdy, by the way. That's *Vie*-ola, not *Vee*-ola, like the instrument. *Vie*-ola." As if she'd spent a lifetime clarifying this for people.

I tried not to look at the cat. "Ms. Purdy, we're hoping you might be able to help us solve a killing that we're investigating for our show."

Her eyes glowed like cathode-ray tubes. "Does that mean I'd get to be on TV?"

Finally! Someone genuinely eager for fifteen minutes of fame. Though in her case, it might only rate fifteen seconds. I was tempted to use her for the astonishing backdrop.

"It depends on what you can share that might be relevant to this case." I withdrew a clipboard from my overstuffed purse. "How long have you been the manager here?"

Her ensuing struggle to guess the correct answer betrayed the same panic as a woolgathering student called upon in class. "Going on nineteen years," she said finally, as if bracing herself for the disqualifying buzzer. "Rent's cheap 'cause of me being manager. Plus, I've spent so much time arranging my things just right. Like I tell my sister: Only way I'm leaving here's in a coffin."

Or if the health department dropped by for a surprise inspection. "Would you happen to remember this tenant from thirteen or fourteen years ago?" I showed her a photo of Amberlee I'd printed off Schultz's web site. "Her name was Amberlee Gormley. She had a five-year-old daughter named Layla."

"Oh. Her." Viola's nostrils flared as if the cat had farted. "Picture don't look much like her. She the one who's dead?"

"So you remember her?"

"Lord, how could I forget?" She pitched her voice like nails on chalkboard. " 'Miss Purdy, the light bulb's burned out. Miss Purdy, the garbage disposal don't work. Miss Purdy, the bathtub drain's clogged up.' Clogged with that long hair of hers, more'n likely."

Encouraged, I flipped to the Internet photo of Schultz. During the one-hour drive from Gypsum, Ahmed had darkened his silver mane with a pencil to make him look younger. "Did this man ever visit her?"

Viola squinted through tortoiseshell frames and stroked the cat. "He does look kinda familiar, now you mention it."

Too late, I saw the trap I'd fallen into. Of course she would say she recognized him, as long as it got her on TV. Which is probably where she'd seen him in the first place, assuming she'd ever laid eyes on him. Rats. I should have brought along other photos and made her pick him from a lineup.

"Do you remember his name? Any specific instances when you saw him? How often did he visit? Ever notice what kind of car he drove? Can you describe his voice?"

Without the softball lob of yes-or-no questions, she struck out with the answers. Another cat, this one a Siamese mix, eeled around the nearest stack of *Ladies' Home Journal,* flung itself against Ahmed's shoe and began to molest it. Ahmed stretched his mouth into a rictus. "Nice kitty."

"How long did Amberlee and her daughter live here, do you remember?"

Sensing, perhaps, her last chance to secure a place in the spotlight, Viola turned cagey. "Well, now, I'm not sure." She licked her chapped lips. "Suppose I could look it up in my ledger, the one where I keep track of rent payments." A put-upon sigh ruffled the cat's fur. "You see, my time is awfully valuable, and I'm not sure whether—"

"You've got a ledger going back fourteen years?" I asked.

"Not the same ledger, of course. Every so often I have to start a new one. But I think I might have the old ones around here someplace."

"May we see it?"

"Well, I'm in the middle of eating my supper right now and it might take me hours and hours to dig it up and I'm probably not supposed to show it to you without a search warrant, anyway . . ."

She stuffed the twenty into her bra.

"Follow me," she said.

Glancing fearfully upward, we trailed her and the cats through the claustrophobic labyrinth of moldering publications. Occasional side canyons branched off to unseen destinations. Bathroom? Bedroom? Or merely access routes to distant provinces of her prized collection?

The litter-box stench was growing stronger. I tried breathing through my mouth, but that made it worse.

Eventually the passageway opened into a small clearing crammed with a round dinette table, single vinyl chair, and half a dozen more cats. The cats left as soon as they saw us, abandoning the open tins of beef-and-liver Friskies plunked across the tabletop. One of them fled from the chicken tetrazzini microwave dinner sitting on a plastic flowered mat.

Ahmed's face was a study in horror.

When Viola dropped to her bony knees and scuttled beneath the table, I recoiled to imagine what warped kind of human-to-feline mind transfer we were witnessing. Then I realized the ledgers were stacked under there.

Viola emerged, skinny butt first, clutching an imitation-leather volume. "Let me see now." She shoved aside food cans to deposit the ledger on the table. Licked her thumb to facilitate each page turn. "Here we are." She pivoted her glasses from nose to forehead to peer closely at the crabbed entries. "Moved in September 1, 1994. Moved out . . ." She traced across with her finger. "June 11, 1995."

She jutted her bony shoulder forward when she caught me peeking over it. "I told her, don't even bother asking for the rest of June's rent back, 'cause you didn't give a month's notice like you're s'posed to. Got all huffy, of course. 'Fine,' she said. 'Just give me back my security deposit.' " Viola chortled. "Shoulda seen her face when I informed her she wasn't getting that back, either."

"She left the place a mess?"

"Wasn't that. Landlord only mails the refund to whoever paid it in the first place."

"Somebody else paid Amberlee's security deposit for her?"

"Same fellow who paid her rent all along."

I edged sideways for a better view of the ledger. "Oh, right. What was his name again?"

She body-blocked me. "Sorry. Afraid that's confidential information."

Another twenty into her bra. Peanut-butter-and-jelly sandwiches for me the next two weeks.

She hunched over the ledger, tapping her crooked incisors. "Can't quite read my own writing."

I interpreted this as a squeeze for more cash, until she stepped aside to point. "You make that out?"

After a few seconds' eye-focusing, the name of Amberlee's sugar daddy leaped up from the page. Yow! Not the one I'd expected.

"Would you mind if we borrowed this ledger?"

"Oh, my. No, that wouldn't be possible. Can't let you remove it from the premises."

"What if we take a picture of it?"

Viola gave me a prim-librarian frown. "Wouldn't that be some kind of . . . what do they call it? Copyright violation?"

Either a better poker face or a fatter wallet might have convinced her, but her internal Geiger counter detected the excitement I was emitting. She wasn't about to hand over her potential ticket to fame and fortune without protracted negotiations.

"We'll be in contact," I said, scribbling down my various phone numbers. "Maybe we can set up an interview next week."

The cats had started slinking back. Viola closed the ledger and crawled under the table again. The fragrant one-two punch of liver and kitty outhouse was making me woozy.

"Let's get out of here," I whispered to Ahmed. "Before there's an earthquake."

Despite one nasty moment involving a wrong turn, we managed to escape the maze of periodical piles. Outside, Ahmed's complexion retained a greenish tinge. "We did not inquire which of the current tenants resided in this apartment complex at the same time as Mrs. Schultz and her daughter."

I was doubled over the second-floor railing, purging my system with more than one cleansing lungful of dry desert air. "Ran out of money," I wheezed. "Anyway, we need a different photo to show people."

"Ah, yes, I see. So they have to identify the correct one. That way we can be certain they are not claiming to recognize the Reverend Schultz so that we will go away and stop bothering them."

"That, too," I said. "But it's not what I meant. The lineup needs to include a picture of the man who paid Amberlee's rent."

"But I thought—"

"It wasn't Schultz," I said, plucking a cat hair off my lip. "It was his lawyer. Davis Litvak."

A brush fire had broken out in San Bernardino National Forest, backing up traffic through Cajon Pass. By the time we got back to Santa Monica, it was past dinner time. Neither Ahmed nor I felt like eating. After I dropped him off, I sat in my car with the dome light on to check the date on the divorce papers McGuire had copied for us.

Amberlee's marriage to Curtis had officially ended June 9, 1995. Two days later she'd vacated the Victorville apartment, in such a big rush, she'd been willing to forfeit more than two weeks' rent. Admittedly, someone else's money.

Was it possible she'd dumped Curtis for Litvak? Followed him from Gypsum to his boss's next scheduled appearance? Amberlee claimed it was Schultz who'd lassoed her heart from the stage of that revival meeting. Had it actually been his hulking protégé?

For a social climber like Amberlee, Litvak didn't seem much of a step up from Curtis. Besides, how did she then end up married to Schultz? The Reverend had to have been the object of her desire all along. When they met, his career was starting to take off and he couldn't risk any whispers about an affair with a married woman. Would have made sense to use Litvak as a go-between to hide Schultz's connection to Amberlee. Litvak was an attorney, after all. It was his job to conceal his client's shenanigans.

I paged through the divorce papers one more time. Not a single reference to Amberlee's attorney, as if she'd opted for a do-it-yourself divorce. Except Amberlee didn't strike me as the type to slog patiently through a legal self-help book, then endure the drudgery of figuring out how to complete the necessary forms. Had Litvak handled all the paperwork behind the scenes, keeping his name off a public document that would otherwise contradict the virtuous fiction that Schultz and Amberlee hadn't met until she was a free woman?

I mashed the papers back in my purse, switched off the interior light, and aimed the Explorer toward home.

So right after Jake dies, Amberlee files for divorce. Cools her heels in Victorville for nine or ten months while Schultz—indirectly—foots the bill. Blows out of town with Layla two days after her divorce is final. All of which proves . . .

Nada. Food for thought, though.

Air blowing through the car vents carried the charred smell of the Malibu blaze. I was desperate to hop in the shower, rinse smoke and dried sweat from my skin, shampoo away any airborne cat-pee molecules still embedded in my hair. Yet the closer I got to home, the more I eased up on the gas pedal.

Truth was, I had conflicted feelings about returning to a dark, empty house that had been broken into only the day before. It was a miracle I'd dozed off last night, with wind rattling the windows, leaves skittering across the roof. Dane slept like the dead. I'd had to stay alert for both of us.

I turned onto Ashland. Half a block away, I noticed every light in my house was on.

I veered over to the curb, heart thumping like Dane's stereo system. The logical components of my brain scoffed that no self-respecting burglar/rapist/murderer would tip off his presence with such a high-wattage display. The illogical components screamed *Run!*

No emergency vehicles flashed their lights in my driveway. Good sign or bad?

Maybe Dane had come home for something he needed at Jeff's, then forgotten to turn the lights off when he left. Frequently he operated as if unaware the switch worked both ways.

I ruled out fleeing to Jeff's or sleeping in my car all night, which left me no alternative.

Cell phone in one hand, tire iron in the other, I sidled along the hedge bordering our front yard, half hoping someone on the neighborhood watch committee would spot me and call 9-1-1.

I raised my head enough to peek in the closest living-room window.

What I saw sent me running back to the Explorer. Ninety seconds later, I dumped my purse on the dining-room table and called, "What are you doing here?"

"Starving. How come there's never anything good to eat in this house?"

I walked over and settled on the arm of the couch, where

Dane sprawled watching *Hellraiser* for the umpteenth time. "How about a peanut-butter-and-jelly sandwich?"

He poked a fingertip down his throat and made a pretend-gagging sound.

"Why aren't you at your father's?"

"He had to fly to Vegas all of a sudden. Some screw-up. They gotta re-shoot a scene where Dad chases this dude into the volcano in front of some hotel."

I reached for the remote and lowered the TV volume. "When did he find this out?"

"Beats me. Soon as I got over there this afternoon, he drove me back here on his way to the airport."

"Wish I'd known. If he'd called me, I could have come home earlier."

"Maybe Dad thinks I'm old enough not to need a babysitter."

I held up my hands in surrender, biting back the retort that apparently he wasn't old enough to fix his own meals. "I haven't eaten, either. I'll see what I can find in the kitchen."

Dane blew a skeptical sound through his nose and turned the volume back up.

I was switching off lights when a minor puzzle occurred to me. I scurried back to the living room. "How come you didn't go to McDonald's or someplace with your friends?"

Shrug. "Bullet went to see Spanking Machine at Bar Sinister with Brandi and Nicole."

"They didn't invite you?"

"Sure. But I'm like, grounded, remember?"

Sneaking out to Denny's yesterday morning had earned him an extension through the weekend.

I processed this: On Friday night, my son had found himself footloose and fancy-free. Unshackled from the bonds of parental supervision. His mother assumed he was at his father's; his father assumed he was at his mother's. Behind this smokescreen of confusion, Dane could have partied with his friends all weekend at minimal risk of discovery.

Yet he'd passed up a chance to accompany his best friend and two of the hottest Goth girls in the senior class to a performance by his favorite local band. Submitting instead to continued house arrest. In a house he considered devoid of edible substance.

I strolled back to the kitchen with a smile tugging my lips. Turned out Dane was right; there was nothing to eat. I grabbed the phone and hollered, "What do you want on your pizza?"

Even with the pillow over my head, I heard ringing.

Conscious thought began to penetrate, as well. Saturday morning. Again I hadn't slept well, eyelids snapping open like broken window shades with each gust of wind, every creak of ninety-year-old house settling.

My cell phone. That's what that noise was. I flung the pillow aside.

"H'lo?"

"Harmony Magnussen?"

"Mmmm."

"Parker McGuire."

It took a second to make the connection. Gypsum. Lawyer.

"I didn't wake you, did I?"

Why do people always ask me that?

I mumbled a noncommittal response.

"Thought you'd want to know," McGuire said. "Somebody fired two .38 slugs into Curtis Gormley last night. Shot the poor bastard down like a dog."

CHAPTER 19

Smoke mantled the Los Angeles basin like a funeral shroud. The Santa Anas had finally died down, but sizzling temperatures continued to bedevil firefighters battling blazes that had torched twenty thousand acres so far.

Periodic incineration actually rejuvenates the grayish-green chaparral that cloaks southern California hillsides. Chaparral comprises a ragtag community of plant life—greasewood, scrub oak, mountain mahogany, flannelbush, buckthorn, deerweed. Some species only germinate in the aftermath of searing heat, others in the presence of chemicals in charcoal left by the inferno. Winter rains usher in a renaissance of spring seedling growth, along with a bumper crop of wildflowers—fire poppy, whispering bells, monkey flower, lupine.

Fire: Beneficial to the ecosystem, disastrous for people who build their homes too close to Mother Nature.

As Dane and I crested Sepulveda Pass, smoke completely veiled the Santa Susana Mountains on the far side of the San Fernando Valley. "Your friend in Malibu," I said. "Is his house in any danger?"

"Styx? Nah. He's way out by Trancas. Fire's near Malibu Canyon. Dad says you can see the flames at night from our house. I mean, his house."

Dane's little slip caused a twang of my heartstrings. Only it wasn't a slip, was it? Until a year and a half ago, it had been our house—Dane's home for a third of his life, until I'd dragged us both from under his father's roof. Swept away by a maelstrom of anger and grief, I'd never paused long enough to ask Dane what he wanted.

Today he'd readily agreed to accompany me. Of course, the alternative was to serve another day of punishment trapped inside the same walls he was ready to climb.

I didn't dare leave my son home alone, for fear Curtis Gormley's murder had something to do with me. With the case I was investigating.

Someone had already broken into our house. Who's to say he, she, or they wouldn't be back, armed this time with a .38 handgun? If the killer had shot Curtis to keep him quiet about Jake's death, I might be the next blabbermouth on his list. Or her list.

The horrible irony was that Curtis had refused to talk, except to deny any involvement in the killing. However, he'd acted awfully nervous. How had McGuire described his late client? Scared shitless. With good reason, it now seemed.

"Sure you don't want any of these?" Dane offered me a near-empty bag of fries. We'd provisioned our journey at Tommy's Hamburgers, a local institution famous for slathering chili on everything. Mere mention of the name could make me salivate, but McGuire's call two hours ago had killed my appetite.

My prime suspect, dead. Was my snooping responsible? Whenever a wave of guilt swamped me, I focused on the fact I could be next, and fear took over for a while.

I glanced again in the rearview mirror. The two-lane desert highway unfurled behind us straight as a rifle barrel. About a quarter mile back, the nearest vehicle shimmered like a mirage in the heat rising off pavement. My hands gripped the wheel tighter. Was that the same car I'd noticed after we exited the freeway at Mojave?

Don't get paranoid, Harmony. Maybe the driver was going to

Red Rock, too. Still, it seemed odd he hadn't passed me, or dropped back into the distance.

"Tell me again why we're driving all this way out to the boonies? Like, they don't have phones?"

Because I had to reassure myself Curtis's death was the result of some unrelated personal grudge—maybe a drunken quarrel over money. Either that, or confirm I'd put our lives in danger. "I need to question Sheriff Salazar. Phones are too easy to hang up."

"What, he won't talk to you?"

"Last time he tried to stonewall me. I haven't figured out if he's hiding something or doesn't like TV people."

"Oughta get Dad out here. Caldwell knows how to squeeze the fuzz."

I angled Dane a look over my sunglasses. "Yes, and it rarely involves calling them 'the fuzz.' "

"Yeah, yeah."

Confronting Salazar was something I anticipated with the same enthusiasm as a root canal. Until this morning I'd half forgotten his ultimately futile attempt to prevent me from seeing the Gormley file. If his goal had been to conceal evidence, I still had no clue what. Evidence of his own incompetence? Would a seasoned detective spot the trail markers of a botched investigation?

On the outskirts of Red Rock, a giant likeness of Salazar's grim, square-jawed kisser glared down at passing cars from a new election billboard. He looked like the kind of guy you'd hire to scare off your teenage daughter's no-good boyfriend. Or sic on a deadbeat's kneecaps with a baseball bat.

Maybe when Jake died, Salazar had deliberately squashed facts that contradicted Amberlee's version of events. Why? Heck, take your pick. Money. Sexual favors. Political pressure. Maybe Curtis or Amberlee was Salazar's favorite cousin.

Which would explain why he had acted so tight-lipped, why the minute I'd left his office he'd picked up the phone and instructed the Records clerk to ditch the Gormley file. Had his next call been to warn Amberlee? Was that why she'd agreed to an interview, to steer me away from the truth? Or—

Switch it around. What if someone had called to warn Salazar about Amberlee's interview? Someone worried about what she might have said. Someone who knew Salazar had equal cause for concern.

The sheriff already faced a scandal-plagued election. High enough stakes to risk stealing the interview tape? If so, he certainly ought to be an expert at burglar skills.

Across from the Fremont County Public Safety Center, the heat had fried the bank thermometer's brain, scrambling its display to a random pattern of dots. My dashboard clock read 1:16 when I pulled into the parking lot. I stepped from the Explorer onto hot gooey asphalt that conjured up images of La Brea Tar Pits.

Next to the bank was a supermarket. "Can I go over there and get dessert?" Dane asked.

"Don't tell me you're still—yes, okay. Why don't you stay there where it's air-conditioned? I'll pick you up out front when I'm done."

I watched him saunter off with a mixture of love and wonder. Where did he store calories on that lanky frame? And did black clothing pose a danger of heatstroke?

By the time I reached the glass doors of the public safety building, the soles of my sandals were scorched. Ruling out shorts and tank top as unprofessional, I'd opted for the Banana Republic version of foreign correspondent: wrinkled khaki blouse and slacks, loose-fitting with lots of pockets. The strap of a canvas tote bag was slung across my chest like a bandoleer. All I needed was a pith helmet and plane ticket, and I'd be fully equipped to cover any trouble spots in hot desert climes.

Maybe if I looked the part, Salazar would answer some of my questions.

Entering the air-conditioned building was like plunging into an alpine lake. My skin tingled with goosebumps, partly from fear I might run into the woman whose house I'd claimed was on fire. Records clerks didn't work weekends, did they?

A signboard propped at the foot of the staircase directed reporters to proceed back outside and around the building to the rear entrance. I started up the steps toward the sheriff's department, but backtracked to study the sign more closely. The sheriff would be holding a press conference at one o'clock to announce the latest findings in the Curtis Gormley shooting.

Correction: Was in the middle of holding a press conference, because it was already after 1:20. I hustled into the sweltering outdoors again, shortcutting across a pristine lawn. Would the murder of a small-time troublemaker merit a press conference if there wasn't an election less than a month away, prompting the candidate to make a big show of fighting evildoers?

The rear parking lot was jammed with sheriff's cruisers and other county vehicles. The entrance into the building had a sign warning "No Unauthorized Personnel Allowed." A podium had been set up in front of it, facing several dozen metal folding chairs arranged on a shady swath of pavement.

Salazar must have finished his spiel. He stood at parade rest behind the small cluster of authorized personnel waiting their turn at the microphone. The folding chairs were sparsely occupied. Only a couple of video cameras, one from a network affiliate in Bakersfield, the other operated by a kid who was probably covering the story for his journalism class. Fremont County orbited in the outer reaches of the Los Angeles television market, but apparently the murder of some schlub nobody liked, in a town nobody'd heard of, didn't rate sending out the satellite van.

Ken Tatum was stationed at one end of the front row, scribbling furiously while a female deputy fielded questions. She prefaced each reply with a wary frown at the microphone, as if it might bite her.

I slid into a seat next to a guy in a frayed bow tie and short sleeves who looked like a burned-out Jimmy Olson. After a brief search for my notepad, I leaned over and whispered, "What have they said so far?"

"Shhhh!"

A few heads turned. All of them flushed and sweaty.

Somebody asked, "What was the victim wearing?"

If the questions had deteriorated to this level, clearly I'd missed all the good stuff.

A hand shot up in front of me. "Bob Ziminski, *Antelope Valley Press*. Who were the victim's next of kin? Have they been notified?"

The deputy glanced over her shoulder, got the nod from a freckle-faced deputy I recognized from my last visit. She turned back, lowered her mouth cautiously to the microphone. "His mother and stepfather in Arizona have been notified, yes." She pointed to my upraised hand.

"Harmony Magnussen, *Cold Case Chronicles.*" More heads swiveled this time. "Do you suspect any connection between Curtis Gormley's death and the reopening of the investigation into the 1994 death of his infant son?"

Murmurs rustled the crowd like a listless breeze. Jimmy Olson blinked at me. The kid with the camcorder swung it in my direction. The female deputy aimed the same look at me she'd been giving the microphone.

Salazar stepped forward to rescue her. "First of all, let me make it clear that the case Ms. Magnussen refers to has not—

repeat, *not*—been reopened. Little Jake Gormley's death was thoroughly investigated at the time and resolved to the satisfaction of all authorities involved. There is no mystery about how he died, despite the efforts of a certain tabloid TV show to exploit a terrible tragedy for the sake of Nielsen ratings."

Tabloid show? Ouch. "You didn't answer my question," I said, trying to keep my voice from quavering. "Is there a possible connection between Jake's death and his father's?"

Salazar's mustache bristled as if to signal the imminent eruption of obscenities. "No," he said through clenched teeth. "This concludes the press conference." With a stiff-necked about-face, he hauled open the door and disappeared into the building. The remaining officials scurried after him, leaving Freckles to wrestle the podium inside.

"Nice work," Jimmy Olson said. "I'll have to remember that trick, next time some press conference drags on too long."

"You're welcome. No charge."

Metal chair feet scraped against pavement as fringe members of the fourth estate began to circle me like a pack of hungry coyotes. One grandmotherly type who looked like a representative from her church newsletter curled her lip at me and muttered, "Disgraceful."

Other stares seemed more curious than hostile, but I didn't have time to defend myself now. Besides, one of the coyotes might decide to launch his own investigation and scoop me.

Ken Tatum was already wheeling out of sight. I chased after him, and in this heat even that minor exertion was enough to discourage pursuers. I caught up with him at his van. "Ken, hi. You got a minute to fill me in?"

"What, you're late for class and now you expect me to share my notes?"

"I didn't know about the press conference. I came here to talk to Salazar, but I have a feeling he's not going to be available to answer my questions."

Ken dragged a hand over his beard to expose a grin. "Not exactly a fan of your show, is he?"

I mopped my forehead with a fast-food napkin I found in my tote bag. "So what happened to Curtis?" I asked, edging sideways so Ken wouldn't have to squint into the sun.

"Seems he was shot to death last night, couple hundred yards up the road from Desert Acres. Sometime between eleven-thirty and midnight." Ken lifted the notepad from his lap and used it to fan himself. "A passing driver found him lying near his car. Salazar wouldn't release the driver's name because his female passenger wasn't his wife, but everyone in town knows who it was."

"Curtis was where, on the shoulder?"

"Middle of the right lane." Ken checked his notes. "Theory is, the killer blocked the road with his own vehicle, then shot Curtis when he got out to investigate. One .38-caliber bullet to the head, another that entered the side of his chest, probably as he fell. The engine of Curtis's pickup was still idling when they found him."

"An ambush?" Lying in wait was a ticket to the death chamber in California.

"Looks like." He grazed knuckles along his jaw. "One of the pickup's headlights was smashed. They found broken glass in the parking lot outside Curtis's favorite watering hole."

"The killer deliberately broke his headlight first, so he could tell it was Curtis's truck coming?"

"Or she. Clever, huh?"

"Were there any witnesses to the shooting?"

Ken shrugged one of his weight-lifter shoulders. "Pretty deserted out there that time of night."

"What about people who live in Desert Acres?"

He snorted. "You've seen the place, haven't you? Gunfire on

a Friday night isn't exactly something that would rouse the residents to glance out their windows." He maneuvered his chair to open the van's driver door. "One or two people might've heard something, but they're a little fuzzy about when. Cripes, it's like an oven in there."

"How did the cops come up with the time frame?"

He tossed the notepad onto the passenger seat. "Last time anyone saw Curtis alive was around 11:15 P.M., when he left The Quarry."

"You mean the mine?"

"A bar, in Gypsum. Where they found pieces of his headlight." A bead of sweat trickled down Ken's temple and plopped onto the collar of his polo shirt. "It's a fifteen, twenty-minute drive from there to Desert Acres, depending on how much you slow down for that sonofabitch curvy section."

Something grim in his eyes reminded me that was where his brakes had once gone out, costing him the use of his legs. "Sheriff have any suspects yet?"

"Not that he's willing to share."

"No possible motive?"

"Curtis inspired murderous thoughts in a lot of people." Biceps bulged as Ken gripped his chair wheels. "Look, I need to get back. I'm putting out an extra edition for tomorrow."

"Sure. Listen, thanks. I owe you. I really appreciate your help." Without offering any in exchange, I turned to walk away from the van, sensing Ken Tatum was a man who preferred to wage his struggles in private.

"Wow, just like on TV!"

The ultimate standard of reality. From the left-hand shoulder, Dane and I gazed through the windshield at the chalk outline that delineated the former position of Curtis Gormley's toppled corpse. Fifteen feet away, another outline showed where he'd left his truck.

The cops had strung yellow crime-scene tape atop a barricade of orange construction cones, but the effort seemed halfhearted. Passing vehicles had knocked over several cones and torn yellow streamers flapped like tattered pennants as wind scoured chalk particles off the pavement.

We'd stopped first at Desert Acres, where I'd reenacted deputies' door-to-door interrogations and come up with the same result: zilch. Nobody saw nothin'. A couple people mighta heard somethin'. Lots of headshaking when I asked who might have wanted Curtis dead.

I shuddered. Dane's reaction to the murder scene wasn't so different from mine. Hollywood has turned the chalk outline into a powerful image of violent death. Seeing this ominous symbol cross the boundary that separates make-believe from real life chilled me with a visceral shock I hadn't anticipated.

A walking, talking human being, someone I'd actually met and spoken to, reduced to this ghostly scrawl of dust.

"This creeps me out," I told Dane. I couldn't imagine any useful information to be gleaned from closer inspection. "Let's go."

I clicked on my turn signal and checked behind for traffic. A black sedan was leaving Desert Acres. I waited for it to pass. After initially slowing, it sped up, creating wind shear that blew over another cone when it whizzed by. A Lexus with tinted windows, pulling out of Desert Acres? Probably stolen.

Crouched on the far edge of Gypsum was The Quarry, a dilapidated boozing establishment fronting the gravel road that meandered out to the mine. Convenient for workers desiring to drop in after their shifts, maybe blow their paychecks on cheap whiskey and watered-down beer.

At 4:30 on a Saturday afternoon, the undersized parking lot was already crammed with high-mileage cars and dented pickups. I found an empty space at the back, told Dane I'd leave the key in the ignition so he could turn on the air con once in a while.

"Can't I come in?"

"It's a bar. You have to be twenty-one."

"No prob. I'll show 'em my fake ID." He rolled his eyes at my expression. "Kidding, Ma. Look, I really need to take a leak."

"Well, I suppose to use the bathroom." A wild-haired patron stumbled out the back exit, fumbled with his zipper, began to urinate on a dumpster. I turned to Dane. "Promise me you won't touch anything in there."

We bypassed the shortcut and trekked around to the front entrance. Compared to the westering sunshine slanting against its metal roof, The Quarry's interior was dark as a bottomless mine shaft. Dane vanished into the murk while I stood next to a cigarette machine and waited for my eyes to adjust. From the slurred exclamations and maudlin toasts making rounds up at the bar, I gathered Curtis's drinking buddies were holding some sort of wake for him.

Grungy brown curtains were drawn closed over the windows, whether out of respect for the dead or to hide the housekeeping from health inspectors, I wasn't sure. Feeble light dribbled from a few dim-wattage bulbs attached to low rafters, supplemented by the sickly glow of neon beer signs. Decayed remains of old sawdust littered the floor, mixed in with all the detritus that had fallen on it since they'd scattered it fresh sometime in the last century.

The loud crack of a cue ball echoed from the back room. Nearby a woman clutching a beer bottle slumped with her head on the fake-wood tabletop, sobbing. I took a deep breath and headed toward the bar, braving the miasma of spilled beer, stale peanuts, sweaty bodies, dried vomit. The state of California had outlawed smoking in bars, but none of the outlaws in here seemed too concerned about a raid.

"That sorry-ass SOB Curtis." A burly unshaven guy showing three inches of hairy beer gut was hoisting his near-empty mug when I pushed through to one end of the counter. "God, I'm gonna miss him!"

Cheers went up. No one paid me any attention, including the bartender. Either it was too dark or they were too drunk to recognize me as the TV person who'd been asking all the questions around town.

Fortunately, I knew how to get this bunch to talk. "Bartender," I called. "A round of drinks for everyone, in memory of my good buddy Curtis."

An hour later I'd been propositioned, pinched on the butt, and found a black hair floating in my beer. But I hadn't learned anything significant about Curtis's last few hours on earth. No, he hadn't acted nervous. Hadn't reported any sinister strangers lurking around his trailer. Hadn't mentioned his kid's death—last night or any other night, for that matter. Most folks around here had pretty much forgotten he was the father of that baby who died.

I made my farewells. Restrooms were down the same hallway as the back exit. One whiff steered me out through the front door. Fortunately the hair discovery had limited my consumption to half a light beer.

Dane was lounging on the fully reclined passenger seat, chatting into his cell phone. It felt like a hundred degrees in the car. "Gotta go," he said, like he'd suddenly made me for an enemy agent. He flipped the phone shut. "You been smoking, Ma?"

I sniffed a fistful of blouse. "Oh, God, I reek, don't I? Come on, let's go home."

"What about dinner?"

"We'll pick up something on the way."

"Pizza?"

"Chinese."

"Mexican?"

"Deal. Put the seat up, please."

The sun had dropped behind the closest mountains. Though not yet true dusk, I switched on headlights as we cruised through town.

"Man, this place is like, Nowheresville. What do they do for fun, sit around and watch cows?"

"I don't believe there are any cows around here." As we left Gypsum behind, the road started its downward grade. Ahead of us, a descending series of hairpin turns jutted from the rocky mountainside. "There's a movie theater."

"Yeah? How many screens?"

"Two, I think." I downshifted to let the engine slow us and avoid overheating the brakes.

"Two? That's all?"

"How big a multiplex do you think a town this size can support?"

He cocked his thumb. "Exactly my point."

"Look at all the advantages, though. Fresh air, beautiful desert scenery—"

"Snakes."

"Okay, I could do without the snakes."

I braked as the next curve approached. Braked harder. Suddenly, my mouth went dry.

I stomped on the brake pedal this time. Drove it right to the floorboard.

Nothing happened.

CHAPTER 20

I yanked hard on the emergency brake. Nothing.

Adrenaline surged through my bloodstream. When I tried to shove the transmission into park, the shift lever wouldn't budge. Reverse. Impossible. First gear. *Come on, come on . . .*

Finally I managed to force it into second. The engine screamed as compression fought the pull of gravity. We were no longer accelerating, but still traveling too fast. Way too fast.

I took the curve with both hands bolted to the wheel like iron claws. Dane's head whipped toward me. "Ma, what . . . ?" At the sight of my expression, he went dead silent.

The Explorer's tires squealed against pavement, kicking up gravel like machine-gun fire when momentum carried us too wide onto the narrow shoulder. I fought to stay in our lane, but as we flew around the next curve, a car winding uphill was forced to swerve out of our way. The Doppler shift of angry honking quickly faded behind us.

With a teeth-rattling jolt, we caromed off a low metal guardrail. Beyond it, the terrain fell away in a steep drop-off. To our left was the side of a mountain. If I hit it, we could loop upside down like a roller coaster. Or ricochet back across the road and over the cliff.

Another curve. Another. Still miles from where the road leveled out on the desert floor. The muscles in my arms were corded like steel cables. *Hang on, hang on . . .*

Now I deliberately cut corners wherever I could, crossing

210

double yellow lines to make the sharp turns shallower. Hoping against hope an oncoming vehicle didn't suddenly swing into view, though at this point a head-on collision might be our best bet.

My heart was slamming against my ribs so hard I could barely breathe. Swamped by terror, one cold, detached compartment of my brain continued to analyze the situation, consider options, make decisions. Above all else, if I could see a way to save Dane, I would take it. Period.

Sweat dripped into my eyes. When I blinked it away, I glimpsed one of the tanker trucks from the mine lumbering down the hill ahead of us. As we closed the distance, the Explorer's image reflected off the back end of the shiny silver tank, expanding at a terrifying rate.

I slammed the horn in an abrupt, desperate warning, then clamped both hands to the wheel and swung into the other lane. If a car was approaching, I wouldn't see it until too late. Where would I go, anyway? Trapped between a wall of sedimentary rock and several tons of rolling gypsum. I didn't dare breathe. The big rig loomed so close Dane could have reached out and touched it.

The driver blasted his horn as we zoomed past, startling me. I nearly lost what little control I had. Up ahead, an arrow shaped like an upside-down U warned drivers not to take this turn faster than twenty miles an hour. I didn't dare shift my gaze from the road to check the speedometer. Not that it made any difference. My foot still mashed the brake pedal against the floor, as if there was a hope in hell the malfunction might suddenly fix itself.

We barreled into the curve, headlights slashing out into nothingness, my hands locked on the wheel in a death grip. Tires screeched, then lifted from the pavement. I heard Dane gasp. Felt the Explorer start to skid. *This was it, this was it . . .*

The road straightened some. Enough. Wheels hit solid ground. No time for relief before we were sailing around the next curve. And the next.

Wishful thinking, or was the gradient less steep now?

There! Looming up on the right, something besides thin air: a saddle ridge connecting two hills, a sort of staging area for bikers and four-wheelers. Trails crisscrossed the rock-strewn terrain, disappearing over the far side. A few people were loading ATVs onto trailers scattered in the fading daylight.

If I veered off-road at this speed, we could very well flip over. On the other hand, we were both wearing seat belts. From previous trips I was almost certain the road would again dive sharply after this relatively level stretch.

"Hang on," I rasped through clenched teeth.

We left pavement and bumped across the shoulder, careening wildly as we hit the uneven ground. I dodged the largest boulders, but something hit the undercarriage with a deafening clunk!

Heads turned, jaws dropped as blurred faces watched us stagger across the rough landscape. The sandy soil dragging at the tires began to slow us.

We pitched down the side of a narrow gully, and before I could crank the wheel, slammed into the opposite embankment. We lurched forward like crash-test dummies, seat belts cutting into hip and collarbones.

The engine died.

Flung backward, we sat motionless.

Silence assaulted my eardrums like pressure underwater. For a few moments the only sound was the tick of heated metal, the hiss of steam from beneath the hood.

"Wow, Ma." Dane's voice came out a little shaky. "Awesome driving."

I burst into tears. Then flung my arms around my son and

hugged him as if I could never let go.

Dane got his wish—pizza for dinner. In lieu of red-checked tablecloths and candles dripping wax down the sides of old Chianti bottles, the ambience consisted of oil-stained concrete, the smell of axle grease, the pressure-cooker chatter of an air wrench.

In the cramped waiting area of Fontana Auto Repair, we stacked up dog-eared issues of *Popular Mechanics* to make room for the cardboard pizza box. Meanwhile, Noreen's son Travis inspected the crippled Explorer. "Might as well go someplace and have yourselves a nice meal," he'd suggested, pointing down the street with a socket wrench. "Time you come back, I'll have had a chance to check out the damage."

But my legs felt too rubbery to walk anywhere. I wasn't in the mood to talk to anyone, rehash our brush with death, face people staring at us. Besides, Travis and his son were missing their own dinner, thanks to me. When he recommended the local pizza parlor, I asked what their favorite kind was and ordered extra.

The first help to arrive after my 9-1-1 call was the female deputy I'd sandbagged at the press conference this afternoon. This afternoon? Seemed like days ago. Once I reassured her we were uninjured, she radioed to cancel the ambulance from Red Rock, then summoned the closest mechanic for a tow.

Travis had arrived twenty minutes later, accompanied by a cute little blond boy with a cowlick. I recognized them both from photos I'd seen at Brittany and Justin's house, although Zack was missing several more teeth. With Dane and me squeezed into the cab of the tow truck, Travis held the eight-year-old on his lap and let him "drive" back to Gypsum. High on my list of Dumb Things Parents Do, but I was too busy biting my nails to lecture him.

Through the grimy window in the waiting area, I could see Zack out in the double-bay garage, working the lever that moved the hydraulic lift up and down. Fortunately, not the lift my vehicle was perched on.

Travis walked in as Dane was reaching for the last slice. I swatted his hand away. "More pizza?"

"Thanks." Travis wiped his hands on a greasy rag, then stuffed it in his jeans pocket. He was a few years older than his brother Justin. Early- to mid-thirties, deep-set brown eyes, the almost-too-perfect, slightly jaded features of an aging teen idol. His thick shock of dark hair was swept back as if he'd been riding a Harley all day without a helmet. Even the short-sleeve shirt with "Travis" stitched over its pocket couldn't diminish his laid-back cool. James Dean. Elvis. The Fonz.

The coolest part was that he seemed as unaware of his appeal as the streak of engine oil across his cheek.

He bit off some pizza, took a moment to reel in cheese strings.

"Did you figure out why the brakes failed?" I asked.

"Yep." He teetered a hand side to side. "Sort of a good news, bad news deal." He chewed, then swallowed. "Good news is, I know what happened. Bad news is, somebody cut your brake lines."

I said, "Are you sure?"

Dane said, "Holy shit!"

"Emergency brake cable, too." Travis dabbed his mouth with a napkin. "Have to report this to the sheriff. They'll want to come out and take pictures, probably."

"Tonight?"

"Let's hope so." With that, he ferried more pizza into his sexy mouth and went to call from the phone in his office.

I dropped my head into my hands and moaned. "I cannot believe this."

"Boy, Ma. Who'd you piss off?"

"Tell me this is a bad dream. Sweet Jesus, we could have been killed, or wound up . . ." Slowly I raised my head. "In a wheelchair."

"Come on, chill. Didn't happen, right?"

Furious, icy resolve straightened my spine like a steel rod. Someone had endangered my kid's life. And that someone was going to pay.

I needed to think. Then talk to Ken Tatum.

Travis was bunching up his napkin when he came out of the office. "Deputy's on her way back. She says to sit tight until she gets here."

With a groan, Dane tossed aside *Popular Mechanics*. "So." Fingers linked behind his head, he said, "You got any cows in this town?"

"They must have sabotaged the car while both of us were inside The Quarry," I said.

The deputy's name was Audrey Gilchrist. Late twenties, sturdy build, dun-colored hair tied back in a short ponytail. Not someone I'd want to arm-wrestle. She narrowed her gaze, sidled it towards Dane. "You and your son have much to drink?"

"Whoa, yeah. Those margaritas were primo."

"Dane!" I stretched my lips in a sheepish expression and shrugged. The deputy didn't blink. "My son only came inside a few minutes to use the bathroom. I had a light beer." She wrote something down. "Half of one, actually."

"Anybody approach the car while you were waiting for your mom?" she asked Dane.

"You mean like, with a pair of bolt cutters?"

I kicked him under the table.

"Nah. Not that I noticed."

"How long were you inside using the bathroom?"

"Dunno. Five minutes, maybe?"

215

"Then you went back outside to wait in the car?"

"Uh, sorta." He studied a hangnail with intense interest. "After I watched some guys play pool for a while."

"You what?"

"How many minutes were you in the bar, total?"

"Dane, I specifically told you to wait outside!"

"Jeez, Ma, it was hot out there! Not like I had a nice cold beer or anything."

Gilchrist's mouth crimped like she was formulating a call to Child Protective Services.

It was after nine P.M., and the repair-shop waiting room had turned into claustrophobic purgatory. A small floor fan whirred uselessly against hot, stuffy air. My rear end had gone numb from the hard molded-plastic chairs. The only available distractions for passing the hours were a bunch of old car magazines and a stale-candy vending machine that ate quarters.

In the first tidal wave of relief to be alive, Fontana Auto Repair had seemed like a refuge. With floodwaters receding, it felt more like prison.

Earlier, with Travis pointing out the severed brake lines, Deputy Gilchrist had taken pictures and dusted the Explorer for prints. Fat lot of good that would do, unless our would-be killer had been cocky enough to dispense with gloves. Who knows? Maybe he figured any fingerprints would be obliterated when the wreckage exploded in a fireball.

In addition to brakes, the repair list had now lengthened to include a new radiator and front axle, which Travis couldn't get until Monday. I killed some time trying to remember how high the deductible was on my insurance policy. Zack had fallen asleep, curled up on the floor in his father's office. It was starting to look like we might have to spend the night there, too.

"Anything else you want to add to your statement?" Gilchrist asked.

I wiggled a thumbnail between my lower incisors. "Someone might have been trying to stop me from asking questions about Curtis Gormley."

"Oh?" She glanced up from her notebook, brows hoisted at a skeptical altitude. "You're saying, someone's afraid you'll find out something official investigators haven't?"

"Well, only because—"

"You're saying with all the resources, experience, and manpower being brought to bear by the sheriff's department, you're the one the killer has to worry about?"

"That's not exactly what—"

"You figure Gormley's killer might have been one of your drinking buddies this afternoon? And you asked such clever questions he decided he'd better sneak out to the parking lot and cut your brake lines? With your son in the car?"

"I'm still working on the whole theory," I mumbled. "Did I mention someone might have been following us this morning?"

"Uh-huh. Dark sedan. No license-plate number, no other description."

"It was a long way behind us. And the sun was reflecting off its windshield into my eyes."

"Um . . ." Gilchrist probed her cheek with her tongue. "Doesn't this contradict your other theory? You hadn't even arrived in Gypsum yet. Wasn't it too soon for Gormley's killer to worry that while the authorities were out bumbling around, the tabloids were going to unmask him?"

Twelve hours ago, who could have predicted the news of Curtis's death wouldn't be the low point of my day?

Since then I'd managed to cheese off the entire Fremont County Sheriff's Department. I'd been sexually harassed by a mob of drunken, blubbering lowlifes. My clothes stank of sweat and smoke and fear, and I'd had to eat pizza with mushrooms because that's what Travis and Zack liked. Oh, yes, and my son and I had come within a guardrail's width of dying.

My nerves were strung taut as piano wire. If the day hit one more sour note, I would snap.

"Got any more quarters?" Dane asked.

Somewhere nearby a car door slammed. Male voices echoed inside the garage. Five seconds later, my ex-husband strode into the waiting room.

CHAPTER 21

"Hey, Dad." Dane's nonchalant greeting immediately made me suspicious.

Jeff crossed to the candy machine in two strides and crooked his elbow around our son's neck. "Hey, yourself. You okay, amigo?"

"Sure."

He turned to where I sat with my jaw hanging open. "How about you, Harm?" he said, scanning me with his Superman X-ray vision.

"I thought you were in Las Vegas," I said.

" 'Hi, honey, I'm fine.' " He dropped from falsetto to baritone. "I was in Vegas. Till I heard what happened."

Wardrobe must have dressed him in that Hawaiian shirt to subliminally remind viewers of *Magnum, P.I.* Dane was studying the paltry candy selection with deep concentration. No need to inquire how Jeff had learned of our near-death experience.

I crossed my arms. "You're making a big deal about nothing."

"You're both nearly killed, and you call that nothing?"

"Someone cut the brake lines, Dad."

"What?" Jeff's tan disappeared. He turned abruptly to the deputy. "Is this true?"

Gilchrist had been observing our exchange like a spectator at a ping-pong match. "Looks like it." She cleared her throat and adjusted her duty belt as she stood up. "Excuse me, but aren't you—"

"Jeff Burdick." He stuck out a hand and flashed his million-dollar smile. "Nice to meet you, Deputy Gilchrist."

"How did you—oh." She touched her badge. She was actually blushing. She shook Jeff's hand, probably thinking she'd never wash her own hand again.

Jeff showed her some more dimple. "Thanks for taking such good care of my wife and son."

"Ex-wife," I said. "And we don't need taking care of."

Gilchrist shot me a daggered glance before turning back to Jeff. "We're not clear yet about what exactly happened, Mr. Burdick," she said, brushing back stray ponytail wisps. "Whoever vandalized Ms. Magnussen's car may have just been trying to scare her. There was no way to guarantee the brakes would fail on that particular section of road."

Terrific. Now our attempted murder had been downgraded to the level of practical joke.

"Please, call me Jeff." Letting her have it with both barrels. "I'm sure it won't take you long to find out who did this. Here, let me give you my number." He dug out his wallet and handed her a card. "Would you mind keeping me personally posted about the status of your investigation, Deputy?"

Would she mind? She fingered his card like it was the key piece of evidence to solving the crime of the century.

"Can we go now, Ma?"

"Go?"

"I'll drive you back to Santa Monica, Harm."

"Wait a sec." I held up my hands. "We're not going anywhere without my car."

"But Dad's got a car."

"And how am I supposed to get back here to pick up the Explorer?"

"The guy said it wouldn't be ready till Monday! What are we gonna do, camp out?"

Travis poked his head through the doorway. "Hey, I figured out why you look so familiar. Caldwell, right?"

"Jeff Burdick." He shook Travis's grease-stained hand in a manly grip.

"Oh, wow. My kid's never gonna believe this. Is it okay if I wake him up? He's sleeping right there in my office."

"Sure. I'd love to meet him." Out came the wallet again. "Listen, I really appreciate you putting in all this overtime on my wife's car. Let me make it up to you, okay?" He lowered his voice to a chummy tone as they headed into the office. "Now, what are the chances you could drop it off in Red Rock when it's fixed? I just flew in there, see, and if you left it at the airport, then Monday when I'm done filming in Vegas, I could pick it up and . . ."

"Ex-wife," I muttered.

Gilchrist sent me a look that could poison a scorpion.

The next morning my neck was stiff, but not from whiplash. I'd strained muscles and tendons clenching my jaw. First when the brakes had failed, later while Jeff lectured me after he drove us home and Dane had gone into the house.

"This is the second time in . . . what, two days? . . . he's been endangered because of this crusade you're on."

"It's not a crusade; it's my job."

"It's not your job; it's the cops' job! Like I said the other day, you should have told the police you still have that tape. Let them figure out what's going on. Stay out of it. And keep our son out of it."

It didn't lessen my aggravation any that part of me agreed. Was I recklessly putting Dane at risk just to prove something to myself? To show my boss, my co-workers—and okay, Jeff, too—

that I had enough smarts, talent, and determination to produce more than coffee?

Then there was Layla. Haunted all these years by the terrible crush of guilt for something she may not have done. Didn't she deserve for the truth to come out? Wasn't Jake entitled to justice?

Layla and Jake weren't my kids, though.

After Jeff left for LAX and the next flight back to Vegas, I collapsed into bed, too wiped out to brush my teeth. It was nearly ten A.M. when I stumbled into the kitchen and found Dane hunched over the Sunday *Times,* littering the Calendar section with flakes of chocolate croissant.

"Where'd you get that croissant?"

"Hey, Ma." He wolfed another bite. "Guess which one of the Seven Dwarfs you remind me of? Here's a hint. Not Sleepy."

"Sorry." I snatched a grease-spotted white sack off the table and peered inside. Then dropped back my head to gaze heavenward. "God bless you." I extracted a cheese croissant and pulled up a chair. "Whatever have I done to deserve such a marvelous child?" I grabbed him by the hair and planted a kiss on his cheek.

"Hey!"

"You're officially ungrounded."

"Good, 'cause I had to walk down to Main Street to get these."

"I notice there's one left."

"Yours. This is my third."

Feeling more cheerful, I reached over to the small TV on the counter. The remote was long gone and the picture tube made everyone's skin tone green, but while I worked in the kitchen I mostly listened to it anyway.

I flipped around until the opening credits of *The Glory Gathering* ascended the screen.

"Whatcha watchin' that for?"

"I'm trying to get a better handle on these people." Due to the one-week delay, this morning's broadcast would be an edited version of last Sunday's service. If any of the major participants had freaked out over Amberlee's interview, I'd have to wait a week to detect anxious expressions.

I turned down the volume. Way down.

Next to the coffeemaker, the answering machine blinked. I whirred French Roast beans in the grinder, then poked the Play button. The first call had come in yesterday morning at 8:27, before McGuire had shocked me awake with the news of Curtis's death. In my rush to get to Red Rock, I hadn't bothered checking for messages.

"Miss Magnussen? This here's Viola Purdy. You remember, we talked yesterday? About a certain former tenant? And you were real interested in a certain ledger? Well, I been thinkin' we really ought to talk further about exactly how much this ledger might be worth to you. Seeing how your show is so popular and all, I'd imagine your budget for such things must be pretty high. Anyhow, why don't you call me back when you get this message and we can discuss it."

Her voice turned coy. "But don't take too long, all right? Who knows? There may be other interested parties. 'Bye, now." Her hang-up cut off a cat in mid-yowl.

I stifled a groan. What were the chances she'd take an IOU?

The only other messages were from Carson, wondering what progress I was making, and Travis Fontana, informing me that Mr. Burdick had already arranged for someone to deliver the part needed to fix my car. I was, Travis assured me, at the very top of his priority list, and even though he usually took Sundays off and his assistant mechanic had quit last week, he'd have the Explorer at the Red Rock airport bright and early Monday morning for Mr. Burdick to pick up.

Caldwell to the rescue. Again.

Braced by a mug of black coffee, I returned Viola's call. Might as well get it over with.

After four rings I heard someone pick up. Then, silence. "Ms. Purdy?"

"No," said a quivery old-lady voice. Good heavens, did Viola have her elderly mother stashed away somewhere behind all those bundled publications? "This is her sister, Alma Ferguson."

"Oh, I see. May I speak to Viola, please? I'm returning her call."

"I . . . she . . . you can't . . ."

All at once I realized it wasn't age but grief making her voice flutter like a wounded sparrow.

"My sister . . . has . . . passed away."

I banged down my mug, slopping coffee. Dane glanced up from the comics. "Viola died?"

"Yes." Sniffle. "Yesterday."

"I'm so sorry." A chill seeped into my bone marrow. "What happened?"

"That's the aw . . . awful part." Sound went muffled as if she'd wadded a tissue beneath her nose. "Her collection fell on her."

"Collection? You mean all those magazines and newspapers?"

"She was so proud of them." Mournful sigh. "We were all set to go shopping yesterday afternoon, only she didn't answer the door when I came to pick her up, so I . . . I let myself in with the extra key and . . . and everything had fallen over and the cats were crying and oh, it was so terrible, there was no place to walk, I had to crawl over all those mountains of paper and then . . . then I found her."

I made a murmur of horrified sympathy.

"And now . . . now the police just called." A sob broke from Alma Ferguson's throat. "They told me someone hit Viola on the head first. That's how she died. Then they must have pushed a few stacks on top of her, and then everything went down like . . . like dominoes!"

I covered my eyes. "What a horrible shock this must be for you."

"Why, I simply can hardly believe it! Here I'd just talked to her the night before, when she called about that phone number, and then boom! She's gone. If we hadn't decided to go shopping the next day, who knows how long she'd've laid there for."

"What phone number?"

"That was why she called Friday, to talk to my son. He's living with me until he gets another job. Eddie's a real computer genius, knows how to find anything on the Internet. See, Viola tried to get the number from Information, only they didn't have it, so—"

"Whose phone number?"

"Some man. No one I ever heard of. Can't recall the name offhand. I let her talk to Eddie, and sure enough, once he got on that computer it only took him a few minutes to find it."

"He gave this man's phone number to Viola?"

"Of course! Eddie called her back right away. She thanked him real nice. Sure hung up in a hurry, though."

"Mrs. Ferguson, I need to find out that man's name and phone number. How can I contact your son?"

"Well, he's helping me . . . oh, wait, here he comes now. He just took another load of Viola's collection to the recycling center. That crabby landlord of hers about pitched a fit when he saw it yesterday. Eddie!" She covered the mouthpiece for a minute.

I grabbed a pencil from the junk drawer and ripped a strip off the newspaper.

"Ma'am? This is Alma Ferguson again. Eddie still had the phone number in his pocket. You want me to read it off?"

"Please."

"Eddie, is that a two or a five?" Alma read off the digits. Orange County area code.

"Could you please ask him the man's name?"

Hand over mouthpiece again.

"Eddie says, Litvak. Davis Litvak. You want him to spell that for you?"

Her words numbed me like a full-body shot of Novocain. "Mrs. Ferguson," I said, "it's very important that you and Eddie tell the police that Viola wanted this man's phone number."

"Oh, we already did," she said. "They asked us when was the last time we talked to Viola."

"Mrs. Ferguson, do you know where Viola stored her ledgers? The ones where she kept track of the tenants' rent?"

"Yes, I believe so."

"You need to show one of those ledgers to the police. It might be the reason someone killed your sister."

"What? Now, why on earth would someone kill Viola because of some silly old record book?"

"There isn't time to explain right now. Can you please see if you can find the ledger that covers September, nineteen ninety-four, through June, nineteen ninety-five?"

"Well . . . I suppose. Hang on a minute."

It took almost five. I envisioned her clambering over the wreckage of Viola's collection, crawling under the table, elbowing cats aside.

She was breathing hard when she finally came back. "It's the oddest coincidence," she said. "But that one seems to be missing."

The bottom dropped out of my stomach. "Maybe Viola temporarily set it someplace else. If you find it while you're clearing out her apartment, could you please give me a call?"

She wrote down all my phone numbers.

"Thank you, Mrs. Ferguson. And please accept my deepest condolences."

"You're very kind." Another deep sigh. "You wouldn't by any chance want a cat, would you?"

After we hung up, I stared into space, trying to fit the pieces together. I drank half my coffee before noticing it had gone cold.

On Friday Viola had spotted my excitement about the ledger. Not one to pass up a moneymaking opportunity, she'd hatched a scheme to sell it to the highest bidder. And who else besides me might be interested? Well, probably the person whose name I'd been so startled to see.

When Litvak's current number turned out to be unlisted, Viola had turned to her clever nephew, Eddie. Then she called Litvak to propose the same sort of deal she'd outlined on my answering machine. Only Litvak responded first. Heard what Viola was selling. Agreed to drive up to Victorville and make her an offer she couldn't refuse.

Being Viola, she would have tried to ratchet up the price by bragging about the TV producer who was ready to pay big bucks.

Poor, greedy Viola hadn't a clue that protecting his benefactor's unsullied reputation might be something Litvak would kill for.

Dane shoved back his chair and stood. "Can I borrow the car, Ma?"

"We don't have a car, remember?"

"Not that one, the rental."

"What rental?"

"The one sitting in our driveway."

I scurried to the back door, opened it, peered out. "Where'd that come from?"

Dane shrugged. "Guy rang the doorbell while you were still asleep. Handed me the keys, said to call when we're done with it. They'll come pick it up."

"The Rental-Car Fairy strikes again," I muttered.

"So can I borrow it?"

"Sorry. Rental-car companies don't allow seventeen-year-olds to drive their vehicles."

"Aw, man, that is so bogus."

"It's common sense. Now, where did you put the—"

"Hey!" Dane stared at the TV. "That's him!"

"Who?" I spun around. *The Glory Gathering* was building up steam for the grand finale. Congregation swaying, choir singing their hearts out. Amberlee had joined Schultz on stage. A motley procession of the newly healed shuffled forward, appearing even less healthy with chartreuse complexions.

"Wait a sec. See if they show him again." Dane swiped the fringe of hair from his eyes for a better view. "There!"

The camera zoomed in on a middle-aged man slumped in a wheelchair, the left side of his face dragged down in the distorted grimace of a stroke victim.

"The guy pushing the chair." Dane pointed. "That's who I saw."

In the split second before the camera switched back to the altar, I glimpsed dark beard, bear-paw hands, shoulders like Hoover Dam. Rolling one of Schultz's latest miracles down the aisle was Davis Litvak.

An ominous prickle tiptoed up my spine. "You've seen that man in person? Where?"

"Yesterday. In that town, uh, whaddayacallit. Nowheresville."

"Gypsum?"

"Yeah, whatever. After I went into that bar to use the john." His Adam's apple jerked as he swallowed. "When I came back outside, I saw that dude hustling across the parking lot."

CHAPTER 22

I called the Victorville police first. The detective in charge of Viola Purdy's case was named Tackett. He perked up when he heard she'd left me a phone message at 8:27 yesterday morning, which helped bookend the time of her death. Then I explained about the ledger. Tackett sounded dubious that fourteen-year-old rental records would provide an incentive for murder.

"Litvak has everything to lose," I insisted, "if it comes out the Schultzes had an affair while Amberlee was still married to someone else." I reeled off alternate scenarios, desperate to convince him. "That's without factoring in loyalty to his longtime mentor. Even if Litvak didn't kill Viola to protect himself, he could have done it to protect Schultz. Or, maybe he told the Schultzes about her extortion attempt, and one of them gave the order to shut Viola up permanently."

Pause at the other end of the phone. "You think a man of God would order his employee to kill someone?"

I bit my tongue. "I think human beings are apt to resort to drastic measures if whatever they value most in life is threatened."

The Fremont County Sheriff's Department was no more impressed by my detection skills.

"Let me see if I've got this straight." Gilchrist's tone transmitted a sour expression. "Yesterday you were convinced someone tried to kill you to stop you from solving Curtis Gormley's murder. Today you're convinced the attorney of a famous tel-evangelist crawled underneath your vehicle and cut your brake lines to stop you from revealing some ancient hanky-panky?"

"The man is a thug! An ex-con! Trained attack dogs cower before him. Look up his record if you don't believe me."

She told me to bring Dane in the next day so she could get both our statements. After I hung up, my first impulse was to bang my head against the wall. Then I thought of at least one cop who'd be glad to hear from me.

I dialed Mark Ellison's cell phone, ignoring my squeamish-ness about asking him favors.

"Mark? You're not in Vegas, are you?"

"Why? You want to meet me at one of those quickie wedding chapels?"

"Ah, I thought because *Caldwell* is shooting there this weekend, maybe—"

"How about the kind where the justice of the peace impersonates Elvis and the organist plays 'Love Me Tender' while you march down the aisle? There, made you laugh. Nope, I'm just lying on the couch, watching the Raiders lose. What's up? You sound serious."

I explained what I needed. "But I hate for you to make a special trip to the station."

"No problem. I'll have somebody fax me the info, then call you back. Is this for work?"

"Yes." Sort of.

"Local case?"

"More or less."

"Guess I better quit before I get a 'no comment,' huh?"

"Mark, I'm sorry to be so secretive, it's just that . . ."

That I didn't need someone else warning me to step aside, little lady, and let the cops handle it. Because even if authorities ultimately reached the same conclusions I had, they weren't moving fast enough.

"It's okay," Mark said. Probably winking. "I like a woman of mystery."

After our conversation, guilt enveloped me like a ratty old bathrobe. How many more requests would Mark indulge without expecting me to reciprocate?

Where feelings were concerned, I didn't think I could.

Dane swung through the kitchen. "I'm outta here, Ma. Don't wait dinner tonight."

From the street, the telltale rumble of heavy metal. "Going somewhere with Bullet?"

For the first time in history, I welcomed his affirmative grunt.

"School night," I reminded him.

"Yeah, yeah."

Seconds later the Dodge roared off like an Atlas rocket, carrying Dane safely out of Litvak's orbit. For now.

I locked all the doors and headed for the shower. When I leaned in to turn on the water, my nose twitched at the distinct smell of smoke. Moment of panic before I remembered the ash-laden pall that had stained the skies for several days. Must have left the window above the tub open.

I whipped aside the shower curtain, planning to step into the shower, and saw the bottom glass louver was missing.

Heart thumping, I stared at the four-inch gap. Could I have forgotten to slide that final louver back into place Thursday?

No way. Not after the break-in had left me feeling so vulnerable. Besides, wouldn't the empty slot have caught my attention during Friday morning's shower?

But yesterday morning I'd left in a mad rush. If someone had recently removed that louver, the closed shower curtain would have concealed it. Last night? I'd hardly been able to keep my eyes open.

Why would someone remove only one louver, though? Unless

they'd been interrupted. Or unless . . .

My blood ran cold, as if the Hot spigot was cranked off.

Assume Litvak had murdered Viola Purdy yesterday morning. To drive here from Victorville would have taken two hours, tops. If Litvak was the intruder who'd broken in Thursday to steal the tape, he already knew where I lived, knew about the bathroom window.

What if he'd been in the process of breaking into the house to attack me when he'd heard us get in the car and drive off? What if his vehicle had been the one in my rearview mirror?

Not knowing whom I might tell about the ledger, Litvak would have been eager to eliminate me as soon as possible. Eager enough to take a chance on severed brake lines?

By now he would have made discreet inquiries, learned I was still alive. At this very moment he might be—

I screamed when the phone rang.

"Harmony? Mark. You okay? You sound out of breath."

"I was, um, outside. You've got the information already? Boy, that was quick."

"We aim to please. Want me to read you the highlights?"

"That would be great."

"Lowlights, I should say." Pages rustled. "Davis Robert Litvak had his first official brush with the law at the ripe old age of eighteen. Probably not the first brush, but his juvie records are sealed."

"I understand."

"Let's see what we've got here. Breaking and entering . . . car theft . . . residential burglary. Spent several years in and out of Ventura County jail."

"Is that where he's from?"

"Oxnard, originally. Mugging arrest when he was twenty-one . . . charges dropped when victim recanted her identification of him. Another couple months in the slammer for beating the shit, uh, stuffing out of his opponent in a bar fight. Next, looks like he skated on an aggravated assault charge when the only witness disappeared."

"The victim?"

"Uh, hold on. No. Apparently, the vic never saw his attacker. A bystander witnessed the whole thing, but before he could testify, he . . . oh, wait, here's a follow-up note. Couple of hikers found the bystander's body a few months later in Angeles National Forest. Somebody'd cracked his skull for him."

I swallowed.

"Okay . . . six months later, different assault charge. This time Litvak's luck ran out. Wound up in Folsom. Kept himself busy while he was there. Got his GED and joined the Aryan Brotherhood."

"The white supremacist gang?"

"Yup. Wanna hear about his tattoos?"

"No, thanks." Layla had already described them.

"Upshot was, guy got paroled after two years when his minister vouched for him. Dietrich Schultz. Why does that sound familiar?"

"He has a TV show Sunday mornings."

"Aha. You going to tell me how this saga turns out? Let me guess. Litvak finds religion and transforms himself into an upstanding citizen."

"Not exactly. He did go to law school, though."

"See? Once you start down the wrong path . . ."

I said, "Ha, ha," though nothing Mark had told me was amusing. Threats to witnesses? Dead witnesses?

Dane was the only person who could place Litvak in the vicinity of my brakes shortly before they'd failed.

An anvil of fear settled on my chest, making it hard to breathe. I thanked Mark and went to take my shower. The whole time under the spray I felt like Janet Leigh.

The police were bound to take their time investigating Litvak. His close ties to Schultz increased the odds of this blowing up into a high-profile case. In the era of Court TV, cops and D.A.s hated to make hasty decisions the media could later second-guess in front of the public.

But while the authorities were pussyfooting around, Litvak would have time for another attempt on my life. Worse, Dane might get caught in the crossfire.

With only my own life at stake, maybe I could have mustered the courage to be patient. Or else taken a sudden vacation abroad. But I wasn't about to sit around biting my nails for another second when my son might get hurt.

Smoldering anger burst into flame. I toweled off and hurried back to the phone.

"Harmony Magnussen to see Davis Litvak."

Outside the Schultz house gates, a disembodied intercom sentry asked if I had an appointment.

"No, but I know he's in there because I called a few minutes ago pretending to be from Fed Ex, and whoever answered the phone told me Litvak was there to sign for a package."

Pause. "I'm afraid Mr. Litvak is not available."

"He'll be available for me. Tell him it's Harmony Magnussen with a camera crew, willing to hear his version of Viola Purdy's death. If he's too busy to talk to us, the story's going on the air anyway. Oh, and he might want to tune in the local news at five."

A strangled syllable erupted. "Let me check with him."

While we waited, Ahmed worried his mustache. "Are you certain you know what you are doing?"

"No. But that's never stopped me before."

"If what you suspect is true, then Mr. Davis Litvak could be a very dangerous man. It is not always wise to corner a viper in his den."

"We're not going to corner him."

With a clank, the iron gates began to open like the jaws of a bear trap. "Follow the driveway and take the first right," the intercom instructed. "Mr. Litvak will be waiting for you in his office."

I shifted the sporty white rental car into gear. Compared to the Explorer, it felt as if my butt was scraping the pavement. "This might be the last time someone lets us in here," I told Ahmed. "Start filming."

We entered the shaded passage between twin rows of Italian cypress. When the ocean burst into glorious view, Ahmed's narration began to mimic the soundtrack of a tourist's home movie. "Off in the distance we can see Catalina Island. Unfortunately, we cannot see it very well because the air is quite hazy this afternoon.

"All of the ships are sailing to or from the Port of Los Angeles, which is called San Pedro, or else the Port of Long Beach. Look! Here comes a very large cruise ship. I am not certain, but I believe it may be the Love Boat."

He swung the camera around. "Now we are approaching the home of Reverend Dietrich Schultz and his beautiful wife. Such magnificence! If I did not know better, I would mistake it for the palace of a very important oil sheik.

"Here we are turning off the main driveway. Through the trees up ahead is a smaller, very attractive building with slate shingles and a chimney that appears to be . . ."

A bedlam of barking drowned out his commentary. He pivoted the camera. "Oh! Now we are being followed by two rather large German shepherds."

"Klaus and Hilda," I said. "Roll up your window."

Ahmed promptly complied. "They do not seem terribly

friendly, these dogs."

Klaus and Hilda were not what riveted my attention at the moment. Parked in front of the guesthouse-slash-office was a shiny black late-model Lexus. A clone of the vehicle that had pulled out of Desert Acres yesterday and sped past Dane and me, headed for Gypsum.

I parked beside it.

"Have I mentioned that I am allergic to dogs?" Ahmed asked. "Perhaps I should remain in the car."

I leaned on the horn until the racket flushed Litvak from his lair. He shouted to the dogs from the porch, dropped them into prone positions with an abrupt hand signal.

"Keep the camera on him," I told Ahmed. "I want this guy to sweat."

From shadows beneath the roof overhang, Litvak glowered at us. Since this morning's church service, he'd removed his tie, unbuttoned his collar, rolled up the cuffs of his long-sleeved white shirt. The crude dark markings of prison tattoos coiled down his forearms. His wrists were the diameter of stovepipes.

He bunched fists against his sides. "Would you please explain the meaning of this intrusion?"

"I think you know," I said, sidestepping the nearest attack dog. "Otherwise you wouldn't have let us in." I waited for Ahmed to catch up. "We'd like to get your reaction to the latest development in the Viola Purdy murder. What do you have to say about the Victorville police naming you their chief suspect?"

Litvak's jaw went slack. "What are you talking about?" Goggling at me. "I haven't killed anyone."

I started up the low flight of flagstone steps. "Phone records show that Viola Purdy called you only hours before she died. Want to explain what you two talked about?"

Litvak regained control of his menacing sneer. "I don't know anyone named Viola Purdy."

"A Jehovah's Witness knocking on doors Saturday morning saw you enter her apartment. How much did you promise to pay her for the ledger?"

"What ledger?"

"The ledger that proves you paid Amberlee Schultz's rent for nine months." I reached the top of the steps and continued advancing. "Except her last name wasn't Schultz back then. It was Gormley. Because she was still married to someone else. You acted as go-between for the man she was having an affair with." Ahmed had the camera practically in Litvak's face now. "Just to clarify his identity for our television audience, Amberlee's adulterous lover was your client, Reverend Dietrich Schultz."

Litvak's skin turned fish-belly pale. "You're delusional." He grabbed for the camera. Ahmed dodged nimbly aside.

I planted myself inside the buffer zone of his personal space. "Viola Purdy was in possession of documented evidence that could have destroyed Schultz's career, and yours along with it. Evidence she planned to sell to the highest bidder. Did the Reverend order you to kill her, or did you act on your own initiative?"

Litvak was breathing hard. Salami and onions for lunch. "I'm going to ask you to leave now."

"No doubt that ledger went up in smoke right after you ditched the murder weapon." I shook a finger at his nose. "If you were smart, you'd have burned the suit you were wearing, too. Ever watch *CSI*? The FBI can match cat hairs, you know."

Litvak shifted back a step. Snail trails of sweat crawled down his forehead. I'd probably just tipped him to destroy incriminating evidence, but building a court case against him wasn't my objective. Besides, he'd never be able to vacuum every single cat hair out of his Lexus.

"The Santa Monica police and Fremont County sheriff want

to chat with you, too," I said. "My neighbor saw you trying to break in my bathroom window yesterday. And some guy who came out the back exit of The Quarry to relieve himself on a dumpster noticed you fiddling with the underside of my vehicle." I pointed toward the Lexus. "He followed you and wrote down your license plate number."

Litvak flushed the color of raw meat. A vein pulsed at his temple. "Get out," he said through clenched teeth.

"Come on, be a sport. We're only about fifteen minutes ahead of the cops. If we capture your arrest on tape, think how much money we could sell it for."

"Klaus! Hilda!" He gestured with a violent swipe of his hand.

The dogs growled. Ahmed whimpered. But held the camera steady.

With one last snarl, Litvak backed into the guesthouse and slammed the massive oak door. I stuck my hand in my purse. As the dogs charged up the steps, I flung a fistful of hamburger over their heads. "What's that? What's that? Good dogs! Yum-yum. Fetch!"

It took another two pounds of ground chuck, but Ahmed and I made it safely back to the car. Between us and the dogs, quite a bit of panting was involved.

I retraced our journey down the driveway at enough speed to prove we weren't intimidated. After the estate gates had clanked shut behind us, I turned at the next corner, made a U-turn and parked.

According to my watch, we staked out the gates for nineteen minutes. Was Litvak taking time to burn his suit in the fireplace?

Ahmed said, "I do not mean to cast doubt upon your honesty, but was everything you said true? About the phone records? The cat hair? The witnesses? Because if all of that is true, I do not understand why the police have not yet arrested this man."

"I may have exaggerated a bit." The gates swung open. "But

maybe they'll arrest him now."

The dark Lexus barreled past, driver invisible behind tinted windows. Litvak might not be headed for jail, but at least he was headed far away from my son.

I picked up my cell phone. Detective Tackett answered on the second ring. "Breaking news," I said. "Your suspect is pulling an OJ."

CHAPTER 23

Next morning I pleaded my case before Carson.

"Two people I questioned have died already," I said. "Doesn't that prove I'm onto something?"

"It might prove you're a menace to public safety," he said. "I'm not sure it proves any connection to a kid's death fourteen years ago." He sighted down a letter opener at me. "That is what you're investigating, isn't it?"

"Look, evidence strongly suggests that at the time Jake died, his mother was involved with Schultz. I think it all ties together somehow." I felt awful enough about the tragic events I'd set in motion. If it turned out they weren't related to Jake . . .

"Litvak presumably killed Viola Purdy to cover up Schultz and Amberlee's affair," I said. "But what if that affair is the key to an even more damaging secret?"

Carson contemplated this. After some thumb-tapping, he nudged a plate of muffins across his desk. "Want one? My wife made 'em. Bran."

"No, thanks."

"Don't blame you." He regarded them with a glum expression. "Supposed to be good for your heart or your colon or one of those organs." He pushed the plate aside. "What about this other guy, the baby's father?"

"Curtis? He was definitely scared of something." I swallowed at the memory of the chalk outline, the empty windswept highway. "After Amberlee filed for divorce, someone beat him

240

up, really did a number on him. Next day he made a complete about-face, signed papers agreeing to all her terms." I shook my head. "Whatever they threatened Curtis with, it was enough to panic him fourteen years later, when I came along asking questions."

"This guy the cops are after. Litvak. You think he killed Curtis?"

I shrugged. "If Curtis knew more about Jake's death than he was telling, either Litvak or the people he works for might have been afraid he wouldn't keep quiet."

"You're implying Schultz or his wife had something to do with the baby's killing."

"Who knows? Maybe Schultz refused to marry Amberlee because she had a handicapped kid. Back then he was becoming famous as a miracle healer. Wouldn't be very good advertising if he couldn't cure his own wife's son."

"You think Schultz might have been the biological father?"

"Seems unlikely he and Amberlee ever crossed paths before that revival meeting. Jake was already eight months old by then."

Carson swiveled his desk chair to gaze at the photos displayed on the century-old brick wall. Mostly of Carson shaking hands with people like Walter Cronkite, Bill Moyers, Ken Burns. You could date the pictures by the distance Carson's hairline had receded.

My heart sank. Carson hated looking people in the eye when he gave them bad news.

"You've done excellent work on this," he said. "Maybe your instincts are right. We could be passing up the blockbuster story of the year." He wormed a finger beneath the noose of his necktie. "But I'm going to have to pull the plug on it. We simply don't have the time and money to keep pursuing this. The rest of the season's episodes are already in the pipeline. I can't spare even one person if we're going to meet our schedule. This was a promising idea, Harmony, but—"

"Two more days," I said. "Give me two more days."

"We can't afford—"

"I'll take the time off without pay. If I haven't proved by Wednesday morning that an innocent five-year-old got blamed for killing her baby brother, I swear I'll burrow back into my cubicle like a good little gofer and never, never, ever ask to produce anything again."

"Come on." Carson blew a stream of air through his lips. "I'm not trying to squash your ambition. You know I encourage my staff to make full use of their talents. This just isn't the right time."

"Two days," I said. "Unpaid leave. I'll work all next weekend to make up for it."

With a sigh, Carson retrieved a packet of Tums from his drawer and polished off the last one. "The next two weekends," he said.

"Deal."

"Deal."

I nabbed a bran muffin on my way out. Couldn't afford to pass up free food anymore.

Overnight a low-pressure system had brought cooler temperatures and higher humidity to southern California. Though several blazes were still charring the hillsides, firefighters had at last gained the upper hand. By the time I hit the desert, skies were smog and smoke-free, scattered with fast-moving puffballs of white cloud.

I called Jeff after I exited the freeway. "I'm on my way to Red Rock," I told him. "Have you picked up the Explorer yet?"

"Nope. I'm still in Vegas. The pilot I hired is flying me over this afternoon."

"If I switch vehicles, can you pick up the rental car instead?"

"Sure, babe."

"Okay. And . . . thanks. For arranging the rental. And driving us home the other night."

"Glad to help out," he said. "Any time. I just wish you didn't mind it so much."

"Yeah. Well. Anyway, thanks again."

"Don't mention it. I'll talk to you—"

"Jeff? I've been, um, thinking." I cleared my throat. "How would you feel about discussing some changes to our arrangement? Regarding Dane, I mean."

In the background I heard what sounded like a door closing. "What kind of changes?"

I took a deep breath. "So he can spend more time with you. I think he'd like that."

"So would I," Jeff said. "Absolutely. Let's talk about it real soon. You serious?"

"I want what's best for Dane."

"Me, too, Harm."

"I know."

Another voice. Female. Jeff covered the phone while he responded. I couldn't make out words, just the tone. Something about it doused me like a bucket of ice water.

"Harm? Listen, I gotta run. Just leave the rental keys with the old guy in the airport office. We'll talk soon, all right?"

"Sure," I said. It felt like a chicken bone was wedged in my throat.

Passing through downtown Gypsum on my way to Noreen Fontana's house, I spotted Ken Tatum wheeling out of the café. By the time I'd parked and hopped down from the Explorer, he was reaching for the door of the newspaper office.

"Ken!"

He grinned when he saw me. "Your timing's off, lady. If you'd shown up forty-five minutes ago, I'd have bought you lunch."

"Let me guess. Today's special was some fabulous secret recipe handed down by Carmen's grandmother."

He rubbed his belly. "Homemade chile rellenos."

"Which will be sold out by the time I get there."

"Come on inside." He opened the door for me. Certainly seemed in a chipper mood. "What brings you back to town? Tying up loose ends?"

"You could say that." Since loose ends were about all my investigation had produced so far. "I wanted to ask about your accident."

"What accident?"

"The one ten years ago." I pulled up a chair as he circled behind his desk. "When your brakes failed going down the mountain."

He lifted his eyebrows. "Who told you about that?"

"One guess."

Amusement twitched his mouth then faded. "It's been more like fourteen years, amazingly enough. But why on earth would you—oh, wait." Finger snap. "I heard about your adventure the other night."

"I'm wondering whether the two incidents might be connected."

Back up went the eyebrows. "How so?"

"For starters, were your brakes sabotaged?"

A wary look scuttled across his face. "That was never determined. I jumped out right as my car went over the cliff. It hit a boulder and exploded. Burned to a crisp."

Seventeen years of motherhood develops a fairly accurate lie detector. Mine whispered that Ken was holding something back. Perhaps the reason someone had wanted to kill the local newspaper editor. If Ken had uncovered Amberlee's affair with Schultz and planned to publish his scoop . . .

Maybe the motive had been more personal. "Carmen mentioned something else." I dug out my notepad. "That Amberlee's father died when she was young."

"What does that have to do with anything?"

"You told me her father ran off with another woman. That Dolores was so humiliated she left town for a while, then came back and made up the story about her husband dying."

Ken scratched the underside of his beard. "That's what I said?"

"Right here in this office." A seed of suspicion began to sprout. "Kind of odd that Carmen, who knows everything about everybody, is still under the impression Mr. Pombo died."

Ken's gaze slid away from mine. A copy of Sunday's extra lay on his desk. Above the fold a banner headline exclaimed: LOCAL MAN GUNNED DOWN!

"Dolores and Amberlee certainly did a good job keeping their secret all these years," I said. "Amberlee must have really trusted you."

"Yeah, I guess."

I tilted my head. "Seems like a classmate would be the last person she'd confide in, though. Considering how kids love to spread stories." I flipped back through my notes. "Didn't you say you only knew her from school?"

Ken dragged a hand down his face. "Okay," he said with a sigh. "Later on we became friends."

"More than friends, you mean."

He grimaced as if in pain. Took a deep breath and huffed it out. "Yeah."

Suspicion blossomed into certainty. I leaned over and touched the back of his wrist. "You were Jake's father, weren't you?"

He yanked his hand away. "No!" Like the blast of a self-inflicted gunshot. He passed a hand over his forehead. "Yes."

His voice cracked. "Jake was my son. Until that bastard killed him."

My mouth fell open. "Who?"

With twin thrusts of his bodybuilder arms, Ken propelled his chair backward. "You want more details about my accident?" He rolled out from behind his desk. "Fine, here goes. Besides never walking again, I'll also never father another child. Jake was it. The only kid I'll ever have."

He gripped the chair's rubber wheels tight enough to turn his knuckles white. "Jake would be fifteen years old next month, did you know that? Probably in a wheelchair, like me." His mouth twisted. "The spina bifida didn't matter. Amberlee only let me see him a couple times, but you could tell what a sweet kid he was. Smart, too."

He flung out his arms to encompass the stacks of newsprint, the row of file cabinets, the fake wood paneling. "When he got older I was going to hire him to help me here. I could have gotten close to him, played a major role in his life. A boy needs a real father, not some sorry excuse like that son-of-a-bitch who killed him."

A giant fist squeezed the air from my lungs.

"I begged Amberlee to leave him, but she always refused. Not unless I promised to take her away from here. The big city, that was her ultimate dream." Ken's voice took on a raw edge. "But how could I leave town when my father expected me to take over the newspaper? I couldn't disappoint him, not when he and my mother were always there for me."

He clamped his molars together. "Now, every single day of my life, I wish I'd taken Amberlee and the kids and moved away forever."

"Wait." A sick feeling curdled the pit of my stomach. "You think Curtis killed Jake?"

Ken blinked in surprise. "Don't you? Isn't that what your TV show is going to prove?"

I swallowed. "Why would you think that?"

"I overheard you last week at Carmen's. You and your cameraman." He gave a sheepish shrug. "After I came out of the men's room. You said Curtis admitted he lost his temper. He didn't mean to hurt him; he just snapped." A flush darkened his neck. "That son of a bitch."

I flew from my chair. "I never said that! Anyway, Ahmed and I were only speculating."

"But I heard you!" Ken's jaw shifted to a stubborn angle. "You said he'd found out Jake wasn't his, and not long afterwards he killed him."

My hair whirled from side to side. God, what had Ahmed and I said? Bit by bit, snatches of our conversation came back. "Ken." My heart was pounding. "Listen. Curtis never confessed to killing Jake. Ahmed and I were talking about how he got fired that day, after he fought with another mineworker. That's who Curtis insisted he never meant to hurt."

Muscles pulled the flesh taut over Ken's cheekbones, so they stuck out like knife blades. "He still killed Jake, didn't he? Why would Amberlee lie, if it wasn't to protect him?"

"I don't know! That's the reason I'm here today, to try and get to the bottom of this."

Ken's eyes darted back and forth, searching mine. Whatever he saw made him glance away. "You'll have to excuse me," he said. "I've got a lot of work to do right now."

"Ken—"

"Look, I'm busy, okay? I've got better things to do than waste time discussing an animal like Curtis Gormley. He beat Amberlee, did you know that?"

"Yes."

"Asshole got what he deserved." Ken's skin had gone a sickly shade, as if the chile rellenos hadn't agreed with him after all.

"Would you please excuse me?" He pivoted.

As I watched him head for the doorway leading into the back, a monstrous thought clawed its way toward the surface of my brain.

Like the dead struggling to rise from the grave.

CHAPTER 24

Last time I'd tried to question Noreen Fontana, she'd pretended not to be home.

This time I parked around the corner and sneaked next door. With all the dead bodies that kept turning up—one of them almost mine—I hadn't had a chance yet to return the owner's key. As part of my plan, I also brought along the baseball bat I keep behind the seat to give carjackers a good laugh before they shoot me.

The stale air inside the former Gormley residence was thick with dust particles and the odor of small-wildlife droppings. I navigated the obstacle course of trash and rotted floorboards, trying not to breathe.

The room that had been Curtis and Amberlee's sat directly across the driveway from Noreen's house. A sheet of plywood had been nailed outside the window. Too late, alas; most of the glass was shattered, leaving only a few jagged shark's teeth around the edges.

Trying to avoid any un-swept shards, I gripped the bat, wiggled my tush, and took a Babe Ruth swing at the plywood.

The impact made my ears ring. Dust sifted onto my hair and up my nose. I sneezed. Swung again. A loose ceiling tile plopped onto the mangy carpet. Another swing. Scurrying noises filtered through the walls as vermin fled for their lives.

I tiptoed quickly to the back door and peeked out. One of Noreen's curtains moved. Progress.

Back to the bedroom. Grand slam! Kiss that baby goodbye! More airborne crud attached itself to my clothes and skin.

Next time I looked out, Noreen stood in her front yard, skinny arms crossed, frowning as if she couldn't decide which to do first: call the sheriff or march over and give the latest vandals a sharp tongue-lashing.

I stepped under the carport and hurried down the gravel driveway. "Noreen! Hi!"

She clapped a hand to her heart. Whether the alarm on her face was a reaction to my grubby appearance, the baseball bat, or something else, it was hard to say.

"What are you doing?"

"Cockroaches." I pushed hair out of my eyes with the back of my wrist. "Man, I hate those pesky devils, don't you?"

She lifted a hand to her throat. "I thought you were finished over there."

"Nope. Still trying to figure out exactly what happened to little Jake. I was hoping you could help me."

"Oh, no." She retreated a step. "I wouldn't think so. I've already told you everything I know."

"Everything?" I waggled a reproachful finger. "See, I think you left something out before. Something that convinced you Layla didn't kill her brother. Something that made you write her that note."

She dug her nails into her neck. "What note?" The world's worst actress.

"Come on, Noreen. I've already spoken to your daughter, Sherri. Besides, your fingerprints are all over the paper." Bluffing Litvak had worked. Why not try it again?

She stuffed her fists beneath her armpits. "I don't know what you're talking about."

I smacked the bat lightly against my palm. "Withholding evidence is a crime, Noreen. Wouldn't you rather talk to me than the sheriff?"

"You wouldn't—"

"I would." I looked her straight in the eye. "Don't you think both Jake and Layla deserve for the truth to come out?"

A gust of wind pasted the cotton dress to her scarecrow frame. "I . . . I can't . . ."

For several moments the only sound was the relentless peck-peck-peck of the whirligig chicken perched atop her mailbox.

"I was mending one of Justin's shirts that afternoon." Her thin nostrils flared. "No one bothers to sew anymore these days. Clothes got a tiny hole or rip? Just throw 'em in the garbage." She mimed a toss. "Go out and buy yourself brand new ones. Even though just a little bit of thread would save all that money."

I clicked my tongue in agreement. "Then what?"

"All of a sudden I heard screaming. Jabbed myself good with the needle, let me tell you." She flicked an apprehensive glance at the Gormley house. "Not like it was the first time I'd heard screams over there, mind you, but these were so . . . so bloodcurdling. Made the hair stand up on my arms."

She shivered, although the temperature here in the sun was over eighty. "Minute I jumped up and looked out my window, their window slid open." She pointed to the plywood covering I'd used for batting practice. "Then somebody climbed out of it."

My pulse picked up its tempo. "Who?"

She fiddled with a button on her dress, adjusted her glasses, rubbed her beaky nose. All the while she stared into the distance, gaze unfocused, as if waiting hopefully for someone else to answer.

Her lips barely moved when she spoke. "Travis."

"Your son?" Not bothering to hide my surprise.

Noreen sewed her lips shut and nodded.

"Why was he climbing out the Gormleys' window?"

She propped her hands on her bony hips. "To avoid that mean son-of-a-gun Curtis, of course. Have to say, when I heard what happened to him the other night, I didn't exactly rush out to buy flowers for his funeral."

"What was Travis doing inside the Gormley house?"

"It wasn't like that," she snapped, as if I'd accused him of something. "He and Brittany were just talking, that's all."

"Brittany? The babysitter? But I thought she and Justin . . ."

I recalled a snatch of our first conversation. *My oldest, Travis, he was kinda sweet on her himself when they were kids.*

Flash forward fourteen years, to Brittany and Justin's living room. Framed pictures face down on the end table. Pictures of Travis.

Noreen studied her ragged nails. "She had a little crush on him. So what? That was a long time ago. When Travis heard she was babysitting next door, he stopped by to say hello. Just to be friendly. Then Curtis came home when he was supposed to be at work, drunk and spoiling for a fight, as usual. Travis figured he'd better hide until he could sneak out. Curtis always had it in for him, see. Travis didn't want any trouble."

Envisioning the layout, I tried to position people like game pieces. "Where did Travis hide?"

"In the bedroom closet." She waved vaguely at the boarded window. "He was going to tippy-toe out the back, soon as he heard Curtis changing channels in the living room. Only then Amberlee drove up."

The driveway offered a clear view of the back door.

"Brittany skedaddled right away, but Travis got trapped. What happened was Layla wandered into the bedroom and started playing right there in front of the closet."

Mentally I moved a tiny Layla figure.

"Then Dolores showed up, and Travis heard them all yelling. He was afraid, though, that Layla would tell on him if he tried to make a break for it." Noreen summoned a weak smile. "Boys will be boys, won't they? Always getting themselves into goofy predicaments."

I shuffled around the adult pieces. "So Travis escaped through the window right after the screaming started?"

Her smile faded. "He had no idea what was happening, of course. Just figured he'd better take his chances and get out of there."

"Did Layla or anyone else see him?"

"Nope. Just me. Eventually I pried the whole story out of him, even though he didn't want to talk about it."

I squinted. "And you never told this to investigators."

"Travis didn't know anything about how that baby died!" Noreen flung her arms skyward. "Why should he get dragged into it? People were always blaming him for things. If those deputies had found out he was in that house, you can bet they'd have caused trouble for him."

I probed my cheek with my tongue. "How old was Travis back then?"

"Twenty." As if daring me to deny it.

"And Brittany was fifteen."

"It wasn't like that!" Though I could see in her face it had been.

Even if Brittany had consented, it still would have been statutory rape. Travis could have gone to jail. Pretty compelling reason for Mom to keep her mouth shut. Maybe there'd been another.

"Noreen." How to phrase this diplomatically? "Were you afraid Travis might have hurt the baby?"

"What?" Her eyes bulged. "No! Dear Lord, the last thing that boy would ever do is harm a hair on that baby's head! Why, you should see how kind and gentle he is with his own boy, Zack. No. No. Travis had absolutely nothing to do with that."

I frowned. "Then why are you so sure Layla didn't kill Jake?"

Noreen sputtered like a pressure cooker. "Because Amberlee came and took her out of the bedroom! While Travis was still in the closet! He heard her talkin' real nice, tellin' her, 'Come along, Mama's got a big surprise for you.' "

"So it must have been later when—"

"There was no later, don't you see?" Noreen wrung her hands. "Soon as they left the room, Travis ran for the window. Only it was stuck, and at first he was scared it wouldn't open. But it wasn't more than a minute after Layla went off with Amberlee that he heard those screams. That little girl didn't have time to smother her brother!"

I felt a jolt, like a rusty key had unlocked the dark, twisty corridor leading to what really happened that day. If Travis's account was true, then Amberlee's wasn't. She couldn't have walked into Jake's room and found Layla holding a pillow over his face.

"That wretched woman lied." Noreen curled her lip in a snarl. "Way I figure, had to be either her or her no-good husband who killed the baby, then made that sweet child take the blame."

My father raised me to be as honest and uncompromising as a Minnesota winter, to tell the truth even when the consequences might prove harsh. All my life I'd looked down my nose at people who lied. Who'd have guessed I had a natural talent for it?

Poor Noreen. Burdened for years by the guilty knowledge that her silence had allowed a baby's killer to go free and ruined an innocent child's life. Then, an unexpected chance to repair some of the damage she'd done.

YOUR NOT THE ONE WHO KILLED HIM.

Noreen would have been shocked when her daughter told her

what Layla had become. Her conscience must have nagged her to write the anonymous note. After all this time, what harm could there be? Just to be safe, she'd dropped it into an L.A. mailbox before the end of her visit with Sherri so the postmark couldn't be traced to Gypsum. A prostitute would hardly be on cozy terms with the police, anyway. Who could have guessed Layla would bring the note to me?

I still needed to verify Noreen's story with Travis. She claimed, however, that after devoting all of Sunday to fixing my Explorer, he'd taken today off, asking Grandma to pick up Zack after school. At this very moment, Travis was out in the desert somewhere, racing dirt bikes with some pal Noreen didn't approve of, judging by her pinched nostrils.

Being of a suspicious nature, I drove by his repair shop to check. A Closed sign dangled from the entrance.

With only today and tomorrow to solve the mystery of Jake's death, I couldn't afford to wait around. Fighting off flashbacks, I made a nerve-rattling, white-knuckle descent of the mountain and headed for Orange County.

A brief Page 5 article in this morning's *L.A. Times* had noted that the Victorville P.D. planned to question the attorney of televangelist Dietrich Schultz in connection with the suspicious death of a local apartment manager. Unfortunately, the attorney's present whereabouts were unknown.

For now, it appeared the authorities were keeping under wraps any unsavory link to the Schultzes themselves. When I pulled up to their estate just before sunset, the usual celebrity-crime media circus was nowhere to be seen. Just a lone Newport Beach patrol cop parked in front of the gate.

When I ignored his move-along wave, he got out of his cruiser, strolled over, motioned me to roll down the window. "Sorry, ma'am. You can't park out here."

"I'm here to see Amberlee Schultz."

"Yeah, right." So young to be so cynical. "You and a dozen other reporters."

"I'm not a reporter. This is a personal visit."

He shook his head. "Reverend and Mrs. Schultz have left strict instructions not to be disturbed."

"What if I'm in desperate need of spiritual guidance?"

He almost cracked a smile. "Sorry to hear it, but you'll have to leave. The city has temporarily suspended parking along this street."

"Here's the deal." I lowered my sunglasses. "As you've no doubt been informed, the Schultz attorney has flown the coop. I'm his replacement. People like the Schultzes get very upset whenever they don't have a lawyer within finger-snapping distance. Now, I will assure the Reverend and his wife that you are doing a masterful job of guarding their privacy, but either you or I will be getting on that intercom within the next thirty seconds to inform Mrs. Schultz that Harmony Magnussen is here." I shoved my sunglasses back on. "Your choice, officer."

If he hadn't been a rookie, it never would have worked. Even so, I was terrified the din of my heart knocking against my ribs would give me away.

Finally, all those acting classes had paid off! He backed slowly toward the intercom, hand hovering above his nightstick. I climbed out to follow, prepared to bluff or threaten if Amberlee expressed reluctance to see me, but she instructed the officer to let me in.

The gates opened. He pulled his cruiser off to the side. Driving past, I waved to show no hard feelings.

Now that I'd observed the cliff-top view at three different times of day, I had to vote sunset the most awe-inspiring. Smoke lingering in the marine layer painted a Technicolor canvas above the horizon—luscious shades of burgundy, nectarine, and Pepto-Bismol.

I left a tire track or two on the grass, trying to park as close as possible to the main house. After arranging things in my shoulder bag, I grabbed the baseball bat, jumped out, and ran like hell. No sign of Klaus or Hilda. Maybe Litvak had taken the dogs with him.

The imposing front entrance had been constructed to withstand a battering ram. Chimes echoed inside like the bells of a European cathedral. For an instant I was transported into *The Sound of Music.*

Amberlee beat the maid to the door. "Thank goodness you're here," she said, practically dragging me into the entry hall. Hardly the reception I'd anticipated. "Thank you, Elena." Shooing away a woman in a starched white apron. "Let's talk in Dietrich's study," she said into my ear. "He's at Holy Shepherd, addressing an emergency session of the church council. Not that we have the faintest idea what all this is about."

Nor, apparently, any idea her gray silk blouse was missing a button. Trailing her down the hall, I couldn't help but notice the seams of her tailored black skirt were slightly askew, so the fabric didn't hang right. The funereal color scheme bleached her fair skin cadaver pale, made the beauty mark near her mouth look like a small-caliber bullet hole. At a guess, she hadn't combed her hair since this morning.

With all these signs of distress, it would have been cruel to mention her roots were showing. "I have a few follow-up questions from our interview," I said, pushing the study door most of the way shut. "By the way, did you have Davis Litvak break into my house to steal the tape?"

"Oh, that stupid tape." Amberlee flung herself onto the antique sofa. "I could have killed Mother when she spilled the beans. Dietrich was furious, even though I assured him I hadn't said anything." She pressed her wrist to her forehead like the heroine of a twenties melodrama. "I suppose Davis might have taken it upon himself to retrieve it. He's very protective. I've told Dietrich he oversteps his bounds. Oh, I don't know what to believe about him anymore." She leaned forward, clasping her hands damsel-in-distress fashion. "The police won't tell us anything. Can you explain why they think Davis is mixed up in some sordid murder?"

"Sure," I said. "I told them about the ledger."

"Ledger?" She crinkled her nose in confusion.

"The ledger he stole from your ex-apartment manager, after she tried to extort money for it." I dug a folded newspaper from my shoulder bag, nudged the bag beneath a chair. "Viola Purdy, remember her? From Victorville. Her records showed Davis Litvak paid your rent while you were still married to Curtis."

Amberlee blanched. "That's ridiculous. Why would Davis pay my rent when I didn't even know him then?"

"Same reason he beat up your soon-to-be ex-husband to make him sign away any custody claim on Layla. Your boyfriend Dietrich told him to."

"Oh, no. No, no. You've got it all wrong." She forced a smile. "Reverend Schultz and I didn't meet until after my impetuous marriage to Curtis was—"

"The police know about the revival meeting, too." I leaned the bat against Dietrich's mahogany desk and opened the newspaper I'd snitched from Ken Tatum's archives. "This one." I tapped the ad. "In Gypsum. When you first decided you and Dietrich were soul mates. Look. Next stop on the revival circuit, Victorville." I tossed the paper onto the desk. "Did Dietrich ask you to follow him, or was it your own idea?"

Red stained her cheeks. "How dare—"

"Kind of inconvenient, you already having a husband. Not that it stopped you from sleeping with Ken Tatum. Was that the only reason Dietrich wouldn't marry you?"

"What on earth are you sugg—"

"Wouldn't exactly thrill most men to be saddled with someone else's handicapped child." I skimmed a palm along the smooth grain of my Louisville Slugger. "Especially a man planning to build a career out of miracle healing. People might wonder why he couldn't cure his own stepson. Was that the reason you had to get rid of Jake?"

Amberlee twisted her mouth as if working up a spitball. "I never—"

The door flew open. Schultz marched Layla into the study, his hand shackled around her thin upper arm. "Look who I just found eavesdropping, Amberlee." If his spin-control meeting with flock members had made him sweat, you couldn't tell. Not a wrinkle in his elegant dark suit, not a silver hair out of place.

Layla wrenched away, fiery green eyes fixed on her mother. "How could you!" she shrieked. "I loved him! He was my little brother!" She stormed across the carpet, finger speared forth like an avenging angel's. "You killed him, you murderer! And all this time made me think I did it!"

CHAPTER 25

"Layla, dear." Amberlee managed a nervous titter. "What a surprise. Did your grandmother let you in?"

"Right, like I'd want her in trouble."

Schultz drew his steel-gray brows into stern alignment. "How did you get in, then?"

"That fuckin' secret gate at the end of the fire road, same way I always snuck in and out. Guess you forgot to reprogram that combination." Lipstick curved with scorn. "But don't bother changing it now, 'cause I'm never coming back here."

Her eyes were puffy, her dyed blond curls straggled loose from her ponytail, and crooked stripes of mascara trailed down her hollowed-out cheeks. In heavy makeup and spiked heels, she reminded me of a little girl playing Dress Up Like Mommy. Assuming Mommy's wardrobe included hot pants and a halter-top.

Amberlee cleared her throat. "If you need money—"

"Amberlee!" Schultz barked.

"You think that's the answer to everything, don't you?" Layla wiped her nose on the back of her arm. "No, that is not why I came. I came because I just found out Daddy's dead. Did you kill him, too?"

"Daddy?" Amberlee clutched her blouse buttons and flung a startled glance at Schultz.

"Not him! I'm talking about my real daddy! The one who married you after someone else knocked you up and split, remember? The one who used to watch *Sesame Street* with me, and let me taste his beer, and taught me how to play Go Fish." Her face crumpled. "That daddy."

"Curtis?" Amberlee looked and sounded bewildered. For once, a genuine reaction.

"I went over to her house this afternoon, to see if she found out anything more about that note." Layla glanced at me, lower lip quivering. "Dane told me someone shot my daddy."

"I'm so sorry," I said.

Schultz fingered his clerical collar, cleared his throat. "Ms. Magnussen, exactly what are you doing here?" He glanced at the bat. "Trying out for Little League?"

"What note?" Amberlee said. "Who is Dane?"

Layla whirled on her. "You told me Daddy signed me away, that he didn't want me anymore after you got divorced. I bet that was a lie too, wasn't it?"

"Young lady, don't you speak to your mother like that!"

"Were you in on it, too?" she cried at Schultz. "Did you help hold the pillow over my brother's face?"

Schultz slapped her.

I took a step forward with the bat. "That's enough."

"You're hysterical," Schultz said. "Besides, I didn't even know your mother back then."

"Yes, you did! She said so." Hand pressed to one cheek, Layla pointed at me.

Schultz's ears turned red. "Ms. Magnussen, if I find out you've been spreading false—"

"Never mind, Dietrich." Amberlee sprang to her feet. "Layla, whatever it is you want—"

"How about the truth, for once?" Shoving her face two inches from her mother's. "How could you blame me all these years for killing Jakey? I was a little kid, for God's sake!" Her eyes welled up. "I loved him!"

Amberlee wrapped her arms around her diaphragm, as if fearful of a sucker punch. "So did I."

"You don't love anybody except yourself. Look at you!" Spittle flew from her lips. "Why didn't you just go ahead and kill me while you were at it? Then I wouldn't have had to grow up thinking I killed the one person on earth who really loved me."

With a moan of anguish, she spun on her heel and stumbled for the door.

"Layla, wait!"

"Go to hell!" she screamed over her shoulder. "Both of you!"

"Layla, I didn't kill him!" Amberlee started after her. "He was already dead when I found him!"

Schultz grabbed her arm. "What do you mean he was already dead?"

Amberlee swallowed. Layla's footsteps faded rapidly down the hall. "He was. Dead already. When I came home that day, after you told me we couldn't be together anymore—"

He shushed her with a quick chop of his hand. "Ms. Magnussen, I think it's time for you to leave now."

Rats, just when it was getting good.

"Here's some free P.R. advice," I said, reluctantly retreating. "When the cops catch Litvak, he'll undoubtedly try to shovel all the blame your way. That good old I-Was-Just-Following-Orders defense is still pretty effective these days."

"Davis would never—"

"Even if you're a hundred percent certain of his loyalty, you're both going to come out smelling a whole lot better if you voluntarily tell the police everything you know. Now. Before they come knocking on your door with a warrant."

Bat and newspaper tucked under my arm, I made a big production of closing the door as I left. The power of the press and a big stick. There was something so Teddy Roosevelt about it.

Once in the hallway, I ducked into the nearest closet and counted off ten minutes in my head. One Mississippi, two Mississippi. The closet was pitch dark. Also infested with some kind of expensive potpourri that made me want to sneeze.

At six hundred Mississippi, I checked if the coast was clear, then made as much noise as possible hurrying back down the hall. I rapped on the door of Dietrich's study, barged in without waiting for an answer.

The tableau was one any marriage counselor would recognize, two red-faced people with tight-lipped scowls facing away from each other. Arms folded, steam coming out their ears.

"Really sorry," I said. "I was almost through the gate when I discovered I forgot my purse." I snatched it from beneath the chair and fled before their startled looks unfroze.

Unmolested by dog or human, I locked myself in the car, extracted the tape recorder from my purse, and fast-forwarded to the point where Dietrich had kicked me out of his study. I started my engine and hit play. Just in case someone wised up and warned the cop at the gate to confiscate it before I could hear what Dietrich and Amberlee had said to each other.

First, the sound of the door shutting behind me.

Amberlee's voice. "Don't you think we'd better—"

"Never mind her. What did you mean, the baby was already dead?"

"Dietrich, that hurts!"

"You told me you killed him!"

The Explorer swerved a little toward the rosebushes.

"Please let go of me." Labored breathing. "All right. That day I came to Victorville, you said if we got married, the state would stop paying Jake's medical bills. That you couldn't afford to pay them yourself because you were saving all your money to build a church."

"Yes, yes, yes."

"And since you were supposed to be a miracle healer, people might question why—"

"Fine. Okay. What does that have to do with anything?"

"Dietrich, I was terribly upset when you told me it was over. Then, when I got home, I found Jake lying in his crib with a pillow over his face. He was dead. It was like a . . . like a sign from God! Only I was afraid the police would suspect me because I was the one who found him, you see? What if they put me in jail? Then you and I would never be together!"

Pause, maybe to gnaw one of her knuckles. "I just couldn't take that chance, not when the obstacle that stood between us was suddenly gone, so I . . . I decided to tell everyone Layla did it."

"How could you?"

"Nothing would happen to her! She was too young!"

Silence. "Who did kill him, Amberlee?"

"How should I know?" she snapped. "Maybe it was Layla."

Faint sounds, possibly Schultz tearing his hair out. "Then why did you tell me you killed him?"

"Because when it was all over, when I came to tell you he was dead so now I could divorce Curtis and marry you, you just made up some other lame excuse. Remember?" The sound of desperation leaked around the edges of her anger. "I had to make you marry me, don't you see? We belong together, darling. God has chosen us to do his work and—"

"You told me you killed him, you lying slut! Just like Abraham in *Genesis 22*, you said. Just like Abraham was willing to sacrifice his son to prove his love for God, you swore you killed your son to prove your love for me!"

"Dietrich, I fibbed. For *us!*"

"You blackmailed me into marrying you!" Agitated respiration. "Tell me, Amberlee. When you claimed you hadn't burned that picture, was that another lie?"

"What picture?"

"Don't pretend you've forgotten. You threatened to tell the police you killed the kid because I asked you to. You swore you'd show them that picture of us. You'd describe the birthmark near my—"

"Dietrich, please!"

"I only married you to save my career, you goddamn bitch, and now you've gone and destroyed it!"

I heard the sound of a loud slap.

Impossible to tell who'd dealt the blow.

Moments later I heard myself on the tape, re-entering the room.

I punched the stop button. As I drove out the gate, my wave at the cop was less cheerful than last time. I should have been pumping a victory fist in the air, thrilled by all the dirt I'd dug up. Instead, I felt . . . contaminated.

I drove around streets behind the estate until I found Layla shuffling along a nearby thoroughfare, her thumb stuck out.

"Hop in," I said.

We didn't chat much on the way home. Her face crumpled when I gave her the money from her grandmother. I let her smoke, as long as she kept the window cracked and held the cigarette tip outside.

Dog hair clung to her skimpy shorts, as if she'd recently been romping with a pair of German shepherds.

Was Amberlee capable of cold-bloodedly suffocating a helpless infant? Lying and blackmail, yes. Exploiting her own child's death, sure. But murder?

Her obsession with Dietrich did provide a powerful motive. If it weren't so tragic, it would have been funny, picturing his face as the nature of her trap dawned on him. The hustler out-hustled.

I made four copies of my illegal recording on Dane's stereo system. Soon as the bank opened Tuesday morning, I locked three of them, plus the original, in the safe deposit box where I'd stashed Amberlee's interview tape.

Still no way to prove who'd killed Jake.

If Amberlee had really found him dead like she claimed, he must have died while Brittany was babysitting. At least, while she was supposed to be babysitting.

Today was my last shot. My first destination? Fontana Auto Repair. Though on second thought . . .

Before I caught up with Travis, maybe I should talk to Brittany.

Most of Gypsum seemed to recognize me now. People didn't literally turn around and gawk as I drove through downtown, but it felt a bit like riding a float in the Fourth of July parade. I was tempted to greet all the coffee drinkers eyeballing me from Carmen's with a homecoming-queen wave.

A car similar to the one I'd seen in Noreen's garage was parked in front of the video store. I scrutinized it more closely. Yup, Noreen behind the wheel. She ducked down and pretended not to see me.

Drawn curtains shrouded the broad arched windows at Justin and Brittany's house. I envisioned the darkened living room, Brittany curled up with a pitcher of screwdrivers, light-and-shadow images from the widescreen TV playing across her vacant eyes, her sunken cheeks, her smudged highball glass.

Sprinklers were wasting water on the front lawn, spewing forth geysers of moisture that would evaporate in the late-morning sun before the grass could soak it up. I rang the bell, prepared for a long wait, but this time the quaint spy window swung open almost immediately. Brittany's prison-pale face hovered behind wrought-iron bars, her cheekbones jutting like chunks of gravel, as if some sadist had stretched the skin over them by braiding her hair too tight.

She moved her lips in greeting, eyes electric with tension. Against brown pupils, gold flecks jittered like sparks.

"Brittany, I have a few more questions," I said. "About the afternoon Jake died. About Travis."

"He doesn't know anything about what happened." Her voice teetered, high-pitched and tremulous, as if she walked a tightrope without a net.

"All right." We could debate that later. "But you and I still need to talk about what happened while you were babysitting that day."

She let me in without questioning my sudden interest in Travis. Apparently, the family grapevine had already spread the word that Noreen admitted seeing him climb out the Gormleys' window.

Brittany padded barefoot across the tiled foyer. In the living room she sank into a recliner chair, her waif-like figure nearly swallowed by its vast tweed bulk. Her scoop-neck blouse bared the sharp wings of her collarbones.

I settled on the other recliner. Half a pitcher of sparkling ruby liquid that might have been wine coolers sat on the walnut-burl coffee table next to a tumbler of pink-tinted melting ice. Spunky Mary Richards and gruff Lou Grant bickered on the television set. I didn't bother with the remote, just leaned forward and poked off the power button. Then I said, "Brittany, did Travis rape you that day?"

"What?" Eyes big as coasters. Her gasp wafted a sickly sweet hint of fermented fruit to my nose.

"I know the two of you had sex. The crime-scene investigator found a small amount of blood in Curtis and Amberlee's bed." Compassion softened my tone. "Was that your first time?"

Tears pooled in her eyes. One glistening drop spilled down her pale marble cheek. "Yes," she whispered.

I bit my lip. "Did he force you?"

"No." She slicked wetness from her face with the heels of both hands. "I . . ." She made a helpless, incoherent sound. Lifted her chin. "I have loved Travis Fontana since I was thirteen years old."

"Travis?" The naked, hopeless sincerity of her declaration skewered my heart. "But I thought you and Justin—"

"That came later." She lifted a weary hand, let it flop in her lap. "Justin and I started dating . . . afterwards."

"But if you still loved—"

"It's complicated. Travis was so much older." She glanced sideways, toward the family photos grouped near the couch.

"Okay." I fished out my notepad. "Let's run through everything that happened that afternoon. You got to the Gormley house at what time?"

Her gaze drifted to a Kincade print on the wall. "Around two." The gaze slid out of focus, as if blurring the fairy-tale cottage might conjure up a lost vision of happily-ever-after.

"Curtis was at work?"

"Supposedly." She shrugged. "Now that I think about it, he'd probably gotten fired by then and was out getting drunk someplace."

"Did Amberlee leave as soon as you got there?"

"Within a couple minutes. She was in a real hurry."

"So it was just you and the two children in the house."

"Yes. Until . . ." She plucked her lip.

"Travis got there."

She nodded.

"What time did he arrive?"

Brittany went pink. "As soon as he saw Amberlee drive off."

"He was next door?"

"No. Watching from down the street. He didn't want his mother . . ." She laced her fingers together, tugged. "There was no place we could go to be alone, you see. Travis had wrecked his car. He was still living with his mom. One of my parents was always around . . ." Her mouth curved with embarrassment. "In a town this size, you can't get away with anything. People notice. They talk."

"I know. I grew up in a small town, too."

"I was so excited when Amberlee asked me to baby-sit that I said I'd do it for half my usual rate. I knew she couldn't afford much, and I didn't want her to change her mind." Brittany twisted her diamond as if trying to wrench it off her ring. "It was awful, I know, taking advantage like that, using their bed, but . . ." Her shoulders sagged. "None of that seemed important at the time."

Of course not. What hardhearted soul could condemn her? Certainly no one who'd survived the roller-coaster thrill, the reckless passion, the spellbinding obsession of first love.

"Where were the children while you and Travis were in Amberlee's bedroom?"

"Layla was in the living room, watching TV." Brittany picked at a brass upholstery tack. "Amberlee said I should try and get Jake to take a nap. He was so fussy. So I left him in the kids' room, in his crib."

"Was he asleep?"

"No. Wide awake."

"Did he seem different in any way? Like he was sick or having trouble breathing?"

"Not that I noticed. He was crying." Her voice splintered as tears filled her eyes. "That's something I'll never forgive myself for. Leaving him there all alone like that, acting so selfish just because I was so desperate to be with . . ." She dug her nails into her cheeks. "I thought he'd be okay, that he'd calm down and fall asleep pretty soon."

"Crying babies can be pretty frustrating. Sometimes when my son was little, I felt like I'd do almost anything to make him quiet." In truth, Dane had been an incredibly mellow baby. It was the teenager I sometimes felt like shaking. "You must have been pretty upset when Jake kept fussing. Especially being nervous about what was going to happen between you and Travis."

"That was no excuse." She retrieved a cocktail napkin from the coffee table, blotted her eyes with it. A track of little red crescents dented each cheek. "I shouldn't have left him by himself."

"Did you pick him up? Walk him around? Maybe jiggle him a little so he'd stop crying?"

"No," she said in a dull, clogged voice. "I just left him lying there."

"Awake."

"Very."

"Okay. So then you and Travis—"

"We went into the other bedroom and locked the door." She stared at the picture window as if curtains weren't blocking the view.

"How long were you in there?"

"I have no idea. An hour? Two? It was like time stopped." She blushed. "All of a sudden we heard somebody slam the front door. God, what a terrible moment! We jumped up and threw on our clothes. I whispered to Travis he should climb out the window. Then I sneaked out of the bedroom." She wadded the damp napkin in her fist. "Curtis was in the living room. Drunk. Yelling at Layla. I just wanted to get out of there, so I called goodbye and ran out the front door."

"Did you check on Jake before you left?"

Guilty head shake. "That's why I was relieved when Amberlee drove up right away. I remember hoping she wouldn't ask me to help carry groceries because the last thing I wanted was to go back in that . . ." She frowned.

"What is it?"

"Oh. Nothing, really. Kind of weird, that's all. I got this flash of walking past Amberlee's station wagon and wondering why there weren't any grocery sacks in it."

Because Amberlee hadn't gone to the store that day. She'd gone after Dietrich.

"Anyway, I was glad when she rushed right by me into the house. I scurried home as fast as I could."

"When did you talk to Travis again?"

Dark clouds shadowed her face. "I don't remember."

"Come on, Brittany. You'd just lost your virginity to a guy you were crazy about, and you're telling me you can't remember the next time you saw him?"

She reached for the drinks pitcher, slopped a little over the rim of her glass. "Couple days later, I guess."

"What did you talk about? Skip the personal stuff. I mean as far as Jake."

"We didn't talk about him." She clutched her drink in both hands, poured some down her throat.

"A baby died either while or shortly after both of you were in the house, and the subject never came up for discussion?"

"We broke up, okay?" She had a wet burgundy mustache, like a lipstick tube run amok. "Next time I saw Travis, we broke up. That's all I remember."

"I'm sorry." I closed my notepad, tilted my head. "Why did you break up?"

She studied the contents of her glass. "That's really none of your business."

Good for you, I thought. Except maybe it was. "Thanks for your time," I said. "You've been very helpful."

"You won't say anything to Travis, will you?"

"About your feelings for him?" I stood. "No, of course not. I just want to hear his version of what happened that day."

Alarm stiffened her spine like I'd threatened to go on *Oprah* and broadcast her confession to the world. "Don't waste your time talking to Travis," she said. "I told you. He doesn't know anything about Jake's death."

I slung my purse over my shoulder. "Well, I still need to hear him say that."

"You . . . you can't!" She popped up like a jack-in-the-box. "He doesn't . . . he'll be . . ." She banged her glass on top of the TV. "Please. I beg you. Don't ask him any questions about that day."

"Why not?"

"Because . . . because it'll remind him of what we did." She licked her lips. "He's probably forgotten. It'll make things awkward at family get-togethers if he remembers."

Forgotten? Not a chance. I edged toward the door. "I'm sorry if it makes things uncomfortable, but we're talking about a baby's death here. I think it's worth a little awkwardness to find out what really happened, don't you?"

"Travis can't help! He doesn't know anything."

"What makes you so sure?"

"Because . . ."

Her eyelids fluttered like trapped hummingbirds. A low, desperate keening rose from the back of her throat.

"Brittany?"

"Because . . ."

When she just kept wringing her hands, I turned to go.

"Because I killed the baby," she blurted.

CHAPTER 26

"It was just like you said. I was upset because he kept crying, so I shook him, but he still wouldn't stop. That's when I put the pillow over his face." Brittany pressed fingertips to her mouth. "I just wanted him to be quiet."

I stared at her in silence. She broke eye contact first. I said, "So, Jake was dead before you started having sex with Travis?"

"No. I mean, yes. I mean, I didn't know he was dead. I never meant to hurt him, I just couldn't stand the crying anymore. It was an accident. I've felt terrible about it all these years."

"Yet you let a five-year-old take the blame."

Misery raked her expression. "I heard she wasn't going to be punished or anything."

Except Layla had been punished. Every day of her life since.

"Are you going to tell the police?" Brittany asked.

"Depends." I started across the foyer. "On what Travis has to tell me."

"But you can't talk to him! There isn't any reason to. Don't you see? Now that I've admitted it, you know who killed the baby. You can finish your show now. I'll even confess on camera if you want." She pursued me as far as the door, pleading, weeping, proclaiming her guilt.

Brittany felt terrible about something, all right. But I didn't think it was for killing Jake.

She stood trembling in the doorway as I drove off, like someone poised for flight but terrified the dazzling sun might blind her, the baked asphalt sear the soles of her feet.

As if straining against invisible bars.

"Lemme finish with this, okay?" Travis waved a wrench at the ancient Buick up on the lift. "I promised the guy I'd have it ready today." He pushed dark hair off his forehead with the crook of his arm. "Man, I gotta find a new assistant, quick."

The garage smelled as if someone had used WD-40 spray as an air freshener. Despite all the No Smoking signs, a whiff of stale tobacco lurked beneath the fragrance of petroleum products.

"I'll be in the waiting room," I said. I would have walked over to Carmen's for lunch, but I was eager to speak to Travis as soon as he could take a break. So I spent the next twenty minutes pondering Brittany's confession and ignoring my grumpy stomach.

I was almost desperate enough to gamble on the vending machine when Travis appeared, wiping his hands on a grease-stained rag. "Come on, let's talk in my office."

He grabbed a chair from the waiting room to plunk in front of his dinged-up metal desk. The desk looked like the kind of bargain you can snap up at government-surplus auctions when bureaucrats decide to redecorate. The usual nudie calendar hung on the wall, surrounded by a variety of posters advertising oil additives and other car-care products.

Nearly hidden behind a stack of repair manuals was a framed 5-by-7 of a much-younger Zack, mugging for the camera from the arms of a vivacious blond cheerleader type. Travis's late wife, no doubt.

"Want a soda?" He opened a mini-fridge behind his desk and extracted a Coke.

"No, thanks."

He popped it open, swung his grimy work boots up on the

desk, and drained about a third of the can. "What can I do for you? Car running okay?" Followed by a predictable burp.

"The car's fine, thanks. I really appreciate all the extra time you put in."

"Zack sure got a kick out of meeting your husband the other night. Jeff Burdick. Who'd've ever thought Stone Caldwell himself would come waltzing into my garage?"

I mustered a tight smile, bit my tongue to keep from clarifying that we weren't married anymore. "The reason I'm here is to ask you about the day Jake Gormley died."

"Oh. That." He sobered. "Yeah, Mom said she told you what happened. About me sneaking out the window and all."

"Brittany just told me that she killed the baby."

"What?" Boots thudded to the floor. "You shittin' me?"

"That's what she said."

"Why, that's crazy! Why the hell would she say something like that?"

"I was hoping you could help me figure it out."

"Why, sure, I'll do anything I can, but I just don't get . . ." He shook his head. "Boy, that doesn't make sense."

"Anybody home?" With a rap on the doorjamb, Ken Tatum stuck his head into the office. "Hey, Travis. Sorry to interrupt, but I noticed Ms. Magnussen's car parked out front." He wheeled forward, cocked a thumb at me. "Wanted to catch you before you left town."

I stole a glance at Travis. He sat plinking the tab of his Coke can, looking completely pole-axed. "This isn't such a good time, Ken," I said. "Why don't I stop by the newspaper office when I'm done here?"

"Sure." He shifted into reverse. "Got a few questions for you about this guy Litvak the cops just arrested."

"Davis Litvak? They caught him?"

"Down near Calexico. Driving a stolen car, headed for the

border. One of my sources hinted you might know some stuff that hasn't been made public yet. I was hoping you could help me scoop the competition."

I laughed, mostly from relief. The image of Litvak in handcuffs gave me a warm, fuzzy feeling. "Ken, didn't it occur to you that I'm the competition?"

He scratched beard stubble under his chin. "Oh. I guess—"

"Just kidding. My episode won't air for months." If ever.

An engine rumbled as someone pulled into the empty garage bay. Great, another interruption while Travis dealt with a customer.

"I'll be glad to share whatever I know," I told Ken. "Soon as Travis and I are finished."

"Thanks. You eaten yet? How 'bout I treat you to—"

A humming duet of small motors kicked to life in the garage, accompanied by the harsh rattle of metal grating along tracks. The furrows creasing Travis's brow deepened. "What the hell?"

"What is it?"

"Somebody closing the garage doors." He banged down the Coke can and came around his desk. "Pranksters or something."

Ken winked. "Not like you'd know anything about playing pranks, huh Travis?"

Travis punched him absently in the shoulder as he sidled past the wheelchair. "Watch it, Tatum. Next time you bring your van in for servicing, I'm gonna change all your radio settings."

Ken's amusement faded along with Travis's footsteps. He rolled his chair a little closer, strumming his fingers against the spokes. "Speaking of your show, how's the investigation going?"

An emotionally disturbed woman just confessed to accidentally smothering your son.

"Making progress," I said.

"You find out yet who killed Jake?" He lifted a parts catalogue from Travis's desk, thumbed through it like he might be in the market for a remanufactured alternator.

"No, I still—"

"Ms. Magnussen?" A male voice echoed from inside the garage. Not Travis's, but vaguely familiar.

"Be right back." Ken's gaze tracked me as I left the office and hurried through the waiting room.

Near the hoisted Buick, Travis shifted from one foot to the other, confusion rumpling his good looks. The man next to him with spiky black hair was his brother. Fluorescent lighting gave them both an unhealthy pallor.

"You met Justin, right?" Travis jerked his thumb. "He says he needs to . . . whoa! What the hell are you doing, man?"

Leveling a pistol at me. Small enough to have fit in the pocket of his chinos, yet with a muzzle hole the size of a train tunnel. My feet welded themselves to the stained concrete.

Justin's watchful eyes glittered like obsidian. "She knows, Trav." A maroon splotch soaked the front of his button-down shirt, as if someone had shot him. Or hurled half a wine cooler at his chest.

"Knows what? Look, put that down, okay?"

"About the kid. Jake. She knows Brittany killed him." His tongue flicked like a snake's. "We gotta get rid of her before she tells the cops."

I forced myself to breathe. In. Out. In. Out. Gasoline fumes mixed with the cloying scent of antifreeze only worsened my nausea.

"How come all of a sudden everyone thinks Brittany killed that baby?" Travis pitchforked a hand through his hair. "No way, man. I was there. Don't you think I'd know if she did it?"

"She confessed, all right? To Sherlock Holmes here." A bead of perspiration crept from Justin's hairline. "Mom called me at work, said Magnussen's car was parked in front of our house. I warned her yesterday to be on the lookout."

He rolled his eyes at his brother's troubled frown. In a tone reserved for dimwitted two-year-olds, he said, "I'm not letting my wife go to jail, Trav."

"You can't shoot the lady, for cryin' out loud!"

I was petrified. So was every muscle in my body. Yet buried in the nether regions of my brain, some primitive survival mechanism was spinning furiously. *Garage doors shut. No windows. If he shoots me, though, someone will hear. Wait, I don't want him to shoot me!*

"Come on, you nosy bitch. In the car." Holding the gun pretty steady for a computer geek, Justin jerked his head toward the late-model SUV parked in the other bay.

"What exactly is your plan here?" Travis made a halfhearted grab for Justin's wrist, forcing him to pivot a little. On command from Survival Headquarters, I edged half a step to my left. Toward the spot where Zack had stood while entertaining himself Saturday night.

Justin glared. "My plan is to drive her out into the desert and shut her up. Permanently."

Travis whapped his thigh in frustration. "You're crazy, man! You'll never get away with it."

"Why not? You gonna turn in your own flesh and blood? We can't let her hurt Brittany, Trav."

"Brittany didn't do anything, for chrissakes!" He clamped both hands to his skull. "I told you. I was there. Look, we were fooling around in the bedroom the whole time. I saw the kid myself, all right? And I'm telling you, he was alive!"

Justin snorted. "Not when I got there."

"You?" Travis's jaw went slack. "What are you talking about?"

I sidestepped a little more to the left. My legs had degenerated to the approximate consistency of chocolate pudding.

"Britt never told you I was there, huh?" Justin corralled a gob of spit and hawked it at the floor. "Oh, yeah. Came over to see her while she was babysitting, all set to ask her out to the movies. Screwed up my courage, rehearsed my little speech, knocked on the back door. When no one answered, I went ahead and walked in." Nostrils flared. "Only to discover my big brother was busy fucking my girlfriend in the bedroom."

"She wasn't your girlfriend!"

"She would've been, if you hadn't gone after her. No chick ever looked at me twice long as you were around, right? Bet it gave you a real hard-on, knowing I had the hots for her." His mouth torqued with resentment. "The big stud scores another conquest."

"How was I supposed to know you liked her?" Fist thump to his chest. "Anyway, it wasn't like that. Brittany and I really—"

"Save it. Who cares?"

"Why did you say the baby was dead?"

"Because, you dumbshit, he wasn't breathing, he wasn't moving, and his face was blue. That good enough for you?"

Travis stared.

"I go looking for Brittany, and instead find this kid in his crib with a pillow over his face. I nearly freaked out, man! I cover him back up, start running through the house, and who's the only person I can find? The little girl, Layla. Who informs me—" he switched to sarcastic baby talk "—Twavis and Bwittany are in Mommy and Daddy's room wif da door locked."

Travis pinched the bridge of his nose, leaving a black oil streak that punctuated his bewilderment like an exclamation point. "You found the baby dead? And never said anything?"

"I said something, all right. To Brittany. Soon as all the commotion died down, all the cops and the ambulance left." He cuffed sweat off his brow. "How do you think I felt, finding out she'd been screwing around with you? You didn't love her, not the way I did." Spittle gathered at the corners of his mouth like a rabid ferret's. "I had to show her she was making a mistake. I had to protect her from going to jail."

"But Brittany didn't . . . she couldn't have . . ." Travis dragged a hand down his face, smearing the oil. "I'm telling you, the kid was alive. He was screaming his lungs out when I . . . when I . . ."

All at once an invisible blow seemed to knock the wind out of him. He staggered backward, colliding with the driver's door of Justin's vehicle. Deathbed pale, he flung up an arm as if to ward off further assault. As his knees slowly buckled, he slumped to a sitting position.

I inched sideways. Closer to the red metal tool cabinet where Travis had set down his wrench.

Justin gaped at him. "What the hell's wrong with you?"

Shock glazed Travis's eyes. His complexion was gray as concrete. He dangled limp forearms across his drawn-up knees, as if his bones had turned to clay. If I hadn't been so concerned with my own survival, I might have worried about his.

Justin shifted his stance to keep an eye on both of us. "Trav, come on. Snap out of it. You gotta help me tie her up. Got any duct tape around here?"

Travis gulped for air. Moved his mouth like a fish.

"You having a heart attack or something? Look, we gotta get moving."

His brother emitted a strangled sound.

"What?"

A muscle flexed along Travis's jaw line. "I think I killed him," he croaked in a rusty voice.

Justin frowned. "What are you talking about?"

Travis's chest heaved as if someone had lowered an engine block onto it. "I went in there, to the baby's room. While Brittany and I were, uh . . ." He coughed. "She was all nervous about, you know, and his screaming was making it worse. I told her to ignore it. He was fine. Everything was cool, but she got pretty worked up. Said maybe we ought to stop, she was too distracted worrying about Jake, so I told her I'd go check on him."

His dark eyes went liquid with agony. "I didn't mean to hurt the little guy. But he wouldn't stop crying, so I thought, well, at least I can fix it so Brittany won't have to hear him." The words scraped against each other like worn brake pads. "So I took a pillow off Layla's bed and set it on top of him."

For some reason, he sought out my gaze. "It's not like I held it down or anything. It never even occurred to me he wouldn't be able to breathe. It was only a pillow. I just didn't want Brittany to hear him crying anymore." He buried his face in his callused hands. "It was all my fault. God, when I think how I'd feel if something ever happened to Zack."

Justin's eyes pinballed back and forth, like an adding machine working on new calculations. "Did Britt know about all this?"

"Hell, I don't know."

Of course she did. Travis might not be the sharpest tool in the shed, but the moment Brittany heard Jake was dead, she would have realized how Travis got him to stop crying.

The horror, the guilt, the shame must have turned her life into a nightmare. Year after year, bottling it all up inside. Now it made sense: the drinking, sedating herself with television, the misery in her bloodshot eyes.

I have loved Travis Fontana since I was thirteen years old.

And paid a terrible price to protect him. Not from the law, but from himself.

Justin's calculations apparently added up to a similar conclusion. "Britt let me think she did it." He wiped his mouth on the back of his wrist, as if tasting something bitter. "All these years, and she never even . . . damn!" He kicked an empty plastic bucket, sent it clattering across the floor.

I eased in front of the tool cabinet, afraid he'd hear the

281

jackhammer pounding of my heart.

"Never mind," he muttered. "She and I still have our deal. This doesn't change anything."

Travis lifted his head. "What do you mean?" His cheeks were wet. "What deal?"

"I promised not to tell the cops she smothered the kid." Justin rolled his shoulders like a boxer headed back into the ring. "Her part of the deal was she had to break up with you. Start going steady with me. Then, when we were eighteen, she'd marry me."

My fingertips groped behind my back.

A scrawl of fresh anguish etched Travis's face. "You black-mailed her into marrying you?"

"It was for her own good." Justin's neck stiffened. "Look what a disaster she created, getting hooked up with you. Britt needs someone to take care of her. Someone who really loves her. Who'll never leave her, no matter what."

"I can't believe you did that to her."

Justin rocked the gun sideways a few times. "Don't get all sanctimonious, bro. Who's the baby killer here, huh? Besides, I did you a favor. She's frigid, man. Like trying to get it on with a sack of cold mashed potatoes." His eyes narrowed. "So don't waste time with any stupid ideas about getting her back."

No need to consult Sigmund Freud. Imagine what kind of terrible sexual and emotional scars you might suffer if losing your virginity turned out to be the indirect cause of a child's death.

My hand closed around the wrench.

Travis gouged dirty fingernails into his kneecaps. "How come you never took her away from here? Never moved someplace where she wouldn't be reminded of what happened?"

Justin widened his eyes and pressed a fingertip to his chin. "That would kind of defeat the purpose, wouldn't it?"

Not to mention make it harder to rub Travis's nose in Little Brother's romantic triumph.

"Look, forget all this shit, okay? Now you've got even more reason to help me get rid of her." He jutted the gun toward me. "Come on, move it. Into the car."

I tightened my grip, praying my overloaded nervous system wouldn't short-circuit. I'd have to edge past him at an angle.

Ken Tatum exploded into the garage like a bull from a rodeo chute, straight on a collision course with Justin. The tormented howl that burst from his lungs would have made the inmates of hell shudder. I caught a split-second glimpse of contorted features, lips stretched back over his teeth in determination, veins bulging with effort. His eyes were bottomless caverns of despair, like those of a man who'd lost his soul and had begun to recognize the consequences.

Justin's startled reflexes kicked in. He fired.

Crimson blossomed across Ken's shirt. The gunshot momentarily deafened me, shattered my scream of protest. The burned stench of cordite curled through the air.

The wheelchair's momentum carried Ken forward, knocking Justin off balance. The pistol flew from his hand, skittered across the floor. We both turned to lunge for it, but Justin was several feet closer.

I reached over and flipped the hydraulic-lift lever. With a clank, the Buick began to descend. Justin instinctively ducked and glanced upward. I let go of the lever and dove for the gun.

A whipcord of pain lashed through my shoulder when I hit concrete. Both knees cracked against the floor like billiard balls. Just as my left hand touched the barrel, steel-cable fingers wrapped around my ankle.

I kicked, squirmed, fought for traction. Sweat nearly blinded me. I hauled back the wrench. With a grunt, I whacked Justin's wrist as hard as I could. The crunch of bone was nearly as satisfying as his shriek of pain.

I twisted free, grabbed the pistol, and scrambled to my feet.

Gasping for breath, I stood over Justin. It was the first time in my life I'd held a gun, much less pointed one at anybody. Know what I discovered? Pulling a trigger ain't exactly rocket science.

"You bitch, you broke my fucking arm!"

Travis dashed for the wall phone and dialed 9-1-1.

"Lower the Buick the rest of the way," I said when he hung up. "Then open the trunk."

He snagged the key from the ignition and complied.

"Get in," I told Justin.

"Trav, you're not going to let her—"

"Better do like she says," he said wearily. "Or I might grab the gun and shoot you myself."

"That trunk doesn't have an interior release latch, does it?" I asked.

"Nah, too old."

As soon as Travis slammed the trunk, I ran to Ken.

We untangled him from his toppled wheelchair, laid him on cushions Travis brought from the waiting room. I'm not sure what a good wound would look like, but his looked bad to me.

I gulped down the queasiness in my stomach, fought off the swarm of black dots swirling behind my eyelids, the lightheadedness that made me want to close them and flop next to Ken on the concrete. Travis dug out clean rags so we could try to staunch the bleeding, but it was a hopeless battle.

Ken's lips twitched.

I brought my ear close. "You trying to say something?"

"I . . ." Barely a whisper. "I shot Curtis. Thought he was the one who—"

"I know." I rested a hand on his shoulder. More guilt I'd have to learn to live with. "Try not to talk any more."

"Envelope," he murmured. "Safe-deposit box."

"Okay."

"Tell . . ." He made a gurgling sound as he struggled for breath. "Tell my parents I love them."

"Promise." I squeezed his hand. Then he was gone.

Nine minutes later we heard the sirens.

EPILOGUE

Gypsum Cemetery huddled on a hill overlooking the open-pit mine. Hardly a peaceful setting, what with the round-the-clock rumble of diesel engines, the monotonous beep of trucks backing up, the crashing thunder of rock being transported from one location to another. Then again, the dead probably didn't care.

A cold wind was whirling clouds of white dust around the gray metal buildings on the day in mid-January when I brought Layla to visit Jake's grave. The high desert was overcast, chillier than L.A. We shivered in sweaters and slacks, hugging our ribs, gazing down at the poignant, no-frills inscription.

Minus makeup and the flamboyant streetwalker get-up, Layla resembled the teenager she still was. In one hand she clutched a small teddy bear. "You think it's okay to leave this here?" she asked.

I thought the next big gust would probably send it sailing across the landscape like tumbleweed.

"Sure," I said. "I bet Jake would like it."

She pressed the stuffed animal to her heart, then knelt to prop it against the grave marker, arranging its little paws just right, making sure the bow around its neck was tied straight.

Next to us, a still-raw mound of soil marked the spot where Ken Tatum had been buried last October. In the plot he'd purchased fourteen years ago.

When sheriff's investigators had opened his safe-deposit box, they found an anonymous typed letter that said "Stay away

286

from Amberlee, or next time you won't be so lucky." Addressed to Ken, postmarked the last day of September, 1994. A week following the accident that crippled him, a month after Amberlee had moved to Victorville.

No useful fingerprints, but dried saliva on the envelope flap had been deposited by Davis Litvak's tongue. Remember the old days, when every thug in America didn't know to keep his DNA to himself?

Litvak is currently behind bars, held without bail while awaiting trial for Viola Purdy's murder. Between stops at every ATM between Orange County and the Mexican border, he'd stolen a new getaway car, shaved off his beard, and disguised himself in a hooded sweatshirt he'd bought from a thrift store. Didn't help his case much when he took a swing at the cop who recognized him anyway. You'd think a lawyer would know better.

The D.A. is confident that phone records, plus my testimony about the ledger, will be enough to convict him. Oh yes, along with the cat hair they found clinging to the driver's seat of his Lexus.

Justin Fontana is out on bail while his attorney tries to weasel a deal on homicide and attempted kidnapping charges that will get his client out of prison before he's old enough to collect Social Security. If the case does wind up going to trial, Travis has agreed to testify against his brother.

Travis himself pleaded guilty to involuntary manslaughter. He was still awaiting sentencing that January day Layla and I visited the cemetery. But the county prosecutor wasn't pushing too hard, not on a fourteen-year-old accidental killing by a now-upstanding member of the community who demonstrated such remorse at his first hearing that the judge came up afterwards to pat him on the shoulder.

Zack's going to live with Noreen during the year or so his father will spend in jail. Travis and Brittany plan to marry as soon as her divorce from Justin becomes final.

Jake Gormley's story is scheduled for next season's premiere of *Cold Case Chronicles*. Carson also promoted me to producer.

Sheriff Duane Salazar squeaked out a re-election last November. I persuaded him to appear on the show by promising not to raise the issue of Amberlee's alibi. Since she claimed to have gone shopping that afternoon, how come no one asked to see the groceries?

I wish this episode had a happier ending. Three people died because of me. Some innocent; some not so innocent, but their faces still keep me awake at night.

Layla and I wandered up and down a few rows until we found Curtis's grave. "You thought any more about getting your GED?" I asked.

She shrugged, knuckled a tear from her eye. "Yeah, I guess. My shrink thinks it'd be a good idea."

"Then you could look for a real job. Didn't you say you might like to work in television?"

She fired off a crooked smile at me. "Okay, I get the message."

I dropped an arm around her.

Dietrich and Amberlee Schultz have chosen to continue the devil's bargain of their marriage. Litvak's arrest spattered a little mud on the old pastoral robes, but no one could dig up evidence Schultz had sent Litvak to kill Viola, sabotage my brakes, or commit any other skullduggery.

Amberlee's newly revised version of Jake's death: She was so abused and brainwashed by Curtis that she blamed her own daughter to protect him from suspicion. Donations to Schultz's ministry actually registered an uptick after her breast-beating, tear-filled public performance.

Back in October I confessed my underhanded behavior to Amberlee and Dietrich, revealing I had a tape on which Amberlee admitted she bluffed Schultz into marriage by claiming to have killed her own son. No need to draw those two a picture. Who better understands the power of television?

If a certain Beverly Hills psychologist doesn't keep getting paid in a timely fashion for Layla's therapy sessions . . .

Blackmail. Who knew it was contagious?

ABOUT THE AUTHOR

Karin Hofland lives in Grass Valley, California, with her husband Jim and a Labrador-terrier mutt named Spenser. She enjoys ballroom dancing, puzzle boxes, and Norwegian cuisine. Every morning she solves the *New York Times* crossword puzzle in pen.